# GANBARE!
# WORKSHOPS ON DYING

First edition, 2021
All rights reserved

Library of Congress Cataloging-in-Publication Data: Available.
ISBN-13: 978-1-948830-42-3 | ISBN-10: 1-948830-42-6

*This project is supported in part by an award from the National Endowment for the Arts and the New York State Council on the Arts with the support of Governor Andrew M. Cuomo and the New York State Legislature.*

*This publication has been supported by the ©POLAND Translation Program.*

**BOOK INSTITUTE**

©POLAND

Printed on acid-free paper in the United States of America.

*Cover Design by Daniel Benneworth-Gray*
*Interior Design by Anthony Blake*

*Cover Images: Makiko Omokawa and Thierry Meier*

Open Letter is the University of Rochester's nonprofit, literary translation press: Dewey Hall 1-219, Box 278968, Rochester, NY 14627

www.openletterbooks.org

# GANBARE!
# WORKSHOPS ON DYING

## KATARZYNA BONI

Translated from the Polish by Mark Ordon

**OPEN LETTER**
LITERARY TRANSLATIONS FROM THE UNIVERSITY OF ROCHESTER

Since March 11, 2001, *Ganbare!* has been the most commonly repeated word in Tōhoku, the northwestern region of Japan destroyed by the tsunami that same year. It's displayed on billboards alongside roads, printed in local newspapers, and voiced by government officials, artists, journalists, and volunteers.

All of Japan is calling: *Ganbare!*

Give it your all! Hang in there! Fight! You can do it!

*Ganbare*, Tōhoku!

The line between needing encouragement and needing help is very thin. As the Japanese would say: *giri giri*.

Sometimes, *ganbare!* will motivate you to act. Sometimes, when you hear *ganbare!*, you feel very lonely.

Give it your all. Hang in there. Fight.

## TABLE OF CONTENTS

GANBARE!
WORKSHOPS ON DYING

# Japanese Tales of Horror

During the Edo period, when Japan, having concluded that the world had nothing to offer, voluntarily sealed itself off from the outside, people would play "A Hundred Tales of Horror" on summer nights. Once the heat would recede and you could finally breathe normally, people all over, be it in peasant huts, merchant homes, or in castles, would get together in a dark room, with croaking frogs and buzzing cicadas in the background. The players would sit on tatami mats around a low table with one hundred lit candles. One at a time, they would tell stories of revenge-seekers from the grave, disfigured ghosts, haunted houses, mountain monsters that would kidnap women, or icy maidens who would tempt men and kill them with their frozen breath. Of phantoms tormenting the living, detached ears and bodies painted in protective spells. Or of disembodied heads flying through the night, looking for human blood to quench their thirst. When a player finished a story, one of the candles was extinguished, making more room for ghosts in the space. People believed that the ghosts would appear in their midst when the last candle went out.

# Garbage

In 2012, garbage started to wash up on the shores of Alaska. Among the tangled mass of Styrofoam, canisters, fishing nets, and cracked beams, beach-goers found objects from a different reality.

A plastic sandal.

A porcelain bowl.

A protective helmet.

A lighter.

A wooden figure of a warrior.

A bottle of shampoo.

A volleyball signed with blue marker.

A child's shoe, its laces still tied.

Sharpened pencils.

One freezing February morning, David Baxter found a yellow buoy in the sand that bore a black Chinese character, 慶. He decided to find its owner.

Newspapers reported how, fifteen months after the tsunami, in the city of Minamisanriku, 430 kilometers north of Tokyo, Ms. Sakiko Miura took out a bank loan and opened a new restaurant. The tsunami had wiped out her original restaurant, Keiemeimaru, along with her house and the oceanfront districts of the city. Ms. Miura learned from a television program featuring David Baxter, who lived in Alaska, that he had found a decorative buoy with the name of her restaurant printed on it. The character painted on the buoy—慶—is the first of two *kanji* of her husband's name: Keigo. He died over thirty years ago, leaving Ms. Miura on her own with four children. She worked odd jobs at local restaurants. After her fortieth birthday, she took a correspondence course and finished school. When she was fifty, she opened her own restaurant, Keiemeimaru, which only served specialties from the local market: fish, salmon roe, and other seafood dishes. Ms. Miura's new restaurant is the only building standing in what was previously a residential district of Minamisanriku. Old neighbors, all scattered about in temporary housing, get together here. The yellow buoy sits on a table against the wall. Next to the buoy are flowers and a picture of David Baxter. David Baxter also found seven other people whose things he picked up at the beach. Other objects are waiting for their owners. Pictures are available on a web site called *Tsunami Return*. Among the recent patrons at Ms. Miura's restaurant were David and his family.

## The City That Is Not There

The ground is brown and sodden, gouged by muddy ruts created by passing trucks. Fences, cranes, diggers. Enormous conveyor belts and pipelines resting on five-meter-long supports bring soil to the shore from the mountains one kilometer away. A large-scale construction site.

There was a city here once.

Rikuzentakata.

There were rows of two-story houses with gardens, where plum flowers would blossom in early spring and hydrangea would appear in summer; where maple leaves would shine red in the fall (the leaves are fragile and small, different than what we're used to); and where pine needles protrude from the snow cover in winter.

It was all there. Now it's gone.

There was the main shopping street, with its white arcades protected from the sun and rain by a roof. The locals would call it *shatto dōri*, from *shut*—closed, and *dōri*—street. Young people were leaving for big cities. Old people no longer had the strength. More and more stores were going out of business, leaving nothing but empty pavilions with white arcades.

It was all there. Gone now.

There was a port where small fishing boats would anchor. Rikuzentakata lived off the sea. Tuna, sea bream, butterfish, amberjacks, seaweed, scallops, sea urchins. And those oysters! Meaty and full of flavor.

It was all there. Now it's gone.

There was an elementary school, middle school, high school, town hall, pharmacies, a hospital, a private dental clinic, a baseball stadium, a shopping mall, restaurants, a gas station, a flower shop, railroad tracks, a train station, a small sake distillery, a baker, a tatami mat manufacturer, a coal producer, a few processing plants, a playground, and a preschool.

It was all there. Now it's gone.

There were meadows on a hill encircled by dogwood and azalea, where the entire city would watch a fireworks display in the summer.

It was all there. Now it's gone.

There were gates, fences, gardens, walls, roofs, streets, windows, shop displays, closed shutters, bus stops, sidewalks, and trees.

It was all there. Now it's gone.

There was a city with a population of twenty-four thousand.

It was all there. Now it's gone.

And there was the forest. Seventy thousand pine trees growing on the sandy shore. The smell of pine needles mixed with the sea breeze. People would make special trips here. For a walk among the trees.

It was all there. Now it's gone.

Only one pine tree survived. It was still alive a year after the tsunami, but its roots died in the salt-drenched soil. Experts inserted a steel scaffolding into the dead stump. Twenty-seven meters high. They added artificial branches and leaves made of synthetic resin. It looks like it's alive and well. It will remain standing. The mighty pine tree. The symbol of the city of Rikuzentakata, which will never give up. I always get lost here. My GPS is useless. The new roads haven't been added to the map. But it does show gas stations and grocery stores that no longer exist. I follow the road from the sea to the hills. I retrace the path of the tsunami, which reached ten kilometers inland. I see that there are still houses left standing on the slopes; the wave didn't reach them. And stretched out across the hilltop and on its other side is the temporary city. The town hall, built of connected metal containers, and container restaurants. Container complexes. No distinguishing marks. Down on the shore, work is in full swing. They have to raise the shore by a few meters before they can build a new city here. They are transporting soil from the hills on long conveyor belts. They'll open stores, pharmacies, dental clinics, fruit and vegetable stores, and flower shops close to the sea. And they'll build two protective walls right on the water. The first will be three and a half meters high, the second twelve and a half. And there will be a memorial facing the ocean on top of it. They'll plant seventy thousand pine trees all around. There will be a forest here again in fifty years. A single building remains on the giant construction site: a long apartment block close to the shore. It is five stories high with balconies separated by railings. The glass doors on the fifth floor are closed. Laundry is still set out to dry on one of the balconies, on a plastic rack with many clothespins. Yet from the fourth floor down, all you see is chaos. Broken glass, moldy mattresses, tree branches stuck in the window frames. At the bottom, there's an upended washing machine, and a pine tree stuck in a window, roots and all. The stairway is blocked by a telegraph pole. It's twisted sideways, so you have to bend down to go up. Wires hang from demolished ceilings. Broken dishes are strewn over the floors of apartments, and knives are stabbed into walls. On the topmost floor, cups were left on the tables, ironed clothes were hanging in the closets, and the beds were neatly made. The first wave was the strongest. It ricocheted off the hillsides surrounding the plain on which Rikuzentakata stood. The wave moving in from the sea isn't that terrifying: you're able to float on its surface. But when it recedes, it sucks everything in. Everything whirlpools. The second wave was the highest. It was the wave that pulled people from the rooftops. Some of them survived; they climbed the chimneys. The town hall employees—126 people—were standing on the roof of the building with water up to their ankles. Another two meters and the sea would have pulled them in as well. There were ten, maybe fifteen waves. Who was counting. People said that from a distance the water was rolling over to the point that you saw the bottom of the sea at times.

The first wave is just water—dirty, gray, and foamy. But each consecutive wave contains more and more cars, parts of houses, television sets, tables, chairs, kitchen stoves, mailboxes, bathtubs, street lamps, broken porcelain cups, plush armchairs, tea kettles, toothbrushes, and photo albums. A wall of water with everything that made up the city just a moment earlier. Dead fish, dogs, and people. The ocean backed off from Rikuzentakata at five in the morning. Those people who didn't have the time to run to the hills and weren't pulled in by the water spent the entire night on rooftops. They said they had never seen so many stars in their lives. And when the sun finally rose, they saw rubble covered in sludge. There were no gates, fences, gardens, walls, roofs, streets, windows, shop displays, closed shutters, bus stops, sidewalks, or trees. Only the sky. Intense, blue. Beautiful, they said.

Of the twenty-four thousand inhabitants of Rikuzentakata, seventeen hundred people died. The tsunami changed something that had always been the same—the appearance of the shore. Entire sections of land, where gas stations and produce stores used to stand, were taken by the water. Today the city ends abruptly. The waves took out the trees that screened the villages from the sea; now the inhabitants of those places, even those who don't live that close to the water, are constantly plagued by harsh winds. Cold gusts that smell of the ocean and freeze you to the bone. The wave washed away the round pebbles from the rocky beaches. People remember perfectly the sound those pebbles made when they were shifted by the water. It was a high, whirring sound. Since the tsunami, the only thing they hear is a dull, rattling noise. The rocks don't look the same, the pebbles on the beach don't sound the same, there are no trees to protect people from the wind, and the scenery has changed; instead of the forest line, you see straight to the sea. Nothing in this quiet northern world is the same. Only the crickets sound the same as they did before. People swear they can hear the voices of the dead in their song.

## What Lies Under the Water?

Once every weekend, Masaaki Narita packs his gloves, diving suit, mask, and fins into a black bag. The drive to the ocean takes him half an hour. He crosses a bridge and turns left onto a single-lane road. He passes houses with pitched gray roofs, the building of the closed post office, and a fish market housed in connected metal containers. Beyond the city, the road follows the coast, separated only by a railway track, which is frequented by a small train connecting Ishinomaki and Onagawa eleven times a day. He passes grass-covered hills on the left and the bay on the right. Fishing boats sway on the water. The green expanse of the Oshika peninsula fills the background.

Masaaki drives in silence. He doesn't like any distractions.

He is fifty-eight years old. He has a wife, a big new house with a small garden, a poodle with a bow over its ear, and a fish processing plant which employs a staff of fifty. He started diving two years ago, toward the end of 2013. He had a hard time controlling his body at first. He would exhale too much, have difficulties with buoyancy, or his fins would get caught on the seafloor and whirl up a cloud of sand, which would make the limited visibility even worse. Yet now, with over a hundred dives under his belt, he is in full control of his body.

He parks in front of a two-story house not far from the main road that connects the two cities. It's a diving center. Eight people showed up today, and they will be split into two groups. Masaaki does not take a seat on the couch, doesn't have any tea. He stands to the side, leaning against the wall, listening to the briefing. One group will swim out from the Oshika peninsula; seahorses had been seen there recently, along with a small fish with a comb that imitates coral. The second group will start off from the dock in Takenoura. They will search for octopus, small cuttlefish, and a yellow boxfish. Masaaki is waiting for his buddy, Yasuo. They always dive together. They've known each other for five years, since March 2011, although they recently discovered they had met earlier. They had attended the same elementary school, though in different grades. They are both the same height. Masaaki has an oblong face and thin lips, with black bangs covering his forehead. Yasuo has massive arms; he had served in the Japanese Self-Defense Forces, but just retired and became the driver of a bus shuttling employees to the nuclear plant in Onagawa. He parts his hair to the right, with a gray streak across his forehead. He has a square face, with thick eyebrows and heavy eyelids.

It was Yasuo who talked Masaaki into taking the diving lessons. If one of them can't go, the other dives solo. They don't like to pair up with people who come here for recreational diving. More and more of these people are showing up lately. After all, it's the only diving center in Miyagi Prefecture, if not in all of northern Japan. And there are lots of interesting things to see underwater. Takahashi, the instructor and owner of the center, makes an exception for Masaaki and Yasuo. They can even separate from the group, because they have the appropriate certification. As long as they don't swim too far off.

On the shore, they put on their dry-suits, pull their hoods over their heads, and load the diving tanks onto the boat. Once they leave the dock (it really isn't big, only five boats are anchored to the concrete pier) and go beyond the seawall that protects the shore, they will put the tanks on their backs and jump into the water. Masaaki doesn't talk with anyone. He had agreed with Yasuo on a set of signs, so they don't need to explain anything to each other. He concentrates on his breathing. Anything to keep his mind off the deep black sea below the boat's hull. Because Masaaki does not like the ocean.

He doesn't even like to dive. He finds no pleasure in it at all.

The Pacific is cold even in summer, as if the sun isn't able to heat it up enough. The dark water does not let you see into its depths. The shore is jagged here, a coastline pierced by deep valleys, with twisting bays, islands, peninsulas, capes and tips, on which provident fishermen build temples for sea gods. The most important of them is Susanoo, the son of Izanagi and Izanami—divine beings who created the Japanese land. As they were mixing the expanse of water with a jeweled spear, a single drop of brine dripped from the spear's tip, congealing as it fell. That's how the island of Onogoro was created. It was on this island that Izanami gave birth to other islands: Honshu, Kyushu, and Shikoku among them. The divine pair gave life to many more gods and goddesses, as well as mountains, trees, and rivers. But when Izanami gave birth to the god of fire, she died, burnt from the inside. Like Orpheus, Izanagi searched for his wife in the World of Darkness. All he found though was her rotting corpse. He ran from the underworld, chased by the curses of his love. When he got back to the surface, he stopped at a stream, where he cleansed his tainted body.

As he brought his hand to his left eye, Amaterasu was born, the most important Japanese goddess, the lady of the sun, who lights the earth and gives it life. When he brought his hand to his right eye, Tsukuyomi was born, the god of the moon, master of the night, ruler of the high and low tides. And when he moved his hands to his nose, Susanoo was born, the rebellious god of wind, storms, and typhoons. Caretaker of the ocean.

But one god is not enough for the Pacific. Shinto shrines with red *torii* gates were also erected for a dragon called Ryūjin, the ruler of the underwater world. The goddess of fishery, Funadama, has a special place on the masts of fishing boats. And an endless myriad of often nameless local deities, or *kami*, who look after bays, river deltas, beaches, waves, rocks, and trees, are worshipped in Shinto shrines and temples, or simply before stones that have their symbols carved on them.

Masaaki sits on the edge of the boat, takes a deep breath, and drops backward onto the surface of the water.

Suddenly it becomes very quiet. You only hear the heavy whoosh of air as you inhale and the sound of bubbles as you exhale. You need to calm your breath so you don't lose too much air. Your feet guide you into the depths, pulling your body down as it becomes heavier by the second and starts sinking like a rock. Maximum depth today is fifteen meters. Masaaki and Yasuo keep to the edge of the group, which has just spotted a brightly-colored sea snail. They carefully look to the sides and swim from right to left in straight lines. They stop near a pile of rocks and carefully move the sand aside to avoid creating a cloud, which would take several minutes to clear. But the only thing the rocks were hiding was a flounder and some algae. They catch up with the group, which is now on the lookout for seahorses. Two girls point to something. On the seafloor there's a big tire, covered with coral. Things like that don't make an impression on Masaaki or Yasuo anymore. They've seen sandals, the heels of which were covered with seaweed, and rubber boots, which became a hideout for black-spined sea urchins. They'd seen an octopus snoozing under a mattress, or washing machines that housed blue and yellow sea snails in their drums, and ventilators with rays hiding next to them. They've also found a wallet, a photo album, and a signed school essay.

But all they really want to find are bones.

Emi was born December 10, 1984. Her mother did not let her out of her sight. Her father, Masaaki, marveled over her tiny fingers, neat little nose, and eyes with their distinctive stare. "She's just like you. Like two peas in a pod," the entire family would tell him.

Not too long after she gave birth to Emi, her mother was diagnosed with cancer. The doctors didn't give her much hope. She hurried to raise her daughter. She wanted to leave her with as much advice as possible, everything to make sure that Emi would be happy. But how could she talk about a broken heart and growing up to a child who's only a few years old? The only thing she could do was to spend time with her. As much time as possible. She wanted to remember everything: her first tooth, first steps, first words, first toy, first dance.

Contrary to the doctors' predictions, Emi's mother got well. She decided not to have more children. She gave all her love to her only daughter. Once a year, they would go to Disneyland near Tokyo, just the two of them. They would dress up as princesses and take pictures with Mickey Mouse. They would go to the haunted houses, though they were both afraid of being scared. They would walk down the hall holding hands. They would wait for the parade, lit up with a million colored lamps, and the fireworks over Cinderella's castle. They would finish their day eating slices of pink cake. Then they would come back home with loads of souvenirs: key chains, T-shirts, stickers, refrigerator magnets. Both Dad and Grandma would listen for hours on end to Emi's story about how she met Snow White.

But it was Grandma who took care of Emi. When her mother and father were at work (she—a nurse, he—the owner of a fish processing plant), she would feed the little one, hold her when she was learning to walk, and practice with her the meticulous writing of Japanese kanji (山—mountain, 川—river, 田—rice field, 天—sky, 火—fire, 水—water, 力—strength, 生—life). She was the first one to hear about arguments with her girlfriends and about first loves. And she always had one solution: food. Oh, how Emi loved Grandma's cooking! Rice seasoned with vinegar and mixed with fried mushrooms. Pickled turnip and pickled cherry leaves. Salty egg pudding, with shrimp and a shiitake mushroom cap. Pumpkin marinated in brown miso sauce, soup with sea urchin roe, breaded tofu, salads with mayonnaise. And fish. Raw, steamed, fried in glistening teriyaki sauce, turned into pâté, or grilled. When Emi sat at the table, she devoured everything in sight.

Yet both Grandma and Mom agreed that Emi was Daddy's little girl. He would spend every free moment with her. After work he would take her to the park where they would play, hitting a wooden ball, jumping rope, or looking for four-leaf clovers. She not only looked like him, but had his character as well—conscientious and farsighted. She liked to keep things neat and loved brand-name clothes.

So it wasn't a surprise that when Emi went to college, she did not want to leave home at all, though Sendai, the largest city in the region, was only an hour away from Ishinomaki. She was late paying for her dorm. Reminders appeared in the mailbox. Always so conscientious, it was unlike her. She left to study English literature—in Japanese. She knew how to read in English, like all Japanese students who have mandatory English at school. But she couldn't speak it. Pronunciation is not practiced in class. She would come home every weekend. Although a bit angry with her granddaughter, Grandma would prepare piles of food anyway.

Emi returned to Ishinomaki after two years and started a job at Bank 77 (Shichijū Shichi Ginkō), the largest regional bank in Tōhoku. For her first end-of-year bonus, she bought herself a Louis Vuitton handbag. The rest of the money went to her grandmother and family.

She would leave in the morning and take the lunch Grandma prepared for her: rice, grilled fish, and pickles. Sometimes she would go out for a beer with friends after work, though she preferred to come home and relax, watching Korean soap operas. She would cry when the genius Seoung Jo would reject the advances of Oh Ha, her favorite character, or get emotional when she saw the blossoming love between the rich heir Han Kyul and the modest Eun Chan. And she would dream of a great love for herself. And lots of kids. At least three.

She was slender. She would pull her jet-black hair in a

ponytail that reached to her waist. She took good care of her skin—never exposed it to the sun—so it had a beautiful milky-white color. Always smiling, always cheerful. She would set her problems aside and be there for others when they needed her. She met Susumu through mutual friends. From then on, he was the one who would take her to Disneyland every year.

They married in December 2010. Emi had just turned twenty-six; she had recently been transferred to the Shichijū Shichi Bank branch in nearby Onagawa, her father's hometown. It was a quick wedding at the municipal government office. A ceremony at the temple, in kimonos, was planned for the following fall. Emi started preparations in March. She took her childhood photo album from her parents. She was planning on making slides for the wedding—the story of herself and Susumu before they met.

On March 11, a Friday, spring was already in the air. The sunshine was getting more and more intense: even young shoots were appearing. Everybody was looking forward to the upcoming weekend. Yasuo Takamatsu drove his wife, Yuko, to work. Yasuo had a lot of free time lately. He had just retired, after having a lifetime of serving in the Self-Defense Forces all his life. Transferred between bases: Okinawa, Miyagi, Aomori. His wife and children traveled with him. They had been together for twenty-two years.

They met through a *nakōdo*—matchmaker. Although it's nothing out of the ordinary in Japan, Yasuo hesitates when he speaks about it. Did he already know during the first meeting that they would be married? The thought had crossed his mind. Half a year later, they had their wedding picture taken, dressed as a European couple from the turn of the twentieth century. She was wearing a wide, full-length dress with balloon sleeves and a ribbon on her back, and a hat, from which her veil flowed. She held a green and white bouquet. He was in a dark-gray suit, bow tie, and vest, with white gloves in his hand. They were standing on a Persian rug, with baskets of roses in the background, a vine-covered column and a painted window that let in plenty of painted light. They were serious, upright, shy.

"Our life really wasn't anything special," Yasuo claims. Having breakfast together in the morning and watching TV together at night. Shopping over the weekend or taking trips to hot springs. There was nothing extraordinary. That's how they wanted it. And that's what he misses the most.

He dropped off his wife in front of the Shichijū Shichi Bank building in Onagawa, where she worked part-time.

"What do you want for dinner?" she asked. Yasuo made a face. "Just don't say that you don't care!" she added. Yuko knew that face all too well. But Yasuo liked it when she made the decisions. He weaseled out of giving an answer, waved goodbye, and drove toward home.

At 2:46 P.M., the ground shook. Differently than usual. Instead of moving left and right, it jumped up sharply. Instead of thirty seconds, it lasted nearly six minutes. However, for the people who hid under desks—who heard books, papers, glasses, and dishes fall off shelves, until finally hearing the shelves themselves thud against the ground—it seemed like eternity.

At 2:50 P.M., as the employees of the Shichijū Shichi Bank in Onagawa got off their knees and started to pick up the strewn documents, they heard the tsunami sirens. The manager appeared in the doorway, on his way back from a meeting, and ordered, "Everybody to the roof! I saw the sea moving back!" They had practiced this before. Once a year they would review the evacuation rules. The roof of the two-story building, ten meters above sea level, was designated as a shelter area. They quickly went up the steps. Only one woman grabbed her bag and car keys. Instead of going up the stairs, she headed for the door and added, "I'm going to get my kid!"

Nobody stopped her. An announcement resonated throughout the town: "A tsunami is approaching. Please evacuate to higher ground. A tsunami is approaching. Please evacuate. A tsunami is approaching. It will be six meters high. Please evacuate."

From the roof, the bank employees saw the exposed beach and fishing boats tipped to the side as the sea pulled out from under them. The bank building was only a hundred meters away from the coast. A few hundred meters further inland, on a hill, was the city hospital. A steep access road, a parking lot with an ocean view, and the building nestled up against the side of Horikiri mountain—the evacuation point designated by the local authorities. They were wondering if they should walk up those few blocks. It would only take three minutes. The tsunami was supposed to be six meters high, though. The water would barely reach the second floor, it wouldn't flood the roof. Yuko stood next to Emi and kept telling her that everything would be all right. She took out her phone and sent her husband a message: "Are you safe? I just want to be home."

After the earthquake, low, whirling clouds shrouded the sky. Gloomy gray. As if something had sucked all the light out of Onagawa. Snow started to fall. The men went back downstairs to get the coats. And then they watched from the roof as, off in the distance, the surface of the ocean started to swell.

And bulge. And then it started to hurtle toward the coast.

At 3:10 P.M., the ocean spilled over the seawall. The dirty, foaming water lifted boats and filled the streets. There was no single, giant wave that would spectacularly collapse above the city. Only surging water. As if somebody threw a giant stone into the ocean and the water was now flowing over its edge.

Lighter objects were swept off right away by the wave and taken further into the city. Five seconds later there was enough water to move cars parked on the street. Sirens wailed. More and more water. Higher and higher. Gray mass. Rapid stream.

One meter. Two meters. Three.

Trucks swirled on the surface of the water like plastic toys. Four meters. Five.

Over the course of five minutes, the water reached the third floor of the Shichijū Shichi Bank.

Six meters. Seven.

The water crushed walls, tore off entire floors of buildings with people inside and swept them away. Buildings collided with a loud crash. The Japanese say: *Goro goro. Goro goro. Goro goro.*

Eight. Nine.

From the parking lot in front of the hospital, you had a good view of the thirteen people standing on the roof of the bank. The men were helping the women climb up the ladder to the top of the generator box. Another three meters of life.

Ten. Eleven.

Cars, vending machines, roofs. The wave carried entire houses, as if they were torn away from an anchor. Yet not all the buildings were upended. Those with stronger foundations were simply flooded with water.

Twelve.

The wave started to creep up to the hospital parking lot. People hurried up to higher floors and up the side of Horikiri mountain. The tsunami flooded the reception and admissions areas on the ground floor of the hospital.

Thirteen.

Fourteen.

Nobody watched as the water carried away the bank employees.

The tsunami in Onagawa was fifteen meters high.

Yasuo headed for the city right away. But the road was blocked by a fallen building, along with piles of smashed beams mixed with wall fragments. He saw a fire in the distance. He had to go back home.

He tried calling Yuko. But the phones were down. He assumed she had taken refuge in the hospital. After all, that was an official evacuation point and each and every Japanese person knew those by heart. There was no other option, he thought. He spent a sleepless night in a cold house. There was no power and no heat. There were only aftershocks that kept him up.

He tried to reach Onagawa again in the morning.

This time he was able to enter the city. Or rather, what was once the city. Gutted buildings, exposed steel structures. Boats perched on building roofs. Mangled remains. Dead bodies strewn randomly across the apocalyptic landscape. Dog. Fish. Human.

Yasuo paid no attention to all of that. He just wanted to get to the hospital and look his wife in the eye. Tell her how worried he was about her. Let her know that the children were all right. That their parents were also safe. And that right after the earthquake, her father, who was living with them, cut off the gas and stood in a safe place, in the doorframe. That the house was there, the wave didn't sweep it away. Only the cupboard fell over and her beloved dishes were broken, European china kept for special occasions. But nothing happened to the collection of classical music. He listened to Chopin at night until the batteries in the player went dead. He was thinking about her. Is she warm? Was she soaking wet? Does she have anything to eat? He came to take her home.

The entire first floor of the hospital was covered in sludge. The floor was strewn with patient files, shattered bottles, broken stretchers. The patients were relocated to higher floors, where doctors and nurses tried to keep them alive in spite of the lack of power, water, and medication. Along with them were five hundred people seeking refuge and a roof over their heads. They were sitting on the blanket-covered floor. Older women gathered in the kitchen and cooked rice on a gas stove; not very nutritious, but at least it was hot.

Yasuo spotted somebody he knew in the hallway. He ran up to her. She turned her head away. "Where . . . ?"

She glanced at her shoes. Streaks of mud on her soles, damp and squishy leather.

"You don't know?" the woman whispered. He had to lean toward her to hear, "the roof . . . they all died . . ."

The woman said something more, but Yasuo didn't hear her anymore. "Impossible, impossible . . . impossible!" he muttered. He turned toward the door. He steadied himself against the wall, his hand just above the brownish line that showed the water level. He left the hospital.

He went to the school, the stadium next to city hall, and

the temple on the hill. All of them were designated evacuation centers. Yuko was nowhere to be found.

When the ground shook, Masaaki was on his way home. He was returning from the hospital with his mother-in-law. He stopped the car on the one-lane road along the seaside. He waited a moment; maybe an aftershock will come? He continued on when he heard the tsunami siren. A traffic jam developed on the road leading up into the mountains. He saw the approaching wave in his rearview mirror. It stopped three cars behind him. I don't know what you feel at such a moment. Your own heart beat? Masaaki doesn't remember.

He came home. But there was no home anymore. And along with it, there was no bed, no closet, no table, no computer, couch, TV or refrigerator, no pictures on the walls, no souvenirs from vacations, no dinnerware collected over the years.

He drove to work. But there was no work anymore. All that was left of the fish processing plant were its foundations.

He tried contacting his wife. She didn't answer. The hospital where she worked was located in a different part of Ishinomaki far from the coast. He tried contacting his daughter. She didn't answer her phone. They are safe, he thought. He came from Onagawa, he was born and raised there and that's where he had his first lessons in evacuation. He knew that the hospital in Onagawa was perched high up. He knew there was a hill behind the hospital. He knew that the Shichijū Shichi Bank was only a few hundred meters away from the hospital. He had peace of mind.

He left his mother-in-law at the school on the hill, another evacuation center, and went to check if anything happened to his employees. He employed fifty people at his plant.

He managed to contact his wife two days later. He didn't find out that his daughter Emi was taken away by the tsunami until Monday, March 14.

Of the thirteen bank employees who sought refuge on the roof, only one person survived. The clerk was fished out of the open sea a few hours later, hanging on to a wooden beam and frozen to the bone.

The woman who ran off to get her child instead of escaping to the roof survived as well.

The families of the twelve missing employees learned about each other very quickly. They would pass each other every day in the place where the Shichijū Shichi Bank once stood. They didn't have to say anything to each other, they simply searched together. They waded in the sludge, picked up dirty boards, and tried to lever up fragments of smashed walls.

They would pass Japanese Self-Defense Forces units (the very next day, the government had sent out 192 planes and twenty-five ships with 107,000 soldiers, who are not officially soldiers; that's nearly half of the Japanese army, which is not officially an army), who were walking around with long poles, checking for bodies beneath the rubble.

They would pass the residents of Onagawa, who counted on finding the remains of their life in the remains of their homes. Some of them would stick a board in the ground with their name written on it in marker, as if to say that *that pile of wood used to be my home.*

Yasuo and Masaaki would return to Ishinomaki when it got dark. And the next day they would return to Onagawa. They would come every single day. They didn't care about the snow, wind and rain.

First one day. A second. A third.

A week.

In Onagawa, the water swept away over five thousand buildings; 70 percent of the city. Every tenth inhabitant of Ishinomaki died. The coastline—the narrow bays, small capes, and steep cliffs, on which provident fishermen build temples for the gods of the seas—only intensified the power of the tsunami. The rushing water would accumulate, reaching heights of up to forty meters and forge its way inland, as far as ten kilometers over a stretch of six hundred seventy kilometers, from the city of Erimo on Hokkaido to Ōarai in Ibaraki Prefecture, just above Tokyo. The three prefectures hit the hardest were Fukushima, Miyagi, and Iwate.

Two weeks. Three.

Good news! The body of a bank employee was found. In the northern part of the bay, under the remains of houses. If one body was found, maybe another would be nearby? They lifted boards, dug through rubble, picked through glass debris, anything to get under the ruins. In the evenings, Yasuo would stare at length at phone, at the last text message from Yuko: "I just want to be home."

Four weeks. Five. Six. Seven.

They found another body! In the south end of the bay, directly opposite the spot where they had been searching. They moved there. They lifted boards, dug through rubble, picked through glass debris. They understood that there was no pattern here: bodies could be anywhere.

They looked for three months. Those who could took time off. Others had no place to work, because the wave devoured processing and manufacturing plants, offices and warehouses.

But after three months, the employers called. They were reopening their businesses. It was time to go back.

Yuko's phone was found in the parking lot next to the bank. Yasuo dried it and put it on a shelf. A keepsake, which would remind him of his deceased wife. Emi's father received a clear plastic case of her business cards.

In June 2011, one hundred divers came to the Sanriku coast. Volunteers from all over Japan. They supported the dozen or so divers from the police who had been working since March. On the seafloor, they would find cars, refrigerators, vending machines, boats, trucks, fishing nets, harpoons, and buoys. And entire floors of buildings. The water took five million tons of garbage with it. Most of it sank near the Japanese coast.

The divers would comb through the underwater city, inch by inch. Anything that could be identified went up to the surface. Recovered wallets, photo albums, personal name stamps, and collections of school essays ended up in government warehouses.

If they found a body, they wouldn't touch it. They would mark the location, swim up to the surface, and inform the police, who were standing on the shore.

A corpse is a corpse. Not a pleasant sight. A beaten-up body, softened by the water. Swollen, pale hands. Blue spots on the chest. Some of the divers refused to go back underwater. Little by little, the volunteers would drop out.

Of the hundred divers, only one was from the region. Takahashi spent half of his life in Australia and Indonesia and didn't come home to visit too often. Even after he returned to Japan, he lived near Tokyo and worked at a diving center in Kanagawa Prefecture. But his roots were in the north. As a child he would play on the beaches of Miyagi, go to Iwate for weekends; he graduated from the university in Fukushima. The tsunami robbed him of part of his memories. He decided to stay, and train professional divers in this part of Japan as well.

He bought a house in Ishinomaki; he and his wife occupy the upper level, and there is a kitchen and living room on the lower level, where he holds dive briefings before going out to sea. He trained instructors. He put up advertisements. Seahorses and small fish with a comb imitating coral.

After a year, the last of the volunteers went back home. The government would send diving teams less and less frequently. So, upon the request of a few families from a town near Onagawa, Takahashi would dive once a month, looking for bodies. The last bodies were found in July 2012. In 2013, even the most resilient families told him to stop. "It's no use," the mothers would sob.

More and more people believed that there was no way any more bodies would be found. Any organic material had decomposed already, they would claim. Those missing must be declared as dead and, against tradition, funerals without bodies would have to be arranged. Those left behind need to make a fresh start.

When Takahashi asked for funding, a local politician stared at him as if he were a madman and replied, "Just stop it." Takahashi didn't even try to explain to him that he was still finding bones. Animal bones, to be honest, but if we're finding the remains of dogs, cats, and cows underwater, human remains have to be there as well. And really, it's not the remains that matter. It's the searching that does.

The months passed and reconstruction started in part of the bay. The place where the port had been was cleaned and leveled. It became an empty, flat plane, now occupied by bustling workers and trucks.

After three years, the debris was no more. The only souvenir from the tsunami was an empty site where Onagawa once stood. That, and the brown line on the first floor of the hospital.

The city was coming back to life.

But for Masaaki and Yasuo, it still was 2011.

Every day, Yasuo would wake up, hoping to hear familiar bustling sounds in the kitchen. Yuko would get up early to prepare his lunch. They would eat breakfast together, the six of them, with their daughter, son, and in-laws. She liked to cook nearly as much as she liked classical music. In the afternoons, after she came back from work, she would reach for her CD collection and iron while listening to Bach. But although Yasuo wore down record after record on lonely evenings, Yuko never showed up. All that was left were memories of skiing trips together or of their trips to Lake Izunuma, where hundreds of thousands of geese and swans would pass overhead in the fall and winter.

Yasuo tried to turn on his wife's salvaged phone. He wasn't counting on much. The phone had been underwater for a few good hours. He was surprised when the display lit up. March 11, 2011 at 3:25 P.M., Yuko had sent a message to her husband that he never received: "The tsunami is enormous."

That's when Yasuo made a decision. He does not want to depend on the government and sporadically-organized diving expeditions. He would learn to dive himself. And he would finally bring his wife home.

Time does not heal all wounds. Time in itself does not have any healing properties. The only thing it can do is pass. It's up to us how we use it.

Masaaki and Yasuo's favorite weekends are those when they are alone with the instructor. No looking for fish and little snails, just the tedious job of combing through the ocean.

They have flashlights, dive knives to cut through lines, and mesh bags to store small items. They dive and they look. They keep looking. Forty, fifty minutes. They methodically move their line of sight, record every pebble and each shell.

Takahashi relaunched his search efforts when Yasuo contacted him in the summer of 2013. The men go out searching once a month. Three weekends a month, Takahashi lets Yasuo and Masaaki join the tourist groups and stay on the sidelines. He knows that they do not like diving with people who come to take pictures of the seafloor after the tsunami. It's no fun for them at all.

Yasuo and Masaaki divided the bay into squares, and they zigzag across it or swim along a spiral. Usually, remains gather in one place, carried by currents. These are the places they look for. Four years after the tsunami, they find only fragments rather than entire objects. The fragments are covered by a thick layer of mud and plant growth, and have sea urchins or crabs living inside them. The sea is recovering.

The deepest part of the bay reaches forty meters; the divers can only be that deep for just under ten minutes. So far, they have searched one-third of the bay. They'll finish in two, maybe three years.

But they don't give that a thought. They sweep across every stone with their flashlight beams. They take care not to touch the seafloor with their fins. Calm breath, slow movements, neutral buoyancy. Each breath is hope that they will finally find bones.

When Masaaki is done diving, he calls his wife. It frightens when her husband goes diving. She firmly clutches her phone in her hand the entire time. But when Masaaki comes home, he is a bit more cheerful. Sometimes he even smiles.

Masaaki does not like diving. He does not like the ocean. And he can't stop.

When underwater, he feels he is closer to his daughter.

For her thirtieth birthday, on December 10, 2014, Emi received a black Chanel bag and silver Rolex from her parents. Something she had always dreamed of. They are in a glass cabinet next to a plush Hello Kitty, a pink teddy bear, and a Mickey Mouse holding hands with a Minnie Mouse, along with a few photos in colorful frames of Emi from her childhood, and her bank employee business cards. Their edges are wrinkled, the thick white paper stained with brown water marks.

Masaaki and his wife still have the photo album that Emi had borrowed (her house was located higher up, the tsunami didn't flood it) to prepare slides for her wedding. They ordered a life-sized portrait from a picture in which Emi is standing sleeveless blue dress worn over a Mickey Mouse T-shirt, her hair pulled back with a red scrunchie.

Masaaki rebuilt his processing plant. Not for himself, though. For his fifty employees. They all survived. He feels responsible for them. He provides them with jobs so they can rebuild their houses, pay off old loans, and pay for their kids' after-school activities. Right next to the plant is a park where he would take Emi when she was little. Not too long ago, he saw a father and child together there. He has to find a different route to work.

Emi's husband, Susumu, with whom she would go to Disneyland, doesn't visit them anymore. During the first year after the tsunami, he practically lived with them. They would spend long evenings together in complete silence. He visited them less and less now. They haven't seen him for months. They know that he showed up in August for Obon, the Festival of Souls. Their neighbor told them he had come knocking at their door—but they had been at the seaside then. They had made their decision. They will live their life remembering Emi. Yet for Susumu, it will be better to simply forget her.

## The Four Tsunamis of Mr. Satō

The first one took his family. Only his great-grandmother survived and he knows all about it from her. The reason people survive is to tell the story.

It was the evening of June 15, 1896. It was the Meiji period; the Emperor returned to power, Japan was gaining strength and was building factories, a telegraph line, railroad tracks and metalworks. Yet in the North, life always ran its own course. *Ura Nihon*, the "back coast" of Japan. The boondocks. Tōhoku is an agricultural region which has been said to supply the capital with rice, soldiers, and prostitutes. The locals built the

Japanese powerhouse, but they did not understand the trend for western clothes, protested against the mandatory attendance of children in schools, and did not believe that the just-introduced constitution would change anything in their world. Only a few decades earlier, the mighty families from Tōhoku supported the shoguns in their battle against the clans from the South, who wanted to restore imperial rule. They chose the losing side. Most of the mighty masters had their land taken away and were converted to regular farmers. Wars and hunger weakened Japan's North. But the locals continued on as always—their everyday life was focused on planting, harvesting, and fishing. That day, people were sitting down to dinner; it was a holiday, the Boys' Festival. Kites in the shape of carp fish were flying above houses, while *mochi* pastries made of sticky rice and wrapped in marinated oak leaves adorned the tables. Because of the holiday, fishermen stayed home, and only a handful sailed out for the nightly catch. And that's when the ground shook. Ever so slightly. Yet strangely. Unhurriedly, as if the large catfish living below the earth's crust only stretched out a bit, but did not thrash its tail. One of those lighter earthquakes nobody pays attention to anymore. Even the dishes didn't fall off the set tables. People sat down to dinner. But, 150 kilometers from the shore, below the dark surface of the sea, the earthquake was very strong, a magnitude 8.5 (the greatest registered quake in the world to date had a magnitude of 9.5). Something really had to anger the catfish. Nowadays, scientists call earthquakes like these, which are strong but nearly undetectable on shore, *nuru nuru*. It's a Japanese word that denotes slipperiness, as if the tectonic plates slipped on each other. But this slowness and lack of suddenness are misleading.

A few decades later, writer and reporter Akira Yoshimura tried to recreate what had happened on the shore. In 1970, he wrote a book called *Umi no kabe. Sanriku engan* ōtsunami [Ocean Wall. The Great Tsunami on the Shore of Sanriku] based on the stories of people who had survived the great tsunami. He writes that "the seawater was beginning to get rough at a high volume, then receding from the coast gradually and picking up speed. It looked like a giant monster rising on his black dress. The water became extraordinarily swollen within the dark off the coast, and then as if the time was just ripe, it turned into a towering wall of water and began to move toward the coast. At that time, the local people near the shore were drinking and dining without realizing the dreadful scenario within the ocean. When they suddenly heard a boom, they looked at each other puzzled. Some thought it was thunder and others thought it was the sound of a cannon booming."

The wave was thirty-eight meters high. It killed twenty-two or maybe twenty-six thousand people. It destroyed nine thousand homes and ten thousand boats. Those few fishermen who had set out to sea that evening didn't even feel the tremors. Or even the wave surging below their boats. When you're far from land, you don't even feel the sea rising. When they returned to their homes just before morning with nets full of fish, they found a heap of rubble on the shore. News of the 1896 tsunami spread all over the world. In September that year, Eliza Ruhamah Scidmore, a geographer and writer, as well as the first woman in the National Geographic Society, wrote about it for the *National Geographic*: "The force of the wave cut down groves of large pine trees to short stumps, snapped thick granite posts of temple gates and carried the stone crossbeams three hundred yards away. Many people were lost through running back to save others or to save their valuables." In Japan, the newspapers would run artist Kuniyoshi Utagawa's woodblock prints showing a wave carrying burning debris, human body fragments, and horse carcasses. And the bare landscape. But the destruction was best depicted by photographs, a new invention in Japan at the time. Photography was probably first used in Japan in 1888 to document the eruption of the Bandai volcano in Fukushima prefecture.

The eruption was so big it blew off the tip of the mountain. Before that, Bandai was compared to Fuji. Now, it's nothing more than a broken mountain. Pictures from the 1896 tsunami show boats lying sideways in meadows, people wrapped in blankets, standing next to the remains of their homes, walls turned into splinters, or men moving wooden beams in the search for bodies. When you compare these photos with the 2011 images, the only differences you see are the clothes, telegraph poles, cars, and walls made of concrete instead of wood. And the fact that the 2011 tsunami was seen by the entire world. Mr. Satō's great-grandmother, who was only a few years old in 1896, lost her whole family then. She would tell her great-grandson over and over, ever since he was a little boy, in her strong northern accent: when the ground shakes, run to the hills. And that *tsunami tendenko*. Everybody on Japan's eastern coast understands this, but how do you translate it? When a tsunami is approaching, save yourself, don't worry about others. Run with all your might, leave your parents, leave your children. It will be here quicker than you think. Before you start helping others, you must first help yourself. A selfish act, without which nobody would have survived to tell the next generations the story. And to warn them that *tsunami tendenko.* Mr. Satō's second tsunami made him come to the realization that life is unpredictable. His father told him about that tsunami. March 3, 1933. It was the Shōwa period, and Japan was picking up the pieces after a four-year economic crisis, during which a wave of protests shook the country. Using haystacks as podiums, peasants would protest against the land owners who wanted to increase their own profits by taking away the farmland they were leasing out. Factory workers protested, and were joined by female silk workers who would walk through the cities at night and throw stones through the windows of textile factories. But since 1933, the country was experiencing an economic miracle based on cotton exports and armaments. Nationalist officers were plotting assassinations to kill politicians and businessmen. As a result, the Army staffed over half of the governmental posts. Japan was getting ready for a war, which the propaganda loudly touted as one against western imperialism. It started with the invasion of Manchuria in 1931 (and the establishment of the puppet state of Manchukuo a year later). And as if it wasn't enough grief that people had lost their jobs and had to return to their family homes, 1931 also saw heavy rainfall that destroyed 20 percent of the crops and left Tōhoku plagued by famine. Poverty was forcing fathers to sell their daughters to brothels in Tokyo, while young men were enlisting in the Army. The North was still supplying the capital with recruits for the Army and women for prostitution. It was a normal March day. Gray sky, gray sea. It was cold, and it snowed in the evening. Whoever could slept under an additional blanket. At 2:31 A.M., people were awakened by a strong earthquake. The catfish was angry, there was no doubt about that. Still half asleep, they dug themselves out from under the covers and instinctively went outside. When the ground shakes, leave the house; you don't want the roof to fall on your head. The earthquake had nearly the same magnitude as the one back 1896—8.4. The epicenter was also located in nearly the same spot, maybe just a bit further from the shore. The fact that the geological causes were different was of no importance; the tsunami that hit the shore thirty minutes later had the same height and power as the one in 1896. But people had remembered the stories their parents told them, so when the swollen ocean spilled over the cities, most of them were already standing on the snowy hillsides. Just like Ms. Tabata, who was eight years old at the time and whose grandfather always told her: you have to run to the hills, even if you are running alone. So she ran, and she didn't look back to see if her parents were there. The girl didn't see her mother being pulled away by the tsunami; she was found battered and broken, and died a few days later. Three thousand people died in 1933. Over one thousand were injured. The tsunami washed away around five thousand buildings and destroyed another seven thousand. In Hongō, a village on the shores of Iwate prefecture, only one house remained out of the hundred that used to be there. It was after this tsunami that some towns started to build sea-walls, while villages with more farmers than fishermen moved entirely to higher ground. Mr. Satō's father survived thanks to his grandmother, Mr. Satō's great-grandmother. She was mindful of the 1896 tsunami when she was building a new house. A beautiful wooden one, with a shingled roof. It was constructed using traditional methods, without nails. The planks were connected by fitting one into the other with bolts. So during an earthquake, the house bends and creaks, but it does not break. On the other hand, a house built with nails will burst from the inside in an earthquake. But the key advantage of Mr. Satō's home is its location. It's situated at least a kilometer inland, and around twelve meters above sea level. He's lived there all his life. In a room with an ocean view, he listened to his great-grandmother's story of the tsunami that came from the sea on Boys' Day, when kites in the shape of carp fish were flying over the entire city. And to his father's story of the tsunami that appeared on a cold March night. The third tsunami affected him directly. It was May 23, 1960, also in the Shōwa period. For the past decade, Japan had been experiencing yet another economic miracle. A country where people had survived off locusts just after the war was now a land of shining steelworks and noisy shipyards. Construction of the fastest railway in the world was underway; it was supposed to cut the time needed to travel from Tokyo to Osaka from eight hours to three. During that period, Tōhoku was supplying the capital with rice, workers, and electricity. Mr. Satō remembers that earthquake very well, although he didn't even feel it. But perhaps he would have been better prepared for it if he had had a television set. On May 22, all the stations were talking about the catastrophe in Chile. It was the greatest earthquake ever registered, with a magnitude of 9.5. It lasted ten minutes. But this time, it wasn't the catfish that was angry, but a human-like Cherufe made of rock and red-hot lava that lives deep below in the Earth's magma. If Cherufe doesn't receive a sacrifice, he will thrash about furiously, causing volcanic eruptions and earthquakes. Fifteen minutes after the ground stopped shaking, waves reaching twenty-five meters hit the Chilean shore. Two million people lost their homes. Nobody knows exactly how many died. Some people claim there were one thousand casualties. Others speak of six thousand. But Mr. Satō had no idea about all of this. In Japan, seventeen thousand kilometers away on the other side of the Pacific, the ground didn't even quiver. He went to sleep. In the morning, he was supposed to go fishing with his friends. The fishermen were the first to notice that something strange was going on. In the early hours of May 23, they were preparing to set out when the water in the ocean started to recede. They raised an alarm. Mr. Satō was awakened by his mother: "Tsunami." They ran up the hills behind their house. Twenty-two hours; that's the time it took the tsunami to cross the entire Pacific. The wave crashed into town just before five in the morning. Eight meters of water. Fifty-two people died in the nearby town. In Japan, the tsunami killed a total of two hundred people and destroyed sixteen hundred houses. Mr. Satō remembers what he saw after sunrise quite well. You go to bed planning the next day, and you wake up in a city steeped in mud. The ocean has a very special relationship with the land here; like lovers, they attract each other and then push each other away. The saltwater flooded the shoreline; Mr. Satō doesn't even know how many times. He had probably experienced around fifty such shin-height tsunamis. But the tsunami from Chile made an impression on him. That's when cities on the east coast of Tōhoku started to build seawalls on an enormous scale. The government decided that since a tsunami could occur at any given moment, they need to be prepared. Bays were cut off from the sea. People screened themselves off from the water with concrete. The seawalls ended up in the *Guinness Book of World Records*. They were the longest. The greatest. The widest. The most expensive. But even that did not prepare the inhabitants of the coast for the fourth tsunami of Mr. Satō. March 11, 2011. The Heisei period: Japan is in stagnation, the famous *bubble economy* has ended, there was talk not only of a lost decade, but two decades. More and more young people were leaving Tōhoku and heading for larger cities. They'd had enough of life on the sidelines. The fact that Japan is getting old and that there are more dogs and cats than newborns in the country can be best observed here. The seaside towns were empty, the main streets lined with shut doors—*shatto dōri*. The fourth tsunami was the most horrifying, although Mr. Satō wasn't scared while it lasted. Only now do his hands sweat when he remembers it all. It changed his entire life; he used to think not much more could change at sixty. First, there was a great thud, and that the ground tilted its angle. It's as if the great catfish had suddenly jumped up. But not at all lightly. None of that *nuru nuru*. Rather, it was a very regular *don don, don don*—loud thuds. And then the water came. Bigger than anybody could have expected. When they heard the sirens, people ran to the schools and hospitals designated as evacuation locations. They didn't see the ocean from inside their shelters. And when the water poured over the seawalls, it was too late for them. The tsunami flooded over half of the sixty-eight evacuation sites where inhabitants had taken shelter. If they would have seen the sea as it was receding and inflating, maybe they would have had time to run to the hills higher up. But, not all the breakwaters turned out to be useless. In the village of Fudai, Mayor Wamura took twelve years to build a sluice 15.5 meters high for just under three thousand inhabitants. He finished in 1984.

People were appalled at how much money he had spent on it. *Thirty million dollars!* And although the tsunami was higher, reaching twenty meters in that location, the sluice reduced its power. One person died; a fisherman who went out to the coast to secure his boat. To this day, people bring fresh flowers to the grave of Mayor Wamura, who died in 1997. But in other places, such as Tarō, where the walls stretched across 2.5 kilometers, the water reduced the seawalls into chunks of concrete that were thrown all over the bay. And in those places where the wave didn't destroy the walls, it would ricochet off them as it receded to the ocean and flow back to the city. Even Mr. Satō's great-grandmother did not foresee such a tsunami. The ground floor of the 120-year-old house, located one kilometer inland and about twelve meters above sea level, was flooded. Mr. Satō's bedroom was downstairs. What if it had come at night, like the one from Chile? Maybe he'd already be dead? It wasn't until the fourth tsunami that he understood what his great-grandmother and father really meant when they said *tsunami tendenko.* When the tsunami comes, you run. You run without looking back. So he ran. His parents were right behind him. His mother was up to her knees in water, while his father was swept away by the wave. He survived, though, because he caught onto a pole. Nobody knows how long he hung there. Maybe thirty minutes. Or maybe an hour. The fourth tsunami took Mr. Satō's gas station. It also took the piece of shoreline where the station had been standing. Along with Mr. Satō's boat. They found it near Tokyo, two hundred kilometers to the south. But why should he bring a damaged boat back home? "Scrap it," he said. He no longer goes fishing with his friends. Volunteers helped Mr. Satō rebuild the ground floor of his house. He found two porcelain bowls in the mud. He kept them as souvenirs. Those people who had heard the call of *tsunami tendenko* feel they need to do something. You can't just simply go back to what was before. So instead of rebuilding his gas station, Mr. Satō joined the ranks of volunteers. They helped him, so he helps in return. He meets with tourists who come for a day or two. They become volunteers. As they would cook fresh seaweed in giant vats, pick apples, or plant rice, he would tell them: *if you're evacuating an office building, use the stairs*. It wasn't until two years later that bodies were found trapped in elevators underwater. Never seek refuge on the highest floor. Or on the roof. You could think that since you're on the fourth floor, you're safe. But you're really only safe when you can keep on going higher. Do not escape in your car. Once the current catches you, it's difficult to open your doors. Mr. Satō doesn't stop talking, although he knows too well that rules will not help, really. In the future, people will hear sirens, but they won't run. Just like on March 11, 2011, when people in some cities decided it was a false alarm. The ground shook two days before, the sirens were wailing then too, but there wasn't as much as a centimeter of water. The warning system has been in place for centuries. Stones were placed in the locations that the water had reached, with a warning carved in them: *The tsunami reached this spot, do not build anything lower than this stone*. In other places, temples were erected along the line of destruction to mark the water level. But what difference did that make? Bushes grew over the stones, and people forgot why the temples were built. Who would have thought about that four hundred years later? People would go back closer to the sea, because it was more convenient that way. In a few villages, stones with such warnings were uncovered only after 2011, during clean-up work. That's why people will come back now, too. The government can plan reconstruction on higher ground, it can draw a line on the map to show where the residential buildings will be. These are not new ideas. They had already proven their worth. Just like in Yoshihama, the village in which all the houses were moved higher up after Mr. Satō's first tsunami. Mr. Satō's fourth tsunami only flooded the cropland there. "But in 30 years, we'll be living near the sea again, closer to the ports, rice fields, closer to the graves of our ancestors," Mr. Satō says. It's just more convenient that way.

## If People Were Dragons

Every single day, the Earthquake Track page reports:

One earthquake occurred in Japan today.

Six quakes during the past week.

Twenty-nine during the past month.

Seven hundred ninety-five during the past year.

The ground shakes here several times a day. Nobody even pays attention to the weaker tremors anymore. Maybe that's why earthquakes appear in Japanese literature less often than we would expect. Instead, described more frequently are twirling cherry blossom petals and the dense green hue of pine forests. Artists do not devote much attention to earthquakes.

The first mention of an earthquake was in the *Chronicles of Japan* in the year 720. The chronicler describes how, in the summer of the seventh year of the reign of Empress Suiko (in the western calendar that was May 28, 599), the Empress decreed worship. The Japanese burnt incense for the unnamed kami who would cause the ground to shake. With time, the kami took on the form of the giant catfish Namazu, who lived in the mudlands underneath the Japanese islands. Only one god from the Japanese pantheon was able to stop it: Takemika-zuchi, a fearsome warrior, god of thunder and the sword, also called Kashima. He brings a stone pole down onto the head of Namazu. If Kashima does not keep an eye on the catfish, it moves its tail and whiskers, thus shaking the ground.

The best description was made by Kamo no Chōmei in *Hōjōki: A Hermit's Hut as Metaphor*, where he recounts a string of unfortunate events that struck Japan toward the end of the twelfth century. First, there were great floods. Then came the great famine. Finally, the great 1185 earthquake that hit Kyoto, the divine city that prided itself on the fact that it was in the safest location in all of Japan.

"Also around the same time, as I recall, there was a great earthquake, and a quite exceptional one at that. Mountain-sides collapsed, damming the streams, and the sea tilted up and flooded over the land. Water gushed from the rent earth, great rocks split asunder and tumbled into the valleys below. Boats rowing offshore were tossed in the waves, while horses lost their footing on the roads. Not a single temple building or pagoda around the capital remained intact. Some collapsed, others leaned and fell. Like thick plumes of smoke, the dust rose. The roar of shuddering earth and the crash of build-ings resounded like thunder. Anyone indoors was sure to be crushed, but we rushed out only to find the earth split open at our feet. Lacking wings, there could be no escaping to the air. Had we only been dragons, we might have fled to the clouds!

Among all the terrors, I realized then, the most terrifying is an earthquake. The dreadful shaking soon ceased, but the aftershocks continued for some time. Not a day passed without twenty or thirty tremors, of a strength that would normally seem startlingly strong. Finally, ten or twenty days later, the intervals between them lengthened—it would be four or five times a day, then two or three, then every second day, then once in two or three. All told, the aftershocks must have been felt for around three months."

Kamo no Chōmei then continues: "Of the four elements, water, fire, and wind commonly inflict harm, while earth causes no great disruptions. Back in the old days, perhaps in the Saikō era, there was a great earthquake that knocked off the head of the buddha of Tōdaiji Temple and caused tremendous damage, but it was not as bad as this. At the time, all spoke of how futile everything was in the face of life's uncertainties, and their hearts seemed for a while a little less clouded by worldliness, but time passed, and now, years later, no one so much as mentions that time."

If people were dragons, they could take to the skies and need not fear any calamities. If they were dragons, perhaps they would also have a better memory. Like Ryūjin—master of the oceans, the grandfather of the first Emperor of Japan—who lives in an underwater palace built of white and red coral. An enormous dragon, with a silvery body covered in scales, fine whiskers, and long horns, that rules over the high and low tides. Its memory reaches far into the past, it can name all the earthquakes that have struck the Japanese islands.

July 9, 869. The Sanriku coast in northern Japan. Over a thousand dead. A tsunami floods the entire Sendai plain.

May 20, 1293. Kamakura (the military capital of Japan during that period). Twenty-three thousand dead.
September 11, 1498. Along the Nankai megathrust. Thirty-one thousand dead. Big tsunami.
December 31, 1703. Edo. Over five thousand dead. The tsunami injures over one hundred thousand people.
May 8, 1847. The famous Zenkōji temple in Nagano, where the first Buddha statue ever brought to Japan is rumored to be hidden. Nearly nine thousand dead. Fires, avalanches, floods. Nearly seventy thousand buildings destroyed.
September 1, 1923. Tokyo. Over one hundred thousand dead. Fires.
January 17, 1995. Kobe. Nearly sixty-five hundred dead. Fires.
March 11, 2011. Sanriku coast. Over eighteen thousand dead. Big tsunami.

Ryūjin, master of the seas, has an excellent memory. He could go on and on, naming all the earthquakes that came after that, even the smallest ones; after all, there are around eight hundred each year. At least two a day.

But people are not dragons and do not have a dragon-like memory. Kamo no Chōmei compares them to bubbles that float upon river pools, only to disappear after a brief moment.

## Mr. Frog Gives Warning

He walks into a bar and before he even orders a beer, while still standing in the doorway, he assesses whether the shelves are firmly attached, how much room there is under the tables, whether the glasses could fall on his head, and where the exits are. It's just his natural instinct. He identifies green zones (safe) and red zones (potential danger). He never sits in a red zone; he'd sooner change bars.

Mr. Frog is an earthquake expert.

His name isn't really Frog, but every time I look at him, I see a frog with a wide mouth. He has a flat face, his hair tucked behind his ears, eyeglasses with thick lenses, and his lips are long, thin, and lively. He's been working with earthquakes his entire life and now he's telling me all about them.

They are impossible to foresee, Mr. Frog proclaims. But when they do appear, you can give due warning. A special system for early earthquake warning uses thousands of seismometers placed all along the Japanese coast. When tectonic plates start to rub against each other, they release energy in the form of waves. The first is the longitudinal wave, referred to as a P-wave (primary wave). Next comes the transverse wave, or the S-wave (secondary wave). Every Japanese child knows this. It's taught at school. The P-wave is quicker than the S-wave, and it's also very gentle. It does not cause any damage, but merely informs us that the S is coming: in other words, the pure energy that destroys everything along its way. The S-wave occurs anywhere from several seconds to thirty seconds after the P-wave.

Those are the seconds that will save your life, Mr. Frog claims.

You'll have enough time to hide under the table. Or cover your head with a pillow.

You'll turn off the stove burner.

You'll move away from the street lamp, display window, or vending machine.

You'll stop your car on the shoulder of the road. You'll get off the elevator. A dentist will stop drilling. A surgeon will interrupt an operation. They'll seal containers with corrosive substances at chemical plants. The automatic brakes of trains speeding at three hundred kilometers an hour will engage.

Pipelines will be cut off at gas plants, and an emergency system will shut down the reactors at a nuclear plant.

In his everyday work, Mr. Frog looks for the border separating life from death.

The questions he tries to find answers to include ones like:

How should two-story buildings be reinforced?

How about seven-story ones?

How can we reinforce not only fragments of the external structure, such as walls and foundations, but also the internal parts, like ceilings, cabinets, or tables?

Mr. Frog, an engineer and earthquake expert, knows everything about them. He manages evacuation programs for schools and helps improve escape routes and warning systems. That's why, when he enters a bar and even before he orders a beer, he makes sure he knows which zone is green and where the exit is.

Given all the advanced technology available for reinforcing and securing buildings, the earthquake itself is not really that dangerous. It's the fire and water that are the threat. Along with the collapsing buildings, falling objects, and landslides.

The most important thing is to know how to act, says Mr. Frog. Because the ten seconds you get thanks to technology is one thing, and practiced, automatic actions are another. But your imagination is important too. Imagine it all in your mind, step by step. What will you do if an earthquake hits when you're at the store, and bottles and cans fly at you from the shelves? And what will you do if you're in the office and binders start falling and wheeled printers start riding all over the room? How will you act if you're at the movies? Or at a shopping mall with a glass ceiling? In your car in a tunnel? Or on a bridge? On the subway? In the mountains? In an elevator? And what if a quake happens at night, and you're in your pajamas? What if you're taking a shower? Or using the toilet?

Use your imagination.

Then start to prepare.

Secure the shelves to the wall before the earthquake comes. Install chains to secure books on each shelf. Place heavy objects on lower shelves: you don't want them falling on your head. Buy house shoes with a thick sole, the kind that shattered glass can't puncture. Get a battery-operated radio and a flashlight, which you'll keep next to your bed. And a fire extinguisher. And a first-aid kit, of course. Make sure you know where the closest safe (green) zones are. Discuss with your family how you will communicate and where you'll meet. Prepare go-bags, where you'll keep a copy of your ID and other documents, cash, socks and underwear, gloves, raincoat, one more flashlight, and one more radio, an additional first-aid kit, a lighter, and a few plastic bags, instant food, any medication and contact lenses. Keep the backpack close to the door, so you can grab it as you're leaving the house. Never run. Panic is not a good idea. Panic messes with your head. It's easier to make mistakes then.

Always keep a stock of water and canned food at home. For at least seventy-two hours.

When you hear an earthquake warning, the first thing you do is open the door, because the doorframe could warp and you would be trapped inside. If you have the time, turn off the gas. Hide under a table. And if there is no table, cover your head with something—a pillow, comforter or bag. Or stand in the doorway. And wait.

When the earthquake is over, extinguish any fires, switch off the fuses, shut off the faucets, close the windows, leave a note on the door for your family, and head for an evacuation site.

On March 11, 2011, the plates rubbed against each other at 2:46:45 P.M. At 2:46:53 P.M., the earthquake notification from the Japan Meteorological Agency reached the prefectures on the northern coast of Japan (Iwate, Miyagi, Fukushima). An automatic alarm went off—in schools, factories, at the television station, at radio stations, and on cell phones.

An earthquake is approaching. You have thirty-two seconds.

The earthquake was so strong that it tilted the Earth's axis, shifted Japan's coast by five meters to the southwest, and lowered it by a full meter. At that time, Mr. Frog was giving a lecture with his students in his office. They hid under the desks. All the books fell off the shelves, a real wave of books, Mr. Frog says with a chuckle. The books blocked the door; it took them twenty minutes to dig through them. What would have happened if a fire had broken out then? Or if a tsunami had come? Indeed, Mr. Frog says with a laugh, you always need to learn from your mistakes. But the tsunami wouldn't have made it there. Too far. And too high.

Thanks to the reinforcement of buildings (which is regulated by a 1985 law, introduced after the earthquake in Sendai in 1978, when over sixty-seven hundred buildings collapsed in the city alone) and repeatedly practiced evacuation procedures, only ninety people were killed in the 2011 earthquake.

Yet the tsunami killed eighteen thousand.

As far as tsunamis are concerned, Mr. Frog has only one recommendation.

Run higher.

Well that's all good, I say to Mr. Frog. We've been sitting here for an hour and a half in your office, which is full of bookshelves and has only one desk. I see that the shelves are secured to the walls, but there are no chains. If the ground starts to shake within the next minute, will we fit together under the desk? And won't a wave of books flood us?

Mr. Frog claims that we'll fit. And that the books won't flood us. Granted, chains on shelves are very useful, but not exactly practical when you are constantly reaching for a book. That's why he placed the bookshelf far from the door, so that the wave of books does not block the escape route. Once we've dug our way out from under the desk and books, we'll be able to escape. As long as we use the stairs and not the elevator.

I always know where it's safe, Mr. Frog tells me as we say our goodbyes.

He's probably right. Because after all, can't frogs sense imminent catastrophe? As far as I know, they will leave an area at least a few days before the earthquake hits.

## The North

In 1689, Matsuo Bashō, a famous haiku poet, sold his house and packed his writing utensils into a backpack, along with a paper overcoat to keep him warm at night. He bid farewell to all his friends and set off on his journey. He didn't think he would ever return from it. People would say that traveling to the North meant betting your life away.

Right after the shoguns from the Tokugawa clan united Japan at the beginning of the seventeenth century—which had until then been broken up into several hundred small feudal states—they established five main roads connecting the new capital, Edo, with the key cities in the country. There were also smaller official roads and many unofficial ones, yet these five routes defined the borders of civilized Japan. Anything that lay beyond them was considered to be the hinterland.

Of the five roads, most important were Tōkaidō and Nakasendō, which led from Edo to Kyoto. The first ran along the Pacific coast, while the second passed through the mountains. The third of the main roads, Kōshū Kaidō, went in the direction of Nagano, passing through a mountain range that the Europeans later called the Japanese Alps. To get to the former capital of Japan, Nikkō, you would take the Nikkō Kaidō, while the Ōshū Kaidō led you north and ended in the city of Shirakawa. Anything further than that was the *Wild North*.

The Tokugawas ensured the comfort of travelers. The routes were eleven meters wide and paved with stones; trees were planted alongside to protect from the sun and wind. If a samurai's horse stumbled on a protruding stone, throwing its master into the mud, the inhabitants of nearby villages would take the blame.

The handful of Europeans who were allowed to travel through Japan during those times would write in astonishment about roads that were crowded like streets in Paris. Traversing them were merchants, monks, small traders, officials, samurais without masters or messengers. But above all others, travelling these roads were *daimyō*, the rulers of former provinces—feudal lords, along with their processions. On the order of the Tokugawas, the *daimyō* had to spend every other year in Edo, and when they would return to their castles (the time and route of their return was closely monitored to make sure they wouldn't meet each other to conspire) they had to leave their families at the court of the shoguns. Their passage along the main routes of Japan was a display of power and wealth: sedan chairs, saddle horses, the Samurai entourage, and hundreds of servants.

The Tokugawas established control points along the routes, where travelers had to present documents issued by local authorities or temples demonstrating the purpose of their journey. In addition to the control points, they built official post stations, or *shukuba*, where travelers could stop for the night. They could give their horses a rest, have a good meal, enjoy some sake, as well as the services of women, *meshimori onna*, who would prepare the futons for the night, and then lie down next to the road-weary travelers (the law allowed inns to have a maximum of two *meshimori onna*—officially referred to as meal-serving women).

*Daimyō*, aristocrats, and high-ranking officials would stay at a *honjin*, an elegant building with sliding doors, a view of the courtyard garden and carved partitions. Less wealthy travelers could expect straw mattresses and fleas.

In addition to the accommodations, each station had tea houses, stables, sake bars, and shops with local wares. And of course, there was the administration office that managed the signboard that displayed wooden boards with proclamations from the capital.

The five main roads of Japan defined the borders of the civilized world. Yet Bashō, who had traveled the southern routes for many years, decided that this time he would cross this border. And he wasn't the only one whose imagination was fired by the North, with its gods and shamans. To the inhabitants of Edo and Kyoto, too, it was mysterious, incomprehensible region. Conquered many times, but never tamed.

On March 27, 1689, Bashō was ready. He left Edo very early, when the moon was still high, but the first rays of sunlight were beginning to chase away the darkness still lurking in the streets. In the distance, he saw the shadow of Mount Fuji. He stopped beneath the blossoming cherry trees in Ueno Park. His friends accompanied him for the first few miles, from then on he was on his own save one travel companion.

After a long journey on foot, he arrived at the gates of Shirokawa, the last city on the northbound Ōshū Kaidō road. Past the gates and beyond was Tōhoku. Bashō wrote that it was at that exact moment that his thoughts finally became sharp and clear.

Bashō returned from the northern lands and published *The Narrow Road to the Deep North*—the first Japanese travelogue that combines literary narrative with haiku. It speaks of moss-covered stone statues that have been standing in the same spot for a thousand years, although nothing in this country is permanent. Of forests that are so dense the rays of the sun never make it to the ground. The pine trees so generously soaked in dew that it's best not to venture in there without an umbrella. Bashō writes about farmers who, bent over, plant rice in fields tucked away in the valleys. About the simplicity of overly loud songs. And about the expression of fear in the faces of fishermen when they prepare their boats in the morning to go out to sea. The poet, a sword on his belt, ventures up to mountain passes that should not be explored without a guide. He visits hermitages where monks use coal to fill the walls with writings, thereby creating fleeting poems. He rests in the shade of a willow near a crystal-clear stream.

He writes about the smell of fresh grass in pillows. About fleas in dirty inns built over hot springs. And about the beauty of islands sprinkled about Matsushima Bay, covered in pine trees with their branches twisted by the salty wind. Bashō spent a sleepless night listening to the wind, watching the clouds sweep across the sky and reading what others had written about the islands. He had dreamt about seeing them long before he left Edo, yet he never wrote any poems about them.

Today, Tōhoku is made up of six northern provinces: Fukushima, Miyagi, Iwate, Aomori, Akita, Yamagata. People here have coarse facial features, dark skin baked by the sun, and cracked skin on their hands. Fishermen and farmers. Strong men, strong women. An accent that is incomprehensible to southerners: hard and rough. And a culture built around sowing, harvesting, fishing, and hunting. Blind shamanesses were village healers. Dried snakes were gods people hung from the ceilings in their homes. Freezing winters, windy summers, temples hidden high up in the mountains, ritual dances to the beat of drums.

Cities aren't too big here, surrounded by rice fields and hills. Wherever you look, you have the green of the trees or the blue of the water. Restaurants with fresh mackerel and tuna sushi. Small houses, each with its own garden, well-kept hedges, evenly-cut cedars, their large branches supported by bamboo poles to keep them from breaking. In late winter, the plum trees blossom and turn a deep purple color. In the spring, pale-pink cherry blossoms appear on black, leafless branches. Daffodils bloom in April, irises in May, and large heads of hydrangeas blossom in June and July. That's when the flowerbeds sparkle in all shades of blue: deep blue, sapphire, cobalt, cyan, azure, navy. In the fall, the mountains blaze with the small, red maple leaves, although the dark greens of the pines and cedars still dominate. And then comes winter. Harsh and severe. The entire northern world transforms into a land of white. It's no surprise that so many legends came to life here, like the one about snow maidens who kill with their freezing breath, or mountain creatures who feed on warm human blood.

It is difficult to describe this place; words cannot convey all the views, all the vast spaces, branches twisted in the wind, deep valleys, gentle slopes, forest trails, ragged shoreline, bamboo groves, rice fields in shades of neon green, the stone *torii* gates hidden between the trees, which lead to the Shinto shrines where the kami live. Kami are the essence of gods, people, animals, plants, natural phenomena, and things that surround us. You can call them ghosts, but how can you name something that you are not able to fully comprehend? Kami are usually gentle, but they can become impetuous and fierce.

That's why it's better to respect them and have them as an ally, and not an enemy.

Even today, people in Tōhoku are still quite aware of this fact.

## Dictionary of Prohibited Words

*Corpse*. A total of 15,894 *corpses* in all of Tōhoku. Add to that 2,562 people lost. A total of 1,656 *corpses* in Rikuzentakata.

*Coffin*. Made from plywood in the best of cases. And if they were out of plywood, the *corpse* was placed on a piece of cardboard and covered with another piece of cardboard. *Homemade coffin*.

*Crows*. They appeared in April. Many of them. Very many of them. It seems that some of the *corpses* had parts of their faces missing.

*Flies*. They appeared in the summer. Fat and sluggish.

*Stench*. The *stench* of decomposing bodies, the *stench* of the humidity and the *stench* of rotting sea salt. The smell of summer in Rikuzentakata.

Mr. Teiichi sits at his desk in his store. This was once the center of Rikuzentakata. Today, it's a construction site: cranes, diggers, trucks. Mr. Teiichi's seeds are housed in a shack with an extension made from mismatched pieces of wood; it's the only store in the neighborhood. You really have to have a reason to come here. Aside from journalists, nearly nobody shows up. Mr. Teiichi's square-rimmed glasses slide down his nose. If customers aren't coming anyway, he may as well write. He's taking it slowly. He chooses his words carefully. He checks each one in the dictionary. Then he confirms it online and only then does he copy the prepared sentences from his notebook to the computer.

He writes in English. There are words in Japanese that Mr. Teiichi doesn't even want to think about, not to mention writing them down. English is safe. Mr. Teiichi does not know any English.

*Monster.* The ocean wave, fifteen meters high, flinging a gray cloud into the air. As it ran rampant, the *monster* destroyed 4,045 buildings. The entire center of Rikuzentakata.

*Snakes.* That's what the waves looked like as they broke the windows in buildings and crawled farther inland.

*Killer.* People who were killed by it were found ten kilometers from the coast.

*Thief.* It stole Mr. Teiichi's house, store, and greenhouse. The only thing it left was the debt.

Volunteers from the Let's Talk Foundation from Tokyo help him write. They first appeared in Rikuzentakata in November 2011 to teach the locals English. They come once a month, check the students' progress and leave materials for studying. Mr. Teiichi attended one class. He learned English in school briefly, like everybody in Japan. But he was not a good student. The volunteers encouraged him to write down all he had experienced. He only wanted to write a single page. A short testimony of what had happened. He started to assemble words into sentences, and sentences into paragraphs.

Instead of one page, he wrote fifty.

He can't stop writing about the tsunami. Although he never actually saw it.

*Providence.* Mr. Teiichi's mother's house is thirteen

kilometers away from the sea. He went there right after the earthquake to make sure that nothing had happened to her. He didn't know that the *monster, killer,* and *thief* was right behind him, only half a kilometer away.

*Seedlings.* The plants that Mr. Teiichi was growing, and the reason he had wanted to turn around and go back while on his way to his mother's house (see: *providence*), to cover them from the snow. His wife made a scene. She is usually a quiet and timid person, but on that day she did not let him return home.

*Blackout.* The reason the gas station en route to his mother's house was closed. Three minutes later, the station was flooded by the tsunami.

*Mope.* An activity done at night, when the power was out and Mr. Teiichi had no news about what had happened in the city center. Mr. Teiichi *moped* about his neighbors, his house, his store, and his *seedlings.*

Mr. Teiichi does not want to say words like *corpse, remains, wreckage,* or *coffin* out loud in Japanese. But you can't run away from words; he repeats them unconsciously, like a mantra. If he doesn't utter them out loud, he quietly says them to himself. He has to write them down, otherwise he'll go crazy. But the words of a foreign language are themselves foreign. A string of meaningless letters. You can pretend they hurt less.

*Prostrate with shock.* The feeling that filled Mr. Teiichi when, from the hilltop, he saw the destruction in Rikuzentakata.

*Habit.* Something that tells Teiichi to listen for the whistling of the train, although he knows that the tsunami bent all the tracks out of shape, and to worry about his computer, although he knows that the wave swept it away. It's like Mr. Teiichi's brain did not understand what had happened.

*Identity.* Something that Mr. Teiichi had lost along with his home, store, certificates, greenhouse, and his *seedlings*, which he cultivated himself get two different varieties of tomatoes and eggplant that grow from the same root.

Mr. Teiichi cannot stop wondering whether the catastrophe could have been avoided. He studies the city's history and digs through the archives for descriptions of tsunamis past. He also measures tree trunks and calculates their age. Salt water kills the roots, so Mr. Teiichi believes that if the tree is older than the tsunami stories, it means the location is safe.

*Harbinger.* He's sure there was one. But people didn't notice it. On the other hand, fishermen claimed that strange things were happening at the beginning of March. Fish were disappearing from the river. And murders of *crows* flew over the houses, ominously cawing.

*Warning.* There was an earthquake on March 9, and the tsunami alarm sounded right after it. But the water in the ocean rose a mere fifty centimeters, and the wave was too small to flood the seventy-thousand-pine-tree-strong forest on the coast.

*Pipes.* Right after the earthquake on March 11, fountains of water gushed from the *pipes.* Everybody was sure that the earthquake had damaged them. But that was a *harbinger* of the imminent catastrophe.

In March 2012, Mr. Teiichi self-published the first edition of his book, *The Seed of Hope in the Heart,* in English. It consists of A4-sized pages bound together, with and a thin cover adorned with a picture of a wonderful pine tree—the SOLE survivor of the seaside forest where seventy thousand trees had grown before. The book is available for purchase at Mr. Teiichi's Seed store. The store is in the same place it had been before the tsunami. Mr. Teiichi rebuilt it with his own hands. He's always there. He looks after the seedlings in the greenhouses, checks the meaning of words in the dictionary, or stares out the window at the enormous construction site with its cranes, diggers, and trucks.

*Planks.* Fragments of somebody's home, which you can use to make a sign saying "It's me, the seed salesman. I'm alive" and pitch it in the spot where your store used to be.

*Rubble.* The place where you pull out broken *planks* and nails that you use to rebuild your store. Before you use the fragments of other people's homes, you need to say a prayer to ask the deceased owners for their approval.

*Wig.* Black hair found while searching through the *rubble*. Along with a strip of meat attached to it. If you find a *wig*, it's best to cover your eyes, go back to the evacuation center, and call the police. The police asked Mr. Teiichi to show them where he had found it. He asked if it was a *wig*. They replied it wasn't.

*Ladle.* A kitchen utensil which, when combined with a piece of bamboo, can be used as a shovel to dig a well five meters deep. Fresh water is needed for the new *seedlings*. Mr. Teiichi wanted to make the barren emptiness green again.

Mr. Teiichi publishes a new edition of the book each year. The fourth edition, enriched with the history of the city, is 137 pages long. The fifth one is in the works.

While waiting for customers, Mr. Teiichi started to write Chinese characters and string them into sentences. The Mandarin version of his book came out in 2014. Not too long ago, he paid a visit to his readers in Taiwan. When we met, he promised that he'd try to write in Polish as well. He translated the introduction to the book and decided that Polish was too difficult after all.

Now he's checking to see whether words written in Spanish are less painful.

*Cadáver* (corpse). A total of 15,894 *cadáveres* in all of Tōhoku. Add to that 2,562 people lost. A total of 1,656 *cadáveres* in Rikuzentakata.

*Ataúd* (coffin). Made from plywood in the best of cases. And if they were out of plywood, the *cadáver* was placed on a piece of cardboard and covered with another piece of cardboard. A homemade *ataúd*.

*Cuervos* (crows). They appeared in April. Many. Very many. It seems that some of the *cadáveres* had parts of their faces missing.

*Moscas* (flies). They appeared in the summer. Fat and sluggish.

*Hedor* (stench). The *hedor* of decomposing bodies, the *hedor* of the humidity, and the *hedor* of rotting sea salt. The smell of summer in Rikuzentakata.

## Cremations

Mourners dressed in black use long chopsticks to pick out bones from the ashes. One after the other, they place them in the urn. They start with the metatarsal bones and end with the skull. The deceased cannot venture out into the afterlife upside down.

When a Japanese person dies, loved ones sprinkle his or her lips with water. Family members cover the household Shinto altar with white paper to make sure that unclean spirits do not force their way in. They set a date for the funeral. You need to be very cautious here, as certain days are better avoided. Their names sound sinister. For example, the second day of the six-day lunar cycle—*tomobiki*—can be interpreted as "take along friends." Nobody wants the deceased to take them along to the afterlife.

A wake is held at the home of the deceased before the funeral ceremony. Family and friends gather to recite Buddhist sutras and burn incense. During the funeral service (91 percent of Japanese opt for a Buddhist funeral), the deceased receives a new name, or a *kaimyō*. That's when the family can finally feel at ease when they say the person's mortal name out loud, as the spirit will not feel summoned to return.

After the farewell, the coffin is transported to the crematorium. In Japan, 99.4 percent of the deceased are cremated—the highest cremation rate in the world. The cremation of an adult lasts about two hours, and requires nearly forty liters of kerosene. The deceased is placed in the coffin dressed in a white kimono, with flowers around the head and shoulders, a pack of favorite cigarettes or candy at hand, and, most importantly, six coins needed to cross the Sanzu River, also called the River of Three Crossings. Family and friends watch as the coffin is slid into the cremation chamber.

The husband, father, or eldest son receives a key. Two hours later, he will use it to open the door to a room where the bones and ashes are placed on metal trays. While they wait, those in attendance relax on couches in an adjacent room; sometimes the crematorium prepares a light meal for them, or sometimes the family simply goes for a walk in the neighborhood. If they don't live too far away and prefer to wait at home, they need to be careful. It's a good idea to take an indirect route to confuse the spirit, which might be following them.

As the family stands over the cremated remains, they are handed long ceremonial chopsticks—one set for two people. The mourners walk up in pairs, examine the bones of the deceased, and transfer them to the urn. The master of the ceremony, who describes and admires each of the bones out loud, hits the skull with chopsticks to break it into several pieces. The head of the family places the hyoid bone into the urn first, because it is the most important bone in the human body. Monks say that its shape reminds them of Buddha during meditation.

Sometimes there are two urns, or even three; one will be placed in the family grave, the second in the temple, while the third is sent to the grave for the employees of the company where the deceased had worked.

Cremation on such a large scale didn't really evolve in Japan until after World War II. Before that, bodies were put to rest in graves. Cremation, which cleanses the soul from impurities and transforms it into a caring, ancestral spirit, a great ally of the family, was something only nobility could afford. But in the 1950s, authorities recognized that burying bodies in the ground was unhygienic and took up too much space, which had always been scarce in Japan. Some cities even issued outright bans on burials, making cremation the only option. Over a million people die here annually.

Before the family brings the urn to the grave, it is set on their Buddhist altar (many homes have both Buddhist and Shintoist altars, therefore blending both religions. Incense is burnt near the urn all day and night. Depending on the region and family traditions, the ashes are placed in the grave one to two months later (usually on the thirty-fifth or forty-ninth day). The family visits the grave of their ancestors once a year, during Obon, the Festival of Souls, in August. The entire country is on the move then; sometimes the traffic jams stretch as long as two hundred kilometers.

The *ihai*, a plaque with the name of the deceased, stays on the Buddhist altar. It is one of the most important objects in the Japanese home. Actually, it's no ordinary object, because after the respective ceremony, the soul of your grandfather or grandmother resides in the lacquered strips of wood. The *Ihai* are set on the household altar according to a strictly determined hierarchy. The family places a bowl of rice next to them and burns incense, especially in those regions where the tradition is still alive—like in Tōhoku. You talk with the deceased like you would with any member of the household; you discuss your plans for the future, you ask for support. They constantly play an active role in family life.

The duality of Japanese beliefs implies that while the deceased remains with the family as an ancestral spirit, the soul must hold its own in the afterlife before coming back to Earth in a new incarnation. Seven days after the ceremonial funeral, the deceased stands on the edge of the Sanzu River. Awaiting the dead are two demons: Datsueba and Ken'eō. Datsueba, an old woman with naked and wrinkled breasts, decayed teeth, and claw-like fingers, strips the deceased of their clothes. If the dead are naked, she strips them of their skin. She hands the clothes to Ken'eō, an old man with a wooden staff, who hangs the clothes on the branches of a giant tree, its bark cracked.

Depending on the weight of their sins, the branch will point to one of three passages across the Sanzu River: a bridge, a ford, or a rapid current that they need to swim across. Awaiting the deceased on the other side of the river are more judges, the most important of which is Emma, the overlord of hell, with bulging eyes and a long tousled beard. Having consulted the opinions of the previous judges, he is the one who makes the final decision about the fate of the deceased. The soul may make it to one of nineteen hells (eight burning, eight frozen, and three isolated) or return to the human world. If Emma is gracious and chooses the second option, the judges after him will consider in which form the soul will return to Earth. Will it be rich, or poor? Beautiful, ugly, charismatic, or cowardly? Will it be a man or a woman? Will it die quickly or will it enjoy a long life? Will it suffer from illness or will the gods give it good health?

On the forty-ninth day after the funeral, the deceased hears the decision regarding his or her future. On the fiftieth day, they will start a new life.

This is unless, on the thirty-fifth day, by the decision of Emma, the soul ends up in one of the hells, where tortures are administered by hairy ogres—*oni*. Their blue, red, and brown skin is covered with scabs. They have five blood-shot eyes and blue lumps on their foreheads, knotty hair, bad breath, sharp claws, and black horns. Their twisted hands hold spiked clubs. They impale people, throw them off cliffs, eat them alive, scorch their flesh, push them into a river full of boiling members, or chop bodies into pieces with burning axes for half an eternity.

The dead can be rescued from hell through prayers recited by the family one hundred days after the funeral. This can also be done on the first and second anniversary of their death; these are the days when the final infernal judges deliver their verdicts for the tormented souls.

There's nothing more that the family of the deceased can do. The soul is on its own.

## Non-Memory

It was maybe March eleventh, maybe the twelfth, or maybe the thirteenth: all those days seem the same to me, I don't remember anything about them. I knew only one thing—if I check one more evacuation center, I'd definitely find them. So, every now and then, I'd grab the phone and dial the numbers. Sometimes I felt they were at home, and just needed to go back there as quickly as possible because they were waiting, worried about where I had been.

But they were still gone.

I don't remember how long we walked through the rubble. It was cold, dark, and snowing. We would trip over broken beams, fall into giant puddles of salt water, tread over gutted buildings, where you couldn't tell what was up and what was down. I can't remember how many times the ground shook; fifty or more? Several hundred? And how many tsunami warnings we heard. Each time, we would leave everything and run up to the hills. We would come back after an hour to continue our search. I remember that we reported them missing; the office had just been closed due to some explosion. The office now consisted of two tables, and working there were people we recognized; we had seen them before on the streets of the city.

All the official registers were taken by the tsunami, so they were registering missing persons on single sheets of paper at one of the tables, and people who had died at the other.

I didn't hear about Fukushima until later, but what did I care?

I was busy fighting for their lives; I checked, I called, I went. But they were still gone, every time. I don't remember when I first stood on the hillside and looked out onto the plain, where my city used to stand. I only remember the buzz of silence in my ears. Somewhere under all that rubble were my children. I started looking in morgues. I don't remember how quickly the boys from the Self-Defense Forces appeared. But they were there; they were climbing the toppled houses, cutting through walls with electric saws, sliding into cracks, and searching for missing people. They waded in mud up to their knees, stabbing the ground with long poles. I think that after about a week, they created a passage through that pile of remains. We could walk between the mountains of what used to be our lives, as if we were crossing an ocean. We found it difficult to recognize the places we used to live. It should be somewhere here, maybe a bit to the left, or a bit to the right? That is, until we saw a piece of a curtain, armchair upholstery, or pot that we had used every day. That's where we'd start to dig, to excavate our memories. Maybe we'd at least find our photos? Maybe our documents? Maybe a keepsake from our wedding, our weddings rings, or the holiday card from our child? At our side, the boys from the Self-Defense Forces were pulling out the bodies of our loved ones from halved houses. They kept them in schools, in bowling alleys, or sports centers. Entire rooms padded with blue tarp, and on it in were rows of bodies covered with plastic; you could only see the faces, so you would walk up and look into every face, hoping that you won't recognize it. I happen to remember that well.

They found my son on March 21. The wave caught him in the woods; he had gone out there with the forest rangers to mark trees to be cut. If he hadn't made that appointment and stayed at town hall, he would have been rescued from the roof along with 126 other people, who watched as the water rose higher and higher. Another two meters and they would have been gone as well. We kept the body at home for ten days. The crematoriums weren't able to keep up, and there was a shortage of wood for coffins. People were cremating their loved ones' bodies placed on planks and covered with cardboard. Over fifteen hundred bodies; they were only able to cremate seven people a day.

In other cities, authorities made a decision: they'd dig temporary graves that they would dig up later. Once the situation was under control, they'd cremate the bodies. And that's when they would be able to let the families transfer the bones of their deceased to urns using ceremonial chopsticks. But the mayor of Rikuzentakata said no. They were low on coffins and fuel, but nobody wanted to bury the bodies in the ground. We started driving to other cities, while our own mayor was supporting us and asking them for access to their crematoriums. I wanted to cremate my son in a coffin, so I took him to Morioki, the largest city in our prefecture of Iwate. He went to university there—he had his team there and his girlfriend lived there.

Over sixty people bade him farewell. I didn't cry when I was picking his warm bones from the ashes, because I knew that he was waiting for me at home. The day after my son's funeral,

I received news from town hall that at three that afternoon they had found my daughter, crushed by debris. We made a coffin for her ourselves. She was at home for three days, until we managed to arrange cremation in the city nearby. That's where she was put to rest. Because we no longer have our family graves. The tsunami took them away too.

## Survival Kit

In 2011, two million Tōhoku homes were left without electricity, and nearly one and a half million without running water. Several hundreds of thousands of people were living in gymnasiums, sports arenas, town halls, or hospitals, where floors were covered with blankets and walls were fashioned from cardboard, though a wall was a luxury item. For the first few days, people slept on bare floors in the same clothes they had on when they had run from the tsunami. The temperature would fall to -5° Celsius at night. Within two days, the government sent out trucks with water and distributed 120,000 blankets, 120,000 water bottles, and 110,000 liters of gasoline; yet many people did not see any transports for over a week. The tsunami destroyed twenty-nine thousand bridges. Roads were blocked. Mudslides came down in certain places. A tuna-fishing boat weighing four hundred tons blocked the access road to Ishinomaki.

There was no power, no heat, no hot water; actually, there was no running water at all; the woods behind the temporary shelters were the toilet, but if going to the woods was too cold for you, you could go behind one of the cardboard partitions and take care of your business in a plastic bag. It smelled. Nobody here had showered in a week.

For the first few days, people would receive one rice ball—one *onigiri*—for the day. Everybody was equally hungry. There was no gas, so no heat. There was no fuel, so no radiators. There was no power, so no light. Unless somebody found some candles. And matches. Everything was lacking. But you can make something from nothing. That's why OLIVE was created. A website where anybody can give advice on how to become a post-earthquake MacGyver.

### WATERLESS TOILET

**Materials:**
- bucket, with lid
- two plastic bags,
- newspaper,
- disinfectant.

**Preparation:**

Line the bucket with the plastic bags, one inserted into the other. Crumple the newspaper into balls and throw them inside; they will absorb the liquid. Spray with disinfectant after use and cover with lid. Change the plastic bags as needed.

### VOLLEYBALL PILLOW

**Materials:**
- inflated volleyball.

**Preparation:**

Release as much air from the ball as you need to achieve a comfortable height for sleeping.

### FLY TRAP

**Materials:**

+ bottle,
+ sake,
+ sugar,
+ vinegar,
+ scissors,
+ string.

**Preparation:**

Mix one hundred grams of sugar with seventy milliliters of sake and fifty milliliters of vinegar. Close the bottle and shake. In the top part of the bottle, cut out a hole three centimeters in diameter. Hang the bottle from the string.

### CAMP STOVE USING CANS AND OLIVE OIL

**Materials:**

+ three cans,
+ aluminum foil,
+ scissors,
+ toothpicks,
+ facial tissue,
+ olive oil / vegetable oil.

**Preparation:**

Roll up the tissue. Fold a piece of aluminum foil into a square. Puncture it with a toothpick in six places and push the rolled-up tissue through the holes (you can also use string). You now have wicks. Cut the cans about three centimeters from the bottom. Take one can, put the wick in it, and add a tablespoon of oil. Set the three tops of the cans around it, creating a trivet. Place a pot of water on top. Light the wicks. The water will boil in ten minutes.

## DISH

**Materials:**

+ bottle,
+ scissors.

**Preparation:**

Cut off the top of the bottle. Cut the bottle in half lengthwise. You now have two plastic dishes.

## TOOTHBRUSHING

**Materials:**

+ salt,
+ water,
+ cup.

**Preparation:**

Pour the water into the cup, add the salt. Rinse your mouth for a minute. Spit it out. Don't swallow the salt water, as you could get sick.

## STRETCHER

Materials:

+ two T-shirts,
+ two sturdy sticks.

Preparation:

Run a stick through the left arm-holes and through the body of first one, then the second T-shirt. Take the second stick and repeat on right side of both T-shirts with the second stick. The shirts should now form a long sling, with the stick-ends as handles.

Before you lay an injured person on it, check to make sure that the stretcher can take the weight.

## BANANA BODY CREAM

Materials:

+ a very ripe banana—so ripe that it's black,
+ cheap *shōchū* (Japanese liquor),
+ aluminum foil,
+ container.

Preparation:

Wash the banana together with the skin. Make seven cuts in it. Wrap the banana in foil, bake it (on the aluminum-can camp stove) until a transparent liquid appears. Collect the liquid in the container. Once it cools, mix with the *shōchū* in a ratio of 1:1. Apply the cream to your face, or your entire body, as needed. You can store it for up to a month. It has enhanced moisturizing properties. And a strong smell.

## HOW TO CONVERT AN AA BATTERY TO D

**Materials:**

+ AA batteries,
+ eight one-yen or ten-yen coins,
+ paper,
+ adhesive tape.

**Preparation:**

Place the coins under the AA battery. Wrap it all in paper and apply the adhesive tape.

**Important:** do not mix one-yen and ten-yen coins! This could cause a short-circuit.

## HOW TO KEEP YOURSELF WARM

+ Put newspapers under your clothes.
+ Wear things that have warm colors. Scientists have proven that they increase your body heat.
+ Put plastic bottles with hot water under your arms.
+ Tie a towel or scarf around your neck.

On the website, people also provide suggestions on how to make a headband from bike tubes, a cup from a plastic bag, a spoon from a milk carton, a kimono from a blanket, a doll from a toilet paper roll, diapers from plastic bags, sanitary pads from the sleeves of a cotton shirt combined with water-proof tape, and a child carrier from slacks. And also how to use smoke to preserve your food and prevent it from spoiling, and how to boil water for a bath in an electric rice pot, for when they finally turn the power on again.

## Grandma Abe

Grandma Abe treats me to coffee; it's so thick and strong that it's practically turned into a solid lump in my cup. It's brewed for fishermen seasoned by the sea. Strong men need strong coffee. We're sitting in a metal container with a concrete floor: it's the temporary fish market in Onagawa, Marine Pal Onagawa. You can see the ocean on the other side of the road.

Even at the market and in galoshes, Grandma Abe is an elegant woman. She has perfectly curled hair, a black shirt, black slacks, and a flat cap on her head. She has an entire collection of flat caps: wool, striped, plush, and leopard-print. She opted for a beige-colored model today. She offers me little fish no bigger than the white of my fingernail to try.

"It's *shirasu*, sardine fry. I marinated it myself," she says as she serves me a helping with some rice.

Not much going on here. Vendors are waiting for customers. Laid out on crushed ice are some silvery Pacific saury, a small fish with an elongated body. It's the pride of Onagawa: local fishermen catch the most saury in all of Honshu. Crabs with tightly-fastened claws wriggle around in Styrofoam containers. Lines of octopus fill the counters. They already have the first scallops and tiny (the season doesn't start until next month) *hoya*, little red creatures with shells that look like a small hoof. The Japanese call them sea pineapples.

Grandma Abe gives me some raw *hoya* to try, explaining that "I sometimes marinate or smoke them, but when they're raw, you get a mix of sweet, salty, bitter, and tart. Goes great with sake. It's too bad you didn't come a few weeks earlier, we've just stopped harvesting *wakame* seaweed, and we have the very best in the world. The Pacific is cold here, the current strong, so our seaweed is succulent and plump. You'd pay a fortune for a kilogram of it in Tokyo. But they'll never be as fresh as the ones you eat straight from the catch. We just immerse it in boiling water and give it a quick stir with chopsticks, left to right. We call that sound *shabu shabu*. They change their color from brown to green. We pour *ponzu* sauce over it. It's based on soy sauce and citrus fruits, and has a sweet-and-sour taste. It's heavenly, you must come back next year, the season ends at the beginning of April. Our local council has introduced strict regulations to guarantee the quality of our *wakame*. After the *wakame*, it's scallop season. You sail out ten minutes by boat and pull out lines full of flat, cream-colored shells. The best ones are for sale. But sometimes, you'll have some on the boat for lunch; raw scallops cut into slices with a splash of soy sauce, the freshest sashimi ever. No, you can never get bored of that taste. Then there's the *hoya*, you've already tried that, would you like some more? In September, we catch sea urchins, their season runs through fall and winter, but the taste changes. The ones caught in September are the best: slightly buttery, sweet, and they don't fall apart. The later ones are too bitter, no taste at all. We wrap up the season with oysters. We don't catch anything in the winter, we clean our lines and plant seaweed seeds on them. And that's how it goes," Grandma Abe says, while she grabs more *shirasu* with chopsticks and adds them to my bowl. "Here you go, try this too, it's *kombu maki*, I came up with the recipe myself. It's marinated saury rolled in marinated seaweed. Almost like sushi, but *kombu maki* can keep for months. I come from Kesennuma, a large port to the north of here. Fishermen from Kesennuma would sail out to catch tuna for several months at a time. The women would prepare food that would not spoil and have the taste of home. That was my model. It took me a year to conjure up the recipe. I changed the proportions, cooking time, types of sauces. Until I finally perfected it. Do you know that the minister gave me an award? That was back in '89.

"Try this, it's a bit sweeter, and that one is a bit more savory; most people serve it on rice, but some people cut it into pieces and eat it like an appetizer. The entire process has twenty-seven steps; come on, I won't reveal all my secrets to you. Okay, so you cut off the head and tail of the saury, gut it, remove the bones, wash it, cook it, fry it, clean it, marinate in a sauce, fry it again, and then you roll it by hand in seaweed, which had been marinated in soy sauce with some sugar. You pack it, scald it, dry it, clean it and put it into cardboard packaging. We do everything by hand. A pot, a pan, and a burner; that's all you need. I rebuilt everything quicker than the government did. My factory was one of the first buildings that went up in Onagawa.

"I won't tell you anything about the tsunami. There's nothing t0o talk about.

"Here, try some of this, it's fermented squid viscera, typically Japanese. And this is really tasty too, it's just marinated mackerel.

"Would you like some more rice? I'll heat some up for you. If we had met at my house, I would've given you some pickled cucumbers and cabbage, but here, at the market . . .

"Wait, aren't you cold? This place is like a refrigerator after all. No, I'm never cold.

"I remember perfectly when the volunteers showed up; they got here very quickly, I think it was the week after. They asked me if I needed anything; the only thing I did need was a bicycle. Two days later I rode my new bike forty kilometers inland. A different world. Normal streets, normal houses. Supermarkets with packed shelves. I would pedal out there stocked with *kombu maki*, and come back with other merchandise. Three months after the tsunami, my business was rolling. What else could I do? People here don't like to just sit around and do nothing. Not too long ago, up there on the hill, in an old shack with a view of the bay, they opened the House of Dreams. Founded by women. Fourteen mothers, a small restaurant, a pleasant little place. The youngest ones, the sixty-year-olds, cook on Mondays, the seventy-year-olds on Tuesdays, and the eighty-year-olds on Wednesdays, and they keep rotating like that. Grilled fish *miso* soup with local seaweed, rice with *umeboshi*, salted Japanese plums, and for dessert, figs, which we eat with the skin. The figs are grown by the *papa chan*—that's what we call the grandfathers who lend a hand at the House of Dreams. No, not with the cooking, no way! They plant vegetables in the garden. Nothing heavy: garlic, chili, and the figs. They wouldn't be able to lift a pumpkin. They're all well over seventy! Though not much older than I am, really. Wait, maybe you'd like some more coffee?

"You'll hear a lot of stories like that here. Not too far from here, on Oshika Peninsula, the wives of fishermen made necklaces from unused fishing nets. Oshika is that green hill sticking out of the water there. In terms of its administration, it's a part of Ishinomaki, but they're closer to Onagawa. Ten years ago, everything got mixed up here, the government introduced some reforms, three cities were combined into one, and that's why you've got three city centers now, along with rice fields, pastures, villages, mountains, and woods in between. Onagawa could have been linked up with Ishinomaki, but we didn't want to. We have our own nuclear power plant, and our government did not want to share the money they were making from it. All right, it's not the power plant I wanted to tell you about, but the fishermen's wives. We local women are bound with the sea. Now these women, from that village on Oshika Peninsula, would breed oysters, scale fish, clean fish, or clean fishing lines and nets. Tough cookies. So it was no surprise that they did not intend to sit around doing nothing. They had no work to do with the fish—they had to come up with something else. So the women started making necklaces from antlers and fishing nets. The stag is a symbol of happiness here. And renewal. It grows new antlers every year. The necklaces are beautiful. They look like Indian amulets, you know, the ones that catch dreams.

But of course, my dear, women are strong here: after all, we are the ones who give life. And each birth is like the climb up Mount Everest. I gave birth four times. After that, I'm ready to go through any catastrophe. Are you still hungry? Because I've prepared a bowl of rice with dried jellyfish in a citrus marinade. And you know what the fishermen are saying? That the oysters are growing bigger. And that the seaweed is richer in taste. Oh, and don't forget to take some rice balls with mackerel. I'll wrap them up for you."

## Expired

The houses were really well designed. Thirty square meters, and there's room for everything. A folding table, washer, stove, kitchen, a bathtub the size of a foot bath, a toilet, two rooms, each with two futons, so an entire four-person family can sleep together. That will keep them warmer at night, especially in the winter, when cold seeps through the metal walls. There are people who don't want to go outside at all. They stay indoors all day with the curtains drawn and they don't talk to their neighbors. Nobody can see what's going on inside, although you can hear everything through the metal walls. Last month, one man committed suicide. He jumped into the river. He was thirty-one years old.

I'm at a complex of temporary housing. It's a large area covered in concrete, with houses arranged in neat rows, one after the other. It's easy to get lost here, every street looks the same. Metal walls, plastic windows; the only greenery are the potted flowers by the doors, intended to recreate the gardens these families once had, before living in these coffins bolted together from metal parts. The walls are so thin that your neighbor practically lives with you. You can hear him echoing the laugh tracks on Japanese TV shows, flushing the toilet, arguing with his wife, and snoring at night.

They were built with an expiration date. Two years. In accordance with standards of humanitarian aid in crisis situations.

The metal walls are cold in the winter; you have to be careful not to touch them. Your morning shower turns into an adventure. In the summer, on the other hand, it's hard to stay inside. Opening the windows doesn't help at all, and you could fry an egg on the roof.

So the people sit outside. They stare at the evenly arranged rows of houses, at the vast space with no greenery.

They're bored.

Local officials try everything. Morning exercises, Saturday tea. Together they mash sticky rice for mochi cookies and make props for a play that tells the story of how bad things are. Maybe they'll feel better then?

The residents try to add some variety on their own. Women meet up—two to five of them, and they fold paper cranes. Or make phone charms from wads of material. Older people wait for Saturday, when the volunteers come. One week it's the monk with coffee, another the masseurs, then the photographers, or an occasional group from Tokyo; none of them know what to do with themselves: they'd like to help, but with what? So they all sit around, bored together.

The inhabitants of the temporary complexes liven up a bit when the conversation turns to the construction of the government-built seawalls. An ambitious project worth a ¥1 trillion ($8.5 billion), consisting of four hundred kilometers of wall that will separate the shore from the sea. A protective wall is madness, people here say. It will destroy nature, they add. We need to be like bamboo or a willow—flexible in the wind, and not stand up to nature with a wall. Why is it a crazy idea? Look at Okushiri Island, which was destroyed by the tsunami in 1993. All of it. Then it was converted into a fortress. Fourteen kilometers of the eighty-four-kilometer shoreline is a thick wall. At its highest point, it reaches 11.7 meters. The houses standing on the shore don't get any light any more. But that's not all! The fauna and flora are changing as well. A small crustacean living on the beach was once blue, now it's turned white. They've protected themselves with that wall, they've built four gates on four rivers, each home has speakers hooked up to an early warning system. They built a platform that has room for four hundred forty people. Around forty evacuation roads with solar-powered road signs lead up to the hills.

They think they're safe. But they've been cut off from the sea. They don't see how it changes color, how it churns, how it reacts. They won't see the danger.

Residents of the temporary housing are also critical of the fact that seawalls are being built instead of apartments. You can't really live on a breakwater, can you? And really, only running away will save you from a tsunami. The government will claim great success, yet wouldn't it be better if they finished the apartment buildings so all these people can move out of here one day? The temporary sheet-metal factories and buildings stand on government land, so you can't build anything here; you'd have to remove the temporary settlement first. And the government itself banned any construction right on the shore. The land in other places is private, and people are building their own houses there. You've still got the mountains, but how can you build anything on the hillsides? Some cities are demolishing summits, smashing hillsides, and creating plateaus. That takes time. But once those houses are finally built (which was supposed to happen in 2013, then in 2014, and then 2015, and now they're talking about 2017, maybe 2018), they'll finally live in comfort. Three rooms with an ocean view, kitchen, bathroom, and normal walls. A bit of privacy, finally. But, they say with raised voices, let's hope that the government makes it before 2020 when the Olympic games are to take place in Tokyo. Even now, more and more people are leaving their jobs here to go build the Olympic stadium.

In 2011, around 68,000 people were moved to temporary housing (out of the nearly 350,000 who were evacuated, although even government statistics seem to be lost here, as some data suggest that as many as 470,000 people were evacuated).

In 2012, 204,000 people were living in temporary housing (out of 330,000 who were evacuated).

In 2013, 179,000 were still residing there (out of 310,000 evacuated). The expiration date of the temporary housing, which was to pass this year, was extended for another two years.

In 2014, 150,000 people (out of 260,000 evacuated).

In 2015, 117,000 people (out of 220,000 evacuated).

The expiration date for the temporary housing was extended once again, by a year or two, depending on the decision of local governments.

In spring of 2016, 65,000 people (out of 170,000 evacuated) were still living in temporary housing. After the great 1995 earthquake in Kobe, it took five years to build 25,000 apartments for all the evacuees.

Tōhoku needs 29,500 apartments. By mid-2015, 11,000 had been built. Some officials are predicting that the temporary housing will still be used until at least 2021. People who were able to, moved out. Those who stayed were retirees or people who could not afford to rent an apartment. Perhaps they're paying off old loans, or maybe they lost their jobs, or maybe they aren't making enough.

In the summer, they sit on benches in front of their houses. In winter, they huddle inside, buried under blankets, and try to heat the cold walls with radiators. They wait. And they feel like second-class citizens.

Expired.

## A White Spot

Post-tsunami clean-up operations involved the help of fire-fighters, police officers, volunteers, and non-soldiers (because what else can you call them, since Japan has no army according to the post-war constitution?). Twenty-four million tons of remains. And probably a few hundred million tons of mud. There were no rules in the post-tsunami world, except for one: clean up everything as fast as you can. Containers from corrosive substances, cables, plastic bottles, and heavy draperies were piled up to be burned.

But you do not burn memories. Local authorities provided access to buildings that had been salvaged and made into temporary storage spaces for memories that had been collected and boxed up. They'll figure out what to do with them later.

Ms. Shimada was the first person to tell Munemasa Takahashi about recovering memories; he in turn launched the Lost & Found project. She had already been looking for them on her own. Right after the tsunami, Ms. Shimada would stand for hours on end in front of the empty space that was once her home. She stared at the ground and did not understand what had happened. She sent her children to stay with family in Sendai, an hour away from Yamamoto. She stayed to help the people living in the evacuation center, cooking soup for them. It wasn't until a week after the first transports with aid had arrived that she joined her children. That was a strange feeling. This was supposed to be her home from now on? She was looking for memories from the very start, during those very first days. What was she feeling? It was hard to express. She would suddenly recognize some little detail and know right away that that was it, she had found a fragment of herself. It was like a feeling of joy flowing from somewhere deep within. She did not find all of her memories. She dug up the last one two years later. She always carries it with her, in her pocket.

The memories gathered by firefighters, police officers, volunteers, and non-soldiers are stuck together, soaked through, and covered in mud. They started to rot when the weather started getting warmer. That's why some cities kept the memories in freezers.

You have to clean them before you give the memories back to the owners. The process is quite simple, though time-consuming. You need to separate the memories that are stuck together. Clean the caked-on mud from them with a brush. Dip them in lukewarm water. No hotter than 30° Celsius and no colder than 20° Celsius. That allows you to get rid of the layer of salt that eats into the silver coating. Then you have to remove the rest of the mud with a small brush. Take out the memory and pin it on a clothes line. Dry it in a dark room where there is no dust. Then you have to number it. Copy any sentences written on the back of these memories or on album pages: "Starting to express wants in broken sentences. Keeps asking to go out. Scared of *daruma* dolls."

Yamamoto. Seven hundred fifty thousand memories.

Ōtsuchi. Three hundred thousand memories

Kesennuma. One million two hundred thousand memories.

Ōfunato. Three hundred fifty thousand memories.

Sendai. Three hundred thousand memories

Natori. Two hundred forty thousand memories.

Onagawa, Rikuzentakata and Minamisanriku. Over four hundred thousand memories.

Once the memories have dried, they are photographed—one photo for each memory. Or the memories are scanned. Then they are put back into the cleaned albums. Those brought in bulk are placed in a box labelled with the location where they were found. Armed with boxes of memories, volunteers visit temporary housing. Maybe somebody will recognize themselves. Some organizations create internet databases, where memories are divided into categories: black & white, vacations, weddings, children, sports. People spend long hours looking over the faces, buildings, clothing patterns. They need to find at least a little piece of something that would connect them with the life that had ended. A confirmation that the cities they lived in had existed. That the people they loved existed. And that they themselves existed. This is how I imagine it: some people talk with others, drinking tea. Others do not say a word to anybody while they swiftly skim through stacks of memories.

Just like Miyoko, a seventy-year-old woman, whose short fingers quickly flip through memories placed in a box. Her gaze is focused as she looks for one detail that will catch her attention. "I was chubbier when I was young," Miyoko says with a laugh to Frank Langfitt, an NPR reporter, who looks on as the woman finds a memory from her daughter's first day of school. It shows the other mothers dressed in kimonos; they sit with their hands in their laps. Miyoko points to one of the women. "Kayo Suzuki. She was washed away as she ran from the tsunami. This is Kayoko Kon. I heard she went back home to get her belongings."

Yamamoto. Seven hundred fifty thousand pictures.

Ōtsuchi. Three hundred thousand pictures.

Kesennuma. One million two hundred thousand pictures.

Ōfunato. Three hundred fifty thousand pictures.

Sendai. Three hundred thousand pictures.

Natori. Two hundred forty thousand pictures.

Onagawa, Rikuzentakata and Minamisanriku. Over four hundred thousand pictures.

The tsunami turned the pictures into abstract works of art. Colors disappeared in places where the bacteria ate the silver particles on the paper. White paper with spots—legs in shorts, folded hands, a piece of a wedding dress, a bouquet, the nose of a big Buddha, an arm in a suit, a brooch, an eye, a child's smile. Some pictures are discolored, others look like somebody had applied a red and yellow filter to them. Or was having fun by using effects like desaturation, freezing, pastels, pencil sketch, oil paints, mosaic bubbles, a watercolor sponge, or film grain. Blurred images. Spots of color and gray blotches like a brush stroke of ink. Scratches like on glass. Yellow streaks. Black streaks. Fuzzy lines. Regular black dots. An orange glare. And in the background, people. At the beach, in business meetings, at a ceremony for the end of the school year, in front of the temple gate, in the park, at home, skiing, at the seaside. The pictures in which you can see at least a part of a building, even a clothing pattern, even a note on the back, are cleaned, dried, and photographed or scanned. Maybe somebody will recognize the roof of the school? The daughter's kimono? The handwriting of a brother with whom they had visited Tokyo in 1954? Maybe thanks to these bits and pieces, people can go back, if even for a moment, to that sun-filled summer when the whole family enjoyed a vacation in the capital? Or once again feel proud of their daughter, who was turning twenty and attending her coming-of-age ceremony? Or as they look at the roof of the school, they'll recall how they won the baseball tournament with their friends?

Ms. Suzuki, why are you crying? What are you worried about, Mr. Honda? That you can't see the face? In Japanese aesthetics, what you can't see is what's most important, you know. In stone zen gardens, the empty space between the boulders creates the tension. In ink paintings, cherry-tree branches reach beyond the sheet of paper. Maybe what's is important is hidden in that very place?

Please keep looking.

## Go Ahead and Complain

Ms. Kobayashi is the first to start. She sets the green beads, which she had been diligently threading onto a string, on the table. She moves aside her unfinished coffee, along with a plate of chocolate cookie crumbs. She sits next to the monk and speaks very softly. Only the monk can hear her.

"I don't have anything urgent today. I just wanted to complain for a little while. Because, for example, yesterday my cake was completely ruined. I was making it for my granddaughter, but the ovens that we have aren't good for anything. The entire house was in smoke in fifteen minutes, and I had to air it out for the rest of the day. The neighbors from other containers smelled something burning and came by to ask if everything was okay. The cake was a charred, black rock. And I had to throw the pan away, too. I didn't try to make another. What kind of conditions are we forced to live in? Everything was drenched in that odor, I couldn't sleep all night. That's no way to live. Those thin walls, the shoddy appliances, the streets filled with identical metal houses! I always get lost there! I don't even go out after dark, because I can't find the way back to my own house; all the streets look the same. That's no way to live!" The monk, Kaneta, nods his bald head in agreement. He carefully observes her from behind his horn-rimmed glasses.

"It's no way to live, Kaneta san," Ms. Kobayashi repeats.

The monk whispers something to her for a longer while. Ms. Kobayashi goes back to the table to get her green-beaded bracelet. The monk places the bracelet on her wrist, firmly embraces it in his hands and closes his eyes. He prays. "That's for good luck, Ms. Kobayashi," he says in a loud voice. And he gives her a broad smile.

Ms. Kobayashi has barely made it back to the table when Mr. Hasegawa walks up to the monk and starts talking feverishly. "I haven't spoken with you yet, Kaneta san, but I thought I'd tell you what's been ailing me. Because I don't think I can take it much longer. My wife's mother has come to live with us. Before, as tradition had it, she lived with her eldest son, but after March . . . well, now, she's living with us. We weren't ready for it. It's difficult to bear. How should I put it . . . I know she's family and all, but a stranger has suddenly come to live with us. And my wife's mother is not terribly happy about the situation either. Each morning she says, 'I want to go home.'

But her home is gone. This is her home now. I just wanted to tell you this, get it out in the open, because it's becoming hard to bear." The monk nods in agreement. He listens carefully.

Next to them, Ms. Yamada is whispering in the ear of a tall monk who is dressed in black.

"I'm very worried. I really don't know what to do. I can't sleep at night, I can't stop thinking about this. My youngest son . . . he just dropped out of college, started working in a restaurant to make some money; that's all good, but I wanted something better for him. I feel guilty. I didn't devote enough attention to him, I've barely spoken to him at all since . . . since . . . since my oldest son . . . his brother . . . he must have really suffered, and I didn't even notice so much time had already passed; how and when did that happen? It's too late for talking now. I'm terribly worried about it, and my husband doesn't even want to talk about it, and I don't know what to do." The monk holds Ms. Yamada by the hand. He nods his head. He listens carefully.

At the next table over, Ms. Fujioka takes a seat next to a monk with a round face, his hands folded on his big belly. He leans over to the older woman and carefully listens to her frantic whispering. "Well, I just can't understand it! He complains to me all day that his back aches, he walks bent over, he can't do anything, but he won't see a doctor. And he just whines that he's in pain. I wanted to bring him here so he could get out and meet people, talk a bit, have a cookie, but he just goes on and on about how it hurts. I made an appointment at the hospital for him, but he canceled it. I don't know how to knock some sense into him. And now, on top of that, the neighbors moved away to a new apartment and he has nobody else to talk to at all. The children have stopped coming to visit, and I haven't seen my grandchildren in two months. It's getting more and more empty around us. He's the only person I can talk to, but he just whines. It's hopeless." The chubby monk nods his head in agreement. He listens very carefully.

Mr. Hasegawa finishes talking, so Ms. Katō walks up to Kaneta. "I know that so much time has passed, but I really can't stop thinking about it. I have to talk about it, I think of them all the time. I was watching from the upper floor of the house as the water was taking them away. They were young and healthy. And me? An old woman. Why did I survive? I was talking a week ago with a young boy here in our complex. He was standing in the window, holding his mother by the hand. But the current was too strong. He feels the warmth of her hand to this day. How many of these stories will I still have to hear? I have to drink to fall asleep. I don't need much. Just a splash of vodka. I don't know where my house is. They took it apart. I don't have a house now. How can I live without a house? How can I stop thinking? Will this ever end, Kaneta san?" Kaneta nods.

We are sitting at a large table fashioned from school desks. Flowers in vases decorate the space. Jazz music is playing from speakers. The monks serve cake and cookies and pour more coffee. They encourage people to work with the beads; it's easier to talk to each other if your hands are busy doing something. And if somebody wants, they can go to one of the monks and complain in private. All they need to do is ask. Yet many of the older ladies complain among themselves over coffee and beads. "I'm telling you, do not marry a Japanese man," advises one woman with a wavy hairdo and a scarf around her neck. "He won't clean, he won't wash the dishes, he won't cook anything. No benefit from a husband like that at all. My husband never washed a single dish throughout his entire life!"

"Oh yes, quite so. And Kaneta is already taken," a woman wearing a black, silk blouse says with a sigh. "He's generally quite taken," an older lady, her hair in a tight bun, chimes in. "He could come here more often, but he has no time at all for us. We're bored without him. We even tried to organize a small get-together ourselves last time. But it's not the same. I prefer to complain to a monk."

Kaneta likes to improvise. A month after the tsunami, he packed tables, chairs, thermoses of coffee, and cake from a nearby bakery into a white van. He drove out to one of the evacuation centers on the coast, an hour away from the town of Kurihara, where his temple is. He parked in front of the gymnasium. He unloaded the tables, pulled out the chairs, put out the cake, and poured coffee into paper cups. He put on some jazz music. He took a board and wrote "Cafe de Monk" on it. The Japanese pronounce it "cafe de monku."

Quite a few monks come along with him, from many different sects and schools: zen, jōdo shinshū, tendai, nichiren, shingon. Kaneta doesn't care about doctrine. It's not religion that matters here, but the willingness to listen. And "Monk" also stands for Thelonious Monk, Kaneta's favorite jazzman: he has a carefree, slightly playful rhythm, but you can feel great sadness in his music. Incidentally, *monku* in Japanese means *to complain.*

The first time round, about thirty people showed up. They helped themselves to cake and had some coffee. They didn't even sit down. Some even took some extra food with them and went home. They considered the monks to be yet another group of volunteers bringing gifts.

That's not what Kaneta had in mind.

So he kept on improvising.

For the next get-together, he brought *ihai*, tablets onto which you inscribe the spirits of your ancestors during a special ceremony. People would search for *ihai* in the wreckages of their destroyed houses. Kaneta placed the empty tablets next to the cookies. He wouldn't say anything; he'd just pour the coffee and wait. They would walk up by themselves. And shyly reach for the tablets. Ask if they can take one. And as the monk would write the name of the deceased on the *ihai*, they would start to talk.

And that is exactly what Kaneta had in mind.

He organized the cafe at least twice a week, in many different places. When people moved from the evacuation centers to temporary complexes, he followed them. He knew the rhythm well; he only needed to tweak it to what they needed. He had to surprise them. Force them to say something. Sometimes, he would simply walk up to a person who was silent and place before them a figure of Jizō, the protector of travelers, pilgrims, unborn children, and the deceased; the deity's stone statues with their rain-washed faces stand near temples, at cemeteries and on the side of roads. Jizō, with a bald head, giant ears, and a kind smile, always appears in places where somebody may need help.

Kaneta would watch. He wouldn't say a word. People would hold the Jizō in their hands and refuse to let go. They would ask if they could keep it. Because it reminded them of somebody. Like with Mr. and Mrs. Abe: Jizō reminded them of their grandchildren. Kaneta sat down next to the elderly couple and listened attentively to their story.

He organized over two hundred Cafe de Monk events over the course of five years.

And he still continues to improvise.

In the guestroom of the Tsudaiji temple in the city of Kurihara, Kaneta treats me to some green tea. We are sitting on pillows at a low table. Hanging on the wall is a scroll with a smiling, chubby face, drawn with thin lines: it's Dōgen, the founder of the Sōtō school, one of the two most important schools of Zen in Japanese Buddhism. Kaneta manages the temple, just like his father, grandfather, and great-grandfather did. The history goes back four hundred years.

But today, he's the one complaining:

"They're like children. Once, I had 120 people at the cafe. What an uproar! I felt like I was in preschool. There was no way to calm them down. I asked them to be quiet; I was nice about it first, but then I had to be more firm. I finally gave up and left well alone. Together with the other monks, we just kept on pouring coffee. And listening to what they had to tell us. Mostly women come, men think that it's too childish. We organized an Osake de Monku twice; we hung a red lantern, put alcohol on the tables, and served grilled meat instead of cookies. They came. But we stopped after the second time. That improvisation did not work out.

"I can't help everybody. In the beginning, I would also drive out to Fukushima; it's only a hundred kilometers south of my temple. But I'm not familiar with their customs or traditions: even their accent is different. I don't know what's important to them or how to attract their attention. It's the same further north, in Iwate. So I focus on what I do know; I make my rounds in Miyagi only. I am aware that complaining cafes organized by monks are being set up in other cities, like Tokyo or Kyoto. And that's a good thing. They're not the same, because those cities are different and people need different things there.

"All you need to do is listen. They share their sorrow and pain with us, and that brings them relief. We take part of that burden onto our shoulders. What do we do with it? We're monks. We listen to an account told by a specific person, but we hear a universal story. It goes through me like through a ripped sack. Although I will tell you that even my wife doesn't see me crying. They'd like me to come every single week. Organize their lives. But that's not the point here. I go see these people to help them stand on their own two feet. People lose the ability to rebuild for only a brief moment, and I help them regain that ability. The first year, they would say nearly nothing. We used up a lot of tissue then. The second year was the same. All you could hear was the sipping of coffee. But I wanted them to express their anger, their sadness, their grief. Without that, you can't move forward."

For two years, he said, they would keep on asking: Why?

Why did I survive?

Why did my daughter die?

Why did it happen?

Why was I rescued?

Why did I lose my entire family?

How do I make any sense of this?

But it doesn't make any sense. That's what it's all about.

"In addition to drinking coffee and having conversations, we started to make clay Jizō figures and Buddhist bracelets, which I bless for good luck. But religion is not the key focus here. We meet for coffee, not for a Buddhist ceremony. Sometimes we sing, sometimes a massage therapist comes to loosen tight necks. Sometimes we have a bonfire and bake potatoes.

"Acceptance started surfacing in the third year. No, not understanding. Acceptance. I may not be able to understand why so many people died on March 11, or why I lost all my belongings; but it happened. It's a reality that we have no way of changing.

"They started to laugh after four years.

"I go less and less often. Once every six months. At the beginning, I tried to visit each location once a month. But already then I didn't think it was a good idea to show up too often. Let them miss you. Let them have something to anticipate. Anticipation means hope and excitement. And it's that, not me, that they really need.

"But a new issue has appeared now; it's the story of our life, because really, as long as we're alive, we'll always have problems. People are moving into the apartment buildings built for them. Over the past four years, they've managed to build a community in temporary housing. Quite often, they did not know each other before and they were brought together by the tragedy and the fact that staying inside the houses for too long was unbearable. Now they're all moving out. And everybody is headed in different directions. They will have four strong walls and a solid, sound-proof door. Doors like that are hard to open. And how many more times can you start over again if you're seventy years old? But I'll go to those new apartment complexes. I'll take set up the tables and chairs, I'll serve some strawberry sponge cake, make some good coffee, put on some Monk, and I'll listen. I'm great at listening."

## Call Me

There are plenty of pictures of it online. It's a white telephone booth, standing in a rose garden on a hill. Inside, the glass walls offer a nice ocean view. There's a classic black telephone with a rotary dial. The cord sways in the wind.

*Kaze no denwa*—the wind telephone. Itaru Sasaki set up the booth in his garden in the town of Ōtsuchi, a month after the tsunami. Anybody can come to have a chat with the people they miss.

Visitors enter the booth, one at a time. They pick up the receiver and put it to their ear. They lean against the wall. They hang their head. Maybe they talk about themselves. Or maybe they just ask questions. They spend many long minutes engaged in a conversation that's carried by the wind.

If you are convinced that you won't hear a thing in a phone that isn't connected, you never will. But if you listen very carefully, you just might get an answer.

All the newspapers, big and small, and not only in Japan, wrote about the wind telephone. Over ten thousand people visited it in the course of three years. They would leave notes in an open book placed next to the phone.

One person wrote: "I finally said *goodbye*."

## Disappointment

Who are you? A journalist? So you came to listen to stories about how people can't sleep at night, because they have nightmares about swollen bodies? You like that, don't you? I can see by the expression on your face. Why aren't you taking notes? How will I know you won't twist and turn my words around? Is that the kind of professional you are? Truly pitiful.

There are four things that I want you to remember. I'll say them clearly and slowly. The first year was a battle. Anything to endure what was going on. To feel safe again. The only thing that people were concerned with during the first year was survival.

The second year was a period of building community. Any ties that were severed were being rebuilt with new neighbors in temporary housing. Everybody wanted to help one another, because each and every person had lost something in the catastrophe. People were sticking together.

The third year was the acceptance of what had happened. That it really had happened and it wasn't going away, and there won't be any miracle. And that you had to do something with the life that had been ruined.

The fourth year was the time to finally move on. People who had money built new houses. Some people moved to apartment buildings built for them. Friendships that had been built over the past four years were severed again. Their lives were back on track. Community was no longer the most important thing. Yet there are people who felt left behind. They didn't have the money, they didn't have the strength, they didn't have the luck.

So remember this and remember it well:

First year—survival.

Second year—bonds.

Third year—acceptance.

Fourth year—disappointment.

What else do you want to hear from me? That children are still talking about their parents in the present tense? "Mom went shopping, Dad is going to the store." A little girl cannot understand that her mom is dead, and her dad's body was never found. When a thirteen-year-old boy heard about the mudslide in Hiroshima that killed several dozen people in 2014, and that they were looking for bodies, he wanted to buy a train ticket to Hiroshima. "Maybe they'll find my mom, if they're looking for bodies there?" Are those the stories you want to hear? Be my guest, we've got plenty of them. Depression, shock, psychosomatic disorders, delusions, disappointments, debt. Ah, yes! And remember, too, that money is important to them. People don't have homes, but they have mortgages. Now that's something you're interested in, right? Human misery. That's why you came here! To sniff out tragedy, while tragedy is what I see every single day! I spend ten hours a day in the office and I listen, listen, listen.

About the house they had just finished building; they had just picked up the keys, and the very next day the house was washed away by the tsunami. The only thing left was the mortgage. The father of the family went crazy. The house is all he talks about, how beautifully it's decorated; he boasts about the sunny spaces, about the square footage, how much money he spent on the tatami mats, how the kitchen was supposed to be equipped, and what was going to be grown in the garden. He lives the life he had before. That's all he has.

Or I listen to stories about that restaurant. The guy spends all he has on it, though he himself is barely making ends meet. He lives in an alternate reality. It will get better soon, he keeps on saying. The tourists will be here soon. And soon, I'll make enough to rebuild my house. Soon, the city will gain a splendor it never had before.

What, not enough for you? There's one more therapist here besides me, a woman working for a non-profit organization. Go pester her. I'm employed by the city, but the officials don't understand what therapy entails either; at the start they gave me seventeen patients a day. I explained to them that I can't have more than five, it's against the standards. So they gave me ten. I fell down the stairs five times. I was in the ER three times. I was hospitalized twice. Although I'm not from here, I understand them. They can't sleep. They see ghosts. They have no motivation to do anything, and tears immediately spring to their eyes. They're ashamed of it. Sometimes, all you have to do is tell them that it's normal. Trauma causes such behavior. There's a name for it. Post-traumatic stress disorder. It's not that there's something wrong with them.

They don't know anything about psychology here, and even less about therapy. If an older woman gets lost in her neighborhood, her husband beats her, because she brings him embarrassment. He doesn't even think that it may be caused by age, or dissociation. They don't know the term "dementia" here. And they don't understand what psychological distance is. They walk up to me on the street to talk about their problems. They knock on the door of the container where I live, and want to vent their feelings. They bring baskets of vegetables from their gardens to our sessions. They would cringe in the States if they saw the extent to which I had to change my therapeutic stand-ards. All that to avoid hurting the pride of the locals. Because they are indeed quite proud. What are you looking at? You doubt my skills? I already told you that I completed my studies in the States! I'm an art therapist! I lived in Seattle for thirteen years. I don't understand why you've brought an interpreter to our meeting, we won't be needing one. I returned to Japan because my mother needed care. She's eighty-eight years old. Tokyo was boring. I prefer clinical work to lectures. I moved here to help the people whose lives were taken by the tsunami. But who here would even think of going to a therapist? Others would start whispering right away that they're off their rocker.

Drinking is a better option. And really, it's an option that most of Japan goes for. It's nothing new that people here drown themselves in alcohol in the evenings. The people who helped search for bodies dull their senses that way. They want to kill the smell of decay. Firefighters who ran away to save their own lives are drowning their guilt. Because fifty-two of them stayed to close the sluice, even though they saw the tsunami approach-ing. Are those the stories you want to hear?

There's no way to get through it without alcohol. People drank a lot here before the tsunami. It's a masculine society. In northern Japan, a strict father is a normal thing. They would even have a competition to see who was able to throw a table further in anger. They would measure the distance in centim-eters. Do you understand that, or do I need to explain it to you in more detail? They held competitions to see who was better in domestic violence.

There will be suicides now. Interested? After the fourth year, people feel they've been left behind. They are disappointed with their lives. Some of them can no longer live in the hope that one day the city will rebuild and things will finally get better. After all, the town is aging, as is all of Japan. Even before the tsunami, young people were already running away from here, the further the better. Now they have even fewer reasons to come back. There are those who say that the catastrophe is an opportunity for the town. That we can rebuild it from scratch, attract people from outside, and breathe some life into this shell. But my patients don't believe it. Those who haven't killed themselves are drinking to their lost hope. Because something has changed in town as of late. The first apartment buildings have been finished, the first families have moved from the temporary housing to their own apartments. Finally, the normal life that everybody has been waiting for. It is finally here. But why is it that this life, put on hold for four years, somehow does not feel right? That's it? That's all? So that's the way it's going to be?

They've waited so long for it, and it isn't that great.

So all they're waiting for now is death.

Enough!

I've told you everything I had to say.

First year—survival.

Second year—bonds.

Third year—acceptance.

Fourth year—disappointment.

I don't want to talk to you anymore.

## What You Dream About in Tōhoku

Late at night, as the city was cloaked in darkness, Nao was walking home. He had a spring in his step, his hands in the pockets of his jacket, and was quietly whistling a tune. The moon scattered the shadows hiding beneath the white arcades of the main street. The clock struck two. Gray clouds covered the sky. Nao livened his step.

He stopped whistling and dug his hands deeper into the pockets. It grew silent. Even the cicadas stopped humming. As he approached the river, he heard quiet sobbing. He looked around. He saw her near the railing in the middle of the bridge. She was sitting on the ground, curled up with her head hanging. When the moon peered from behind the clouds for a brief moment, he caught a better glimpse of the colors of her kimono (orange with green flowers and pink birds), the curve of her white neck and her shimmering, ink-colored hair, held up with a shiny pin. A girl from a good family, he thought. What is she doing here on her own, at this hour? Her shoulders were shaking and her sobbing was becoming louder and louder.

"Hey . . ." he called out quietly.

She didn't react.

"Hey . . . hey! What's wrong?" he asked as he walked closer. She covered her face with her sleeve and wept.

"Hey," he gently called out. "Don't cry. What's going on? Tell me, I want to help you!"

The girl got up and placed her hands on the railing. The flowers and birds on her kimono flickered in the light of the moon. Her pale neck stood out clearly from her black hair and orange collar. Her head hung low, and her shoulders were still shaking as she sobbed silently.

Nao feared that she had come here to throw herself into the river, that she would jump over the railing at any moment. That's what people were doing after what had happened. "Listen to me!" he called to her. "It's such a dark night, that can make anybody sad. Please, stop crying, and let me take you home."

The girl slowly turned around. Her head was down, her face was covered with her hands. Nao placed a hand on her shoulder, anything to keep on talking, to make sure she wouldn't change her mind. "Look, I know . . ."

She lifted her head and he looked at her straight on. A face without eyes, without a nose, without a mouth. Only white skin pulled tightly over her skull. The girl grabbed his wrist, threw her head back, and cackled. He shrieked and tried to pull himself loose, but she held him tight, bringing her eyeless and mouthless face closer to his. He yanked one more time, screaming. He freed his hand. He ran, and his footsteps resounded a drumming, hollow echo throughout the white arcades of the shopping street. A light flickered in the distance. It was the old ramen vendor. He suffered from insomnia, which was why he would sometimes keep his shop open until the middle of the night. Nao ran up to the vendor, who was locking the security gate. Nao looked behind him. Nobody was there. He didn't hear any cackling. He placed his hands on his knees and breathed heavily. He rubbed his wrist where the girl's fingers had left a red mark.

"What happened?" the vendor asked in a rough voice. Nao stared at the ground. He was trying to catch his breath.

"Somebody mug you?" the vendor asked as he secured the padlock on the gate.

"No, no . . ." Nao gasped.

"Then what has you so scared?"

"You wouldn't believe it. It was . . . it was . . ."

"I've seen it all . . ."

"But not this . . . not this! That girl . . . she . . ."

The vendor laughed. He turned away from the gate to face Nao. He lifted his head and yelled, "Maybe it was something like this? Huh?"

Nao looked straight into the face of the ramen vendor, which had no eyes, no nose, and no mouth. Just white skin tightly pulled over his skull. Nao stared at the shopkeeper, terrified. He wasn't able to move an inch. His legs were bolted to the ground. The man came closer and closer, rattling his keys. Nao felt the odor of garlic and grease. Just then, the moon appeared from behind the clouds, and brightly illuminated the pale, mouthless, eyeless head. Nao shrieked. He shoved the shopkeeper and started to run.

He ran as fast as he could, just to get as far away from the bridge and the shopping street. He turned right, then left next to the garbage cans, ran through a passageway between houses, straight into a parking lot, which he cut across. He made a turn and fell into the circle of light in front of a 7-Eleven, one of the more popular convenience store chains in Japan, where you can buy anything, from sandwiches to socks. Nao bolted inside. The three people on staff gave him a puzzled look.

"What's got you running like that?" asked the young man at the checkout. While the woman who was cleaning the coffee machine added, "It's like you'd just seen a ghost."

The man with the mop in hand laughed maliciously and asked, "Did it look like this?" and waved his hand in front of his face. Nao saw how his eyes, mouth and nose began to disappear. The only thing left was smooth skin. He glanced at the register. The woman who had been cleaning the machine turned toward him; her black hair hung over her face—eyeless, mouthless, noseless. The young cashier was chuckling, too. His own mouthless, noseless, eyeless face was shaking with delight.

Nao had no idea how and when he stumbled back to his own front door. He rushed inside without even taking his shoes off. His wife was asleep in the bedroom.

"Haruka! Haruka!" he called, shaking her arm. "Haruka! Haruka! Wake up!" She looked at him with sleepy eyes. She leaned on her elbow. "What happened, dear?" she asked. "You look like you've seen a ghost."

"A ghost? Ghost?!? They . . . all of them . . . they didn't have faces! And that woman in the kimono . . . I thought she wanted to drown herself . . . and she . . . and the ramen vendor . . . and that young guy at the checkout . . . no noses, no eyes . . . nothing . . . empty faces . . . no mouth . . . all you could hear was that laughter . . . Haruka!"

"What are you talking about, Nao? You're scaring me!" his wife exclaimed, moving away from her distressed husband. "You don't mean to say that they all looked like this?" she asked, and as she waved her hand in front of her face, her black eyes, slender nose, and thin lips disappeared. Nao was looking at pale skin tightly pulled over her skull. The sound of chuckling filled the house.

They come out at night, when darkness sets in the cities. You can find them sneaking through the arcades and lurking under bridges or bamboo groves. The *nopperabō* have no faces, they chuckle devilishly and take pleasure in the horror of their victims. Very similar are the *ohaguro bettari*; they are beautifully dressed and wait near temples. They give the impression of being fragile and lost. When you walk up to them, they show their face. The face has no eyes, only a distorted, grimacing mouth with sharp black teeth. Or the *rokurokubi*, which extends its neck at night, and the head floats over its sleeping body. It's really good at stretching, and since it's quite nosy by nature, it can spy on people even several miles away. It likes to make fun of drunks; it appears before them in all its splendor. It knows that nobody will believe their babbling stories anyway. Or it blatantly stares at sleeping men. It waits until they awaken, unsettled. Then it changes its face to that of a person the man had hurt in the past. But these three ghosts are not particularly dangerous. They like to scare people, but they're not interested in killing anybody.

Things are very different with the *jorōgumo*, which appears to its victims as an elegant lady. Tall, graceful, she treads lightly. Her hair is in a bun, with just loose lock grazing her neck. She catches the attention of men on the street. They walk up to her, wanting to show her the way. She quietly whispers something to them, so they have to lean in to hear her better. Then she grabs them with eight arms, traps them in a spider's web, and wraps them in a cocoon, which she will feed on for the next few days. *Jorōgumo*—the woman-spider. Or rather, the spider whore, as the Japanese call her. Then there's the *teke teke*, which gets its name from the noise it makes when its arms hit the street. It's just an abdomen without legs that crawls through the streets on its elbows. It has shining eyes, unkempt hair, and a sickle in one hand. If the victim is not quick enough, the *teke teke* will cut him or her in half at the waist. It cares about one thing only—to make everyone look the same as it does.

*Nopperabō, ohaguro bettari, rokurokubi, jorōgumo,* and *teke teke* have been scaring people in Japan for hundreds of years. Some people believe that they are the souls of tormented people that detach from the body as they sleep, taking on grotesque forms. They try to lessen their own agony by scaring others. They represent people's thoughts and emotions, and most of all, the burning grief, limitless sorrow, deep despair, heavy hearts, and lost hope as they roam the streets of the reconstructed cities of Tōhoku.

But the most terrifying of them all is the *nukekubi*. It weaves through the arcades. It doesn't want anybody to notice it—not right away at any rate. It roams the streets and peeks into dark windows. It stretches its neck to see better, to see children sleeping in cribs, and the parents, cuddled up to each other on the bed next to them. Immersed in deep sleep, they dream colorful dreams of the future. It looks at their peaceful faces, at their chests moving with each steady breath. Its cold eyes open wider, its face contorts. It pushes its nose against the window. The window is open. The *nukekubi* smiles and licks its sharp teeth. Its long, black hair bounces with every move. Only the head floats through the window. The rest of the body is at home, asleep under warm covers, as if it has no idea what the head was up to at night. Meanwhile, the head slips through the open window and floats above the crib. The child doesn't even have time to whimper. All you can hear is a slurping sound, quiet enough not to wake the parents. The *nukekubi* licks its blood-covered lips. It moves to the bed where the pair is cuddled up. Its shining eyes gaze at the man's neck. Olive-colored, smooth skin. In a flash, its sharp teeth sink into his neck. Blood splatters the walls, stains the sheets, and drips onto the face of the sleeping woman. The *nukekubi* faces her and, overjoyed, looks straight into her terrified eyes.

Yoko woke up screaming. She opened her eyes wide, buried her face in the pillow, and, just like when she was a child, she called out to Baku san, a monster with the nose of an elephant, body of a bear, paws of a tiger, tail of an ox, and the narrow eyes of a rhinoceros. "Baku san, I beg you, come and eat my dreams, Baku san, I beg you, come and eat my dreams, Baku san, I beg you, come and eat my dreams," she whispers. It's a childhood spell that you repeat three times. And she doesn't care anymore if the terrifying Baku san sucks away any hope for the future, along with her nightmares. There is no more hope.

She looks at her husband, sleeping on the other side of the bed—as far as possible from her. She gets up, goes to the kitchen, makes some coffee. Her movements are mechanical, kind of rehearsed. Her stare is absent. Her voice is pallid when she starts to speak. "I start my day by dying. I feel like I don't have any skin anymore, no protective layer. My husband leaves in the morning. He comes back in the evening. I prefer when he's not here. We don't have much to say to each other. I get everything confused. Last time, I went out into the snow again in short sleeves and loafers; I didn't notice until I got to the gas station. Is it December already? I was convinced it was May. All the days look the same anyway. Only sometimes, I think I see him on the street. Broad shoulders, short hair. I run after him, I want to take his hand. That's when I see his profile. Not that nose, not those eyes, not those lips. It's not my son. My son was killed by the tsunami. The third year was the hardest for me. Although I transferred his bones to the urn myself, each time I turned the key in the lock, I always hoped to hear his voice. I would set the table for six, I would do the shopping for six, and cook for six. I would make his bed. I would see a checkered shirt in his favorite colors and I'd buy two, for later.

"Our other sons no longer live with us. Our youngest graduated from high school two years ago; he was a freshman in 2011. I don't even know where those three years went, I didn't snap out of it until he left for university, far away from home. Already? And not once did I ask him if he needed help with his homework. He chose food science, but he dropped out after six months. He works in a sushi bar, he turned twenty. A coming-of-age ceremony for twenty-year-olds is organized each year on January 11. He didn't want to go. I don't have the strength to worry about him. I can't wait until the night comes. I want to fall asleep as quickly as possible. Maybe he'll appear in my dreams? Maybe I'll hear his laughter. There's nothing I desire more than to hear my son say 'Mom,' to me, one more time, one last time."

## Who You Will Become After You Die

If you're a woman who dies in labor, you'll become an *ubume*. You will come back to earth to take care of your children. Although sometimes you'll appear at a crossroads, old and senile, with a child in your arms. The child will be too heavy for you. You'll barely manage to hold it. That's why you'll ask passersby in a shrill voice, "Please, please, hold my child for me." And when they take the bundle from you, you'll disappear. And they'll be left with a rock in their arms.

If you died at sea, you'll turn into a *funayūrei*. On rainy days or on nights when the moon is full, you'll rise from the abyss of the sea with a giant ladle that you'll use to pour water into passing boats, only to sink them. During a storm, when the cold rain floods the decks of ships, you'll light a fire in the middle of the sea, to confuse the fishermen. You'll wait for days when the ocean is shrouded in fog; nobody can see you from afar then, so you can sail up close to a lone boat and shake it until one of the sailors falls overboard. You want nothing more than to have all the living join you in the watery depths.

If you died as a small child, you have the chance of turning into a *zashiki warashi*. You'll live somewhere in northern Japan in a big, traditional house with sliding walls made of paper, a fireplace with a cast-iron kettle, and a wooden pathway running along the garden filled with white gravel. You'll have plenty of room to play. You'll leave an impression of your tiny body on the futons set out for the night. You'll leave dirty ash marks on the floor. You'll hum traditional songs in empty rooms. If any of the inhabitants should hear that, the quiet melody will make them happy. In northern Japan they know that your presence brings good luck (though they're rather afraid of you in the south). Sometimes the owner's children will play with you. Then you'll hear them tell their parents about the red-faced child with close-cropped hair.

If you died as the result of an assassination and you have an aristocratic background, you'll become a *goryō*, or a noble ghost. You will possess amazing powers after your death. Your righteous anger and the injustice inflicted on you will give you power over the elements. You will be able to send typhoons and earthquakes to your enemies. You will destroy harvests and demolish houses all over Japan. Just like Sugawara no Michizane, who was demoted by the Emperor to the status of a lowly clerk and banished from Kyoto to the boondocks in faraway Kyushu as a result of a conspiracy plotted by the Fujiwara clan—who, in turn, were rivaling for the Emperor's favor. Sugawara died a lonely death; afterward, lightning struck the main building of the imperial palace several times. The country was plagued by a long drought, followed by an epidemic that took the life of the Emperor's son and the head of the Fujiwara family. And finally, Kyoto was flooded by rainfall lasting several weeks. The Kamo River overflowed and destroyed the city. The Emperor struck from record any mention of Sugawara's exile and restored all his titles. This seemed to soothe the vindictive spirit, but just in case, seventy years after Saguwara's death, the next Emperor declared him a deity. A few years after that, he was given the title of great minister. Today, Sugawara is not only the god of science, literature, and calligraphy, but is also the protector of those who have been unjustly treated.

If you are a mother who has lost her child to war or famine, you will return after death as a *muonna*. Although you want to protect children from evil, the desire to nurture them with your motherly love is even stronger. You put them to sleep with a magic spell and absorb their spirits. Yet sometimes, teeming with caring feelings, you will save the life of a child and allow yourself to be destroyed instead. However, if during your life you did not follow the ways of the Buddha and allowed yourself to be controlled by urges, envy, and greed, after death you will become a *gaki*. Your belly will be round like a ball, while your mouth and throat will be so narrow that no food will be able to pass through it. You will suffer from eternal hunger. Whenever you reach for a bowl of rice, it will burn right in front of your eyes. No food will ever make it to your mouth. You won't be much better off if you cared only about yourself during your lifetime, and if the only thing you thought of was how you could benefit at the expense of others. After you die, you will be condemned to eating human corpses as a *jikininki*. You will feel disgusted with your own self as you tear the meat from the bones of corpses with your teeth. This will last for all eternity, unless there is somebody brave enough to perform a *segaki* for you, or a ritual for hungry and abandoned spirits. And if you die with a heart filled with hate, you will turn into an *onryō*. Your final mortal thought, full of anger and sadness, will not allow you to leave the Earth. You will wander about, seeking vengeance. Just like Oiwa, the rejected wife of a *rōnin*, a samurai without a master, who desired to wed a younger woman. He poisoned Oiwa, but the poison didn't work; it only disfigured her face. Her left eye fell out of its socket, her forehead was covered with lumps, and she lost all her hair. Oiwa killed herself with a sword, but her disfigured face continued to torment the *rōnin*. It even appeared on the day of his wedding, on his new bride's face. Terrified by the sight, he pulled out his sword and cut her head off. Oiwa persecuted her unfaithful husband to the point that he desired his own death.

The dead exist alongside the living in Japan. It's nothing out of the ordinary. Especially between two and three at night, when the veil dividing the two worlds grows thinner, and especially in places where somebody had died a violent death. Especially if the body was never found and put to rest according to rituals. Especially if unresolved matters are keeping the dead near the living. Love. Or hate.

*Yūrei*. Faint spirits. They take on various forms. If they return out of love, without any evil intentions, they appear as they were before death. But those that return for vengeance turn into a specter with a pale, elongated face and tousled hair. Wrapped in a white shroud, they float above the ground with their arms helplessly dangling alongside their bodies.

The good ones shine like fireflies. The evil ones buzz like houseflies.

## Ghosts

It was already dark when, at the very last minute, the headlights of the bus caught the children standing on the shoulder. Children at this hour? A rarely frequented road, between two seaside towns, no school in the area. Maybe they were returning from some party and got lost along the way? The driver opened the door and smiled. The passengers on the bus made room up front. The boys got on one after the other, dressed in festive uniforms, like ones worn for the end of the school year. They didn't say a word to anybody. Their eyes were glued to the floor. They squeezed next to each other on the seats. The driver closed the door and continued down the dark road. Then he glanced at the rear view mirror and hit the brakes.

The front seats were empty.

Ghosts started appearing in Tōhoku roughly five months after the tsunami. Women would hail taxis, give an address, and when the driver started off, they would disappear into thin air. The drivers would continue on to the address provided only to find the cleared foundations of a house washed away by the tsunami. Firefighters would take calls to fires at addresses that no longer existed. While working on the coast, a worker felt somebody pat him on his shoulder. When he turned around, there was nobody there. It wasn't until he got home that his wife noticed a black handprint on his shirt. In front of the remains of a fruit and vegetable shop, people saw customers standing in line at a non-existent checkout. Drivers would tell stories of human shadows running to the hills, as if they were not able to stop reliving the final minutes of their lives. Mothers claimed that their drowned children would come back home to play with their favorite toys; they would move blocks or turn on music boxes. And one woman stopped leaving her house, because she would see the eyes of drowned people in each puddle.

Some people summon exorcists. Others make a special effort to look for ghosts. They drive to the seaside at dusk, wait on the beach, or go where their houses once stood. They want to see their loved ones just one more time. They can't forget.

They constantly feel the pain. The pain of the cold half of the bed. The pain of only one set of flatware on the table. The pain of only one ticket to the movies. The pain of silence in response to a question. The pain of a shopping list found in a drawer, written in her handwriting. The pain that does not let you go. The pain can drive you crazy. So it's better to try to talk to your deceased loved one.

Now that's something you can do. All you need to do is go all the way up to the north of Tōhoku, to the Aomori province, and find an *itako*.

*Itako*—a shamaness, prophetess, medium. Three years of training, waking up at two at night, having cold water poured on their bodies, and memorizing mantras—for toothaches, stomach aches, and aches of the soul. Being an *itako* was once an opportunity only for blind girls. It seems that people who cannot see the outside world find it easier to observe the world within.

They do not go about flaunting their skills. To strangers, they outright deny having any such abilities. They have husbands (current or ex) and children. A regular job. Only the locals know that the woman working at the bakery can help you talk to your late father. The easiest way to meet with an *itako* is on Mount Osore, a cursed, volcanic mountain at the very tip of the Japanese island of Honshu. A Buddhist temple stands in the caldera of the active volcano; worshippers say that it's the final stop before the gates of Hell. This is where the Sanzu River flows. Further on, there are only dead spirits. Twice a year, when the dead are more active, the *itako* pitch tents along the road to the temple. At the request of mourners, they let the dead enter their bodies and answer questions. It used to be that a dozen or so *itako* would come here. Today, there are only two. The others are dead or too sick to spend the entire day sitting in white robes summoning spirits. Of the real *itako*, those who went through the training and can really communicate with ancestors, there are only ten left, maybe twelve.

Ms. Matsuda, who's been an *itako* for the past twenty-five years, is one of the two who come to the festival at the foot of Mount Osore. She meets with mourners more than twice a year. Three times a month, she goes to a hotel where owners of tourist agencies bring people looking to contact their deceased. One coach, thirty people. An individual meeting with the *itako* lasts fifteen minutes.

Inconspicuous, with no makeup, in a white outfit with her hair tied back. She wears a bamboo container with protective coils on her back. In her hands, she holds a rosary of black beads and animal skulls.

Matsuda is like a puppet; she lends her body and mouth to the dead, even to those who have been gone for several hundreds of years. As long as the person who came to ask the questions is related to the deceased by blood or by marriage, she can summon anybody. Even any one of the shoguns. Or Napoleon.

An *itako* needs to clear her mind of any thoughts—she must make room. If the spirit has died recently, the *itako* becomes very sleepy during the session. She finds it more difficult to speak with the recently deceased, as if something was still keeping them on earth, as if they had not yet moved on. But if they have spent some time in the afterlife, things are much easier.

"Date of death?" Matsuda asks. "Relationship to the deceased?"

The rosary rattles and a throaty song follows. The *itako* closes her eyes, and starts to sway. And then the voice comes out of her.

People can ask whatever they want.

"Do you feel pain?"

"How did you die?"

"I'm sorry for my fits of anger. Please don't be upset with me."

"I miss you. Every day."

"Is there anything we can do for you?"

"It's so hard to believe that . . . that . . . that . . ."

"Do you need anything?"

"I just wanted to say goodbye for the last time. And tell you that I love you."

"Where is your body?"

"I'm in pain."

People's personalities don't change after they die. Sometimes they don't want to talk with family. But Ms. Matsuda is effective. Ninety-eight out of a hundred ghosts appear.

Yet with time, the questions started to change.

"Mom, where should I build a new house?"

"Dear, wouldn't it better for me to quit my job?"

"Or maybe I should get divorced after all? What do you think, Dad?"

And one more:

"How can I die to end up where you are? Throw myself into the sea?"

Ms. Matsuda sets the rosary aside and looks the man straight in the eyes.

"If you die, who will care for the grave of your loved one? You have to keep on living for her."

And the others? What kinds of answers do they receive? Ms. Matsuda does not know. When she's in her trance, she remembers nothing.

On the other hand, Kaneta the monk perfectly remembers each spirit he has spoken with.

"I want to kill myself," he heard when he answered the phone in the evening. It's a special line for people who are lonely, for people who need to talk, and for people who are suicidal. Kaneta had it hooked up after the tsunami. He isn't always available; there were times when he saw missed calls on the display. In his thoughts, he apologized to the person he had disappointed. He cannot help everybody.

Yet on that particular night (because people usually call in the evening, after eight, when loneliness becomes unbearable), he was able to answer the phone.

"I want to kill myself," the tired voice of a young woman said.

Two hours later, a car pulled up at the four-hundred-year-old Tsudaiji temple. The woman was not able to get out on her own. Helping her were her mother, younger sister, and fiancé. Kaneta led them to the guest room, where they took a seat on pillows at a low table. Kaneta's wife brewed some tea—a special tea made of fresh, non-fermented leaves. It has a sweet note to it and tastes like spring.

"I want to kill myself," the woman repeated. She was twenty-five years old, had a strong build, dark bags under her eyes due to lack of sleep, matte, shoulder-length hair, and a colorless voice. "I can't take it anymore. I keep on hearing them, they won't leave me alone, they don't want to go away, they talk, they keep on talking all the time, I just can't take it anymore. I want to kill myself."

"What is your name, dear child?" Kaneta quietly interrupted her.

"Yuko."

"Yuko chan," he addressed her affectionately, just like a small child who needs a hug, "when did you start hearing these voices?"

"Oh, I don't remember. It had to be when I was a child," she answered.

"In our family, women hear voices of the dead," her mother interrupted. "The same thing would happen to me, but it stopped when I got married. Yuko's aunt had the same thing, but she managed to control it. Yuko was able to handle it as well, at least for the longest time. It wasn't until the tsunami that bad things started happening," she explained.

"Before, all I had to do was imagine a big solid box," Yuko continued, the words flooding out of her as if she were afraid that she wouldn't be able to say everything. "I would put them in the box, close the lid, and that was it. I was able to go to work, have fun with my friends, talk with my family; but that was before. Now no box and no lid can help. Even a metal safe won't silence them; they keep on talking, they talk constantly, they never stop; they keep on banging about in my head."

Kaneta had met people before who were seeing ghosts. Even before the tsunami. Tortured by bad dreams, haunted by specters seen out of the corner of their eye. Sometimes they would feel a presence that was too close and too intense. Or they felt that something was not right. That there was danger in the air, that the ancestors were worried.

The procedure was always the same: talk it out. Kaneta is not an exorcist. He does not have the ability to chase ghosts away. But he does know how to listen. So he asks: What do you believe in? What is important to you? Did someone close to you die? Did this somebody leave any unfinished business? Where are you from? How did your ancestors die? Did anybody die a violent death? What rituals do you practice? What do you worry about? What do you dream of? Why can't you sleep?

Kaneta keeps on patiently asking until he learns what exactly is tormenting the person seated before him. And once he knows what the problem is, the solution suggests itself—a ritual needs to be performed, the unfinished business needs to be taken care of, a prayer needs to be said for the unsettled spirit. Reassure the spirit and yourself.

Ten people came to him after the tsunami. Each of them spoke differently of the ghosts; some saw them, some heard them, others felt their presence. One man was even possessed by the dead who were angered by his disruptiveness; he had gone to the seaside a week after the catastrophe to check it out. He ate ice cream on the beach, as if he were on a day trip. The dead were furious. They tormented him for three nights. All he needed to do was realize his carelessness, and the attacks went away.

But with Yuko, things were different.

That's because the spirits possessed her body.

Yuko was living in Sendai, where she was born. Her family came from the coast—from Ishinomaki, where half of the city was destroyed by the tsunami. Nobody from Yuko's family, nor any of her friends had been affected. In the past, her ancestors looked after the double mouth of the Kitakami River, the largest river in all of Tōhoku. Is that why Yuko heard so many voices after the tsunami?

Although Yuko did not lose anybody in the tsunami, her father had died not too long ago. Perhaps that provided the spirits easier access to the bereaved woman? Especially since Yuko had been anxious about her father not being at her wedding. He didn't even have the time to get to know her fiancé better. Or maybe he did not approve of her relationship?

Maybe he felt that Yuko had made a bad choice? That would torment her just before she would go to bed. And then she couldn't sleep anyway, because she would start to hear voices.

"Yuko chan, go back home, say a prayer for your father before the altar. That should calm him down. And you as well. And if at any time you feel that something is happening that you can't handle, come back to see me."

The spirits accepted the invitation. Yuko came back twenty-five times.

The third time round, Yuko's fiancé carried her from the car, over the stone pathway through the temple garden, and sat her at the low table; when Kaneta asked what was going on, Yuko answered in a man's voice. A furious, desperate voice. She yelled, "Where is Wakana?! Where is Wakana?!"

Kaneta started the conversation.

"Who is Wakana?"

"My daughter. Where is she? I have to find her!"

"Why do you have to find Wakana?"

"Because the tsunami is approaching! I have to take her from school, before the wave hits!"

Step by step, Kaneta pieced together the facts. The man's wife was supposed to pick up their daughter from school, but she had been stuck in traffic. So he decided to go pick her up himself. The spirit of the man does not know this, but when he was driving out to get his daughter, the tsunami must have washed him away. Seated before Kaneta was twenty-five-year-old Yuko, screaming in a deep voice, "Where is Wakana?!" Kaneta had no idea what to do, so he improvised.

"Where are you now?"

"At the bottom of the ocean."

That surprised the monk, but he didn't let it show.

"Your body is at the bottom of the ocean, so you can't look for Wakana there. Try to move and swim in the direction of the light. Then you can start your search. Do you see the light?"

Silence.

"Do you see the light?"

"No. I see darkness all around me."

"Can you move?"

Silence.

"Can you move?"

"Another body is crushing me."

"Can you move it out of the way?"

"No. I can't. I can't move."

"But you have to move to find Wakana. You want to find your daughter, right?"

"Yes! I must find Wakana."

"So reach out and start to swim until you see the light. Then all you have to do is continue in that direction."

Silence. Two hours had passed since Yuko arrived.

"Do you see the light?"

"It's possible that I can see a bit of light." Wakana's father grew suspicious. "And who are you?"

"I am Kaneta, a monk, the caretaker of the temple in the city of Kurihara."

"Do you have the powers?"

"Yes. My powers are sufficient."

Another hour passed before Wakana's father finally saw the light. Together with Yuko's fiancé, Kaneta carried her from the pillows in the guest room and seated her in front of the altar.

"You are a spirit in the body of a twenty-five-year-old woman, I will try to help you get out. You've quite simply lost your way. Now you will swim toward the light. And I will pray. Do you understand?"

But when they sat down in front of the altar, Wakana's father started to have doubts.

"Will you lead me to the light? Will I find Wakana? Will your powers be enough?"

Kaneta couldn't take it anymore, and said, "Look, you're a father. You know what it means when something bad is happening to your daughter. So just imagine what the parents of this woman are feeling, because you're inside her body and you don't want to leave!"

"I'm sorry . . . I just want to find Wakana."

Kaneta was finally able to start the ceremony; he sprinkled Yuko's head with water, chanted the sutras, and lit the incense. The girl's muscles relaxed, her expression became more gentle, and when she said her thanks, she had her normal, slightly higher voice.

Yuko left the temple at 2 A.M.

Conversations with subsequent spirits always lasted six or seven hours. In addition to Wakana's father, he was also paid a visit by:

A World War II navy veteran.

A girl who made her living as a hostess, entertaining customers at bars with conversation.

A woman who was not able to escape the tsunami.

A high school student hit by a car.

An old man, who left his wife behind when he died and could not forgive himself for it.

And then there was a small boy. A little lad. Maybe five years old. He was calling his mom. Kaneta will never forget that. "Mom, Mommy, don't be mad at me! Mommy, forgive me!" The boy had been taking care of his younger brother, Yo, when the city was hit by the tsunami. "Mommy, I didn't want to! Please, don't be mad at me. I wasn't able to hold on to his hand. I'm sorry, I'm sorry! I didn't want to let go of his hand. Please, forgive me, don't be mad at me for letting him go!"

This time it was Kaneta's wife who started to talk with the boy. She took Yuko by the hand and said, "Don't be afraid, I'm a mom, too. You don't have to be scared. Everything is okay, let's go find the light together."

They had no idea how much time had passed before the boy said that he could see the light and he'd keep going on his own now.

Yuko showed up at Kaneta's temple for the last time maybe about a year ago. She was planning her wedding and a move to the Aichi prefecture, far south of Tōhoku. Together with her were two professors from the university in Sendai, who wanted to study her case. This time the ghost that possessed her was the ghost of a dog. Yuko was throwing herself about, though three men were holding her down. She was growling. Kaneta was unable to ask any questions. A dog wouldn't be able to answer them. So he took the woman to the temple to perform a ritual—light the incense, read the sutras, and sprinkle her with blessed water. She was walking on all fours around the temple, growling, and she even barked a few times. He waited for her to calm down.

It wasn't until later that Yuko told him how the dog had seen his owners leaving in haste. They lived in Futaba, the city where the Fukushima Daiichi power plant is located. They were in such a hurry that they didn't let him loose. And they didn't leave him any food either. Maybe they were counting on coming back soon? He was in agony for a few days. His spirit stayed there long enough to see how a figure in a white uniform approached his body. The person touched the animal's neck, determined that it was dead, and disappeared beyond the fence.

Ghosts have been appearing less and less as of late. They stopped reporting fires. They no longer hail taxis or stop buses in the middle of the night. There are no more lines forming where the supermarket used to be. Children no longer come back to play with their toys.

Rather, the ghosts show up in the dreams of their friends, husbands, wives, and parents.

The Japanese believe that the souls of the deceased will not find peace until their bodies are cremated and put to rest in the family grave. The grave works like a gate—it lets the deceased go to paradise and return to Earth during Obon, the festival of the dead in August. The dead take care of the living. The living take care of the dead.

Yet if, for whatever reason, the rituals are not fulfilled, the ghosts float between the worlds. Sometimes anger keeps them here. Sometimes it's love. They cannot find peace.

Those whose bodies have not been found come back.

Those who have not been identified and their ashes placed in a common grave come back.

Those who did not take care of important matters come back.

Those who are furious come back.

Those who love come back.

Those who are unaware of their own death come back.
Those whose families do not want to let go cannot leave.

# II

## The Shadow

The beach is full of people. They've spread out their beach tow-els, they've taken out their food; they sit and watch the ocean. Kids run around, chasing a ball. It's mid-summer, with the kind of humidity that makes your clothes cling to your body. *Beta beta*, the Japanese say. It isn't until late afternoon that the weather becomes more pleasant. The sun slowly hides behind the horizon, cicadas hum, and the air smells of salt.

The beach isn't very wide and is lined with evenly placed, flat stones at one end. It was built on soil taken from the Pacif-ic. Filling the background is the gray skyline of Tokyo. Not too far away is one of the largest Ferris wheels in the world. On clear days, you can see Mount Fuji from the top.

The sun goes further down, changing the color of the ocean from silver to gold. A ball is dropped by tiny hands and rolls down toward the shore. One of the mothers pulls up her skirt and goes ankle-deep into the water to try to catch the ball before the wave does. Suddenly, she stands up straight. She looks into the sun and shields her eyes. Her skirt is drenched in the salt water. She tucks her hair behind her ear, grabs the ball, and turns to the children. She chases them in the direction of the beach. The mothers pack the food into baskets, while the fathers shake the sand from the towels. Two young girls take a selfie against the Tokyo skyline. Nobody pays any attention to the shadow creeping just below the surface of the water.

It isn't until the black shape blocks the sun that people turn their heads toward the ocean. The monster stands a dozen or so meters from the shore, water dripping from its body. Its skin is covered in scales, with an enormous tail and a row of spikes on its back, twisted claws, sharp teeth, and small eyes in its reptilian head.

A roar thunders over the beach.

When it stops, the silence seems unbearable. Even the cicadas are silent. The black creature takes a deep breath. It looks beyond the beach, in the direction of Tokyo. It exhales a nuclear flame—brighter than the sun.

ゴジラ.

*Gojira.*

Godzilla attacked Japan twenty-eight times (and the shores of America twice). A prehistoric reptile that feeds on radiation. Nuclear tests awakened him from a long sleep, similar to death. He has the power to regenerate, bullets deflect off his hard skin, while airplane gunners only intensify his rage. An enormous force that we try to control. That we don't understand. And over which we have no power.

He appeared in Tokyo Bay for the first time in 1954. He stepped over railroad tracks and train cars, shook buildings, broke windows, started fires. He left smoking debris in his path. The destruction of Hiroshima and Nagasaki, as well as the bombing of Tokyo in 1945, when nearly 90 percent of the city was burned to the ground, was still fresh in the minds of Japanese moviegoers. Older viewers also remembered the great earthquake of 1923, when at least 140,000 people died. Over half a million buildings were destroyed at the time, though some sources estimate it was nearly 700,000.

Ishirō Honda's movie made reference to well-known images.

Godzilla dies from a weapon so terrifying that his creator, Doctor Serizawa, hesitates as to whether he should tell the world at all that he is able to slay Godzilla. He burns all his documents, takes the "oxygen destroyer" underwater, and dies along with the prehistoric reptile. Once Godzilla, who but a moment ago was madly destroying Tokyo, is reduced to nothing but a skeleton, nobody cheers. It's not our success. It's our failure.

The only thing we know how to do is destroy.

Godzilla immediately became a celebrity. He even has his own star on the Hollywood Walk of Fame. He starred in commercials for cars, energy bars, and athletic shoes. With every movie, he gained new powers: in addition to the nuclear force (with varying intensity), a breath of fire, an electrocuting bite, superhuman speed, and even a nuclear-powered thrust that let him fly. He went to battle with a three-headed dragon—King Ghidorah, the terror of the cosmos. He fought Gigan, a brutal cyborg with blades for arms and a chainsaw in its torso (it's the only monster that managed to pierce Godzilla's thick skin). Finally, he fought with his own mechanized clone, the Mechagodzilla. He also confronted Biollante, a bizarre mutant made from the cells of the deceased daughter of a famous scientist, the genetic material of her beloved roses, and a few cells from Godzilla himself. Biollante snaps its sharp-toothed jaws and spits a poisonous spray.

Some of Godzilla's opponents, who were even killed by him, would take his side in subsequent movies; such as Mothra, the giant moth, the armored Anguirus (who, as Godzilla's enemy, confronted him in Osaka, completely destroying the castle there in the process). Or Radon, the enormous radioactive pterosaur that lives in the Aso volcano on Kyushu. For the most part, Godzilla wreaked destruction in Tokyo, but he also razed Kyoto, Okinawa and the Hakone peninsula to the ground. He defended himself (and the world) against space aliens, visitors from the future or creatures inhabiting underwater kingdoms. He even had a son, a small annoying creature named Minya that appeared with him in five movies (Godzilla is referred to as "Dad" here, and is therefore male, although in Japanese and other languages, the creature was agender or female).

Godzilla would always stubbornly return, whether he was thrown into a volcano, the ocean abyss, or frozen, and his heart would melt much like fuel in a nuclear reactor. Godzilla did not always choose good roles; indeed, he would sometimes appear in features that were miserable failures. The more grotesque he would become, the more the public loved him. Yet he really doesn't care about people. They're just these small creatures who only create problems. If Godzilla defends us, it's not because he all of a sudden became good—he does not understand the concept of good and evil. Godzilla is an enormous force that strikes blindly at anybody and anything that threatens him. One of Godzilla' s producers, Shōgo Tomiyama, compares him to the god of destruction. The more we fight him, the stronger he becomes. He feeds on our fear. His only purpose in life is complete annihilation. Something new can only be built on ruins.

Godzilla—the kami of destruction. But also of revival.

We try to tame him. We built monuments for him. Like the one at the entrance to Yūrakuchō station in downtown Tokyo. The small figure with the long tail and open mouth doesn't seem dangerous at all. Just the right size for us, deprived of its terrifying force. We turn him into amulets—brass figures and rubber keychains that you can buy at stalls next to temples and in souvenir shops. The Tōhō Film Studio (producer of twenty-eight Godzilla movies) installed a twelve-meter-tall head of the monster on the roof of its building in Shinjuku, a district full of bars, shops, and neon signs. From below, it looks like the giant reptile is attacking his creators. But if you take the elevator to the roof, you see that it's only a concrete head attached to a stone pedestal.

A pop-culture hero. Tamed. Cut to size. Ridiculed. Turned into a rubber symbol of kitsch. Even when he scares you, he's not that scary.

But these are just tricks. No amulets will help us. When he returns, and he will most certainly return, we will tremble with fear. He will suddenly emerge at the ocean shore. He will block out the sun and the world will once again be petrified.

If we survive, it won't be because of our own courage or resourcefulness, but because our time hasn't come yet.

His shadow will appear first.
It's always with us anyway.

## Kampai!

"Do you like our sake, Kasia san? It's *daiginjō*—the best grade! Made with rice grains polished for a long time until they're reduced by half. No husks, just pure rice. You can feel it in the taste, don't you think? It's fresh and strong and smells like flowers; as if you were drinking spring. Here, let me pour you some more. Actually, I shouldn't really be drinking. They've cut out three quarters of my liver. It was over ten years ago, a gigantic tumor, twelve centimeters. My surgery lasted nine hours. Now I need to watch out for myself. But a little sake once in a while won't do any harm. Okay then, *kampai*! But let me explain something to you; we here in Japan don't really call sake *sake*, did you know about that, Kasia san? We call it *nihonshu*. Sake is quite simply alcohol. From beer to liquor to brandy. Well, but for you, *nihonshu* is sake, so let's leave it like that. You have a lot of funny little customs. I remember the first time I was in Europe, at a conference. I walk into the bathroom at the hotel, and I see another bowl next to the toilet. I didn't know what it was, but after all, one had to be for '#1' and the other for '#2,' because otherwise, why put two toilets next to each other? Ha, ha, ha. I nearly took care of my business in the bidet!"

"Kasia san, don't pay any attention to Hikaru san's foolish jokes. He always makes us laugh. Here, let me pour some more."

"But it's true, my dear Yoko san! After that, I lived in Switzerland and Russia, I got used to you and now I don't eat rice for breakfast, but I enjoy fresh, fragrant bread. And I drink red wine, it's good for the heart. But still, I prefer *nihonshu*—sake."

"Our sake is exceptional. Neither wine nor vodka. I think it's closest to beer. Because it's brewed as well. And it's not that strong at all. From 15-20 percent. The doctor said that he has no idea how that cancer grew so big. And in such a short time. No more than two years. And that's when I remembered the word that I hadn't heard for over half a century: *hibakusha*."

"We're all *hibakusha* here—irradiated from the bomb. Hikaru san, let me pour you a bit more of this; it happens to come from Nagano, from the Japanese Alps. The Europeans called them that because it reminded them of the Alps. Fresh air, crystal clear streams, and snowy peaks. And the sake has a delicate fruity taste to it. Although I never had cancer, my grandson suffers from a low white-blood-cell count and he's constantly sick. Although I will tell you, Kasia san, that although each of us went through that, we don't talk about it at all. Only Hikaru san, once his cancer was cured, started to talk about it. He even went to Israel to give a lecture. But us here . . . we were afraid of meeting you today. These are things you just don't talk about. Oh! Kasia san, you know how to hold a sake cup? Are you sure you weren't born Japanese? Maybe another piece of sushi? Sea urchins happen to be in season now, please try some."

"Yes, yes, Kasia san, Wataru san is right, you absolutely must try the sea urchin! We'll order more right away. Well indeed, we don't talk about it, but it's not a problem for me, because I don't remember much. I was three years old, or not even. I have only one image in my head; three-year-olds don't have memories, so even that is exceptional. I see it very clearly. I'm crouching over the toilet. At the time in Japan, we had old-style toilets: a hole in the ground and that was it. All of a sudden, the walls started coming down like a house of cards. I ran out, yelling *Mommy, Mommy*! I fell into her arms. My mom was wearing a white blouse. Please try this one, it's from Kyoto, it has a delicate taste and pleasantly fills your mouth. The secret is in the water. Because what is *nihonshu* actually, meaning sake? Let me explain it to you. It's cooked rice, a special type that has more starch, you add to that a *Kōji* mushroom, which decomposes the starch into sugar, and yeast which ferments the sugar into alcohol. And water, water, water. When you tour a sake brewery, at the end during the tasting they first have you try the water. It's the water that has the flavor of the entire region sealed in it. Sake from Kyoto is soft and delicate. Very feminine. While the sake from Kobe is full of minerals; it's very robust and manly."

"But I like the sake from the mountains of Fukushima the most. Slightly sweet, but with such a rich taste! They take the water from underwater springs beneath the Bandai volcano. Hikaru san studied in Kyoto. And that's probably why he remembers the local sake so fondly. He's the youngest here, aren't you Hikaru san? Only seventy-three! He pulls our average down, because we're all nearing eighty, a Shigeru san just turned ninety. I remember it all well . . . First there was a bright flash. *Pika!* That's what we say when a blinding light shows up from nowhere. And then a warm orange color that changes to yellow, silver, green. I can't even name them all, they were all so beautiful. It wasn't until a moment later that I heard the sound. *Don!* Just once and that was it. The roof collapsed and the windows were shattered from the blast. Debris from the glass was stuck in my back. I was three and half kilometers from the hypocenter. We all know our distances. It's like a middle name."

"Ha, ha. Hikaru, two point nine."

"Shigeru, two point two."

"And me, Wataru, six kilometers."

"Kazuko, second generation. You know, my mom remembered those colors differently than Yoko san. She said that the entire sky turned light-blue. Like a calm ocean on a sunny day. But she was eleven kilometers from the hypocenter and standing on a hill. She saw a cloud floating above the city. It didn't look at all like a mushroom, but rather like an ice cream cone, the tip a glittering pink.

"Oh good, the waiter. Let's order some appetizers. So what if we've already eaten dinner? Kasia san, you will have the full sake experience. Deep-fried tofu, fried seaweed, gingko nuts, squid tempura. What else could we get? Edamame? Will you try some *shirako*? It's grilled salmon milt. It melts in your mouth. Well yes, milt are the seminal glands. And yes, they have semen. What else have we got here? Some pickles, of course. Ah yes! And please give us sake served in a *tokkuri*, not in a bottle. Kasia san, you don't know what a *tokkuri* is? Well, it's that belly-shaped pot for sake. Do you know that the hole in the neck of the pot has to be as big as your pinkie? Only then do you hear the pleasant *tok tok tok* sound when you pour the sake into your cup."

"I remember much more, my friends, just give me some more of that one from Nagano: it smells of the pine forest and the rain. I was twenty years old, working in a weapons factory hidden in a tunnel near Nagasaki, exactly two point two kilometers away from the hypocenter. The tin walls shook. The factory was located outside of the city, in the hills. I stepped outside. Rice fields were burning. Two women were lying on the road. They could not open their eyes; that's how swollen their eyelids were. They kept on saying that they were cold."

"Yes, people complained of cold, I remember that well. Kasia san, wouldn't you like some more sushi? We didn't order too much. And they were thirsty. A pleading choir of voices was in the air over Hiroshima, calling *Water, water*. But with water or without it, they would have died anyway. There was nothing more that could have saved them. I remember one more thing. Hot asphalt. I was crossing a bridge four hours after the explosion, and the soles of my feet were totally burned. In the hypocenter itself, the temperature was so high that the only thing left of people were shadows on stones."

"I don't remember the light or the boom. But for the past forty years, I've remembered the smell. You know what that smell was? I'm embarrassed to even say it! Barbecued dried squid. Just like the beer snack."

"Ah, and here is our waiter. Kasia san, let's do an experiment; not many people realize that the thickness of the *guinomi*, you know, the cup that you drink sake from, matters. See, this one is thin, made of porcelain, and this one is ceramic, with a coarse texture. I pour the same sake into each cup. Please try it now. Unusual, isn't it? You know why this happens? Because if the *guinomi* is thin, the fluid first hits the tip of the tongue, which detects sweet flavors. And if it's thicker, the sake first touches the back of your tongue and it tastes more bitter. Everything matters when it comes to sake! Not just the water. It matters whether the rice was mixed with barley, if alcohol has been added, if it's pasteurized or aged in cedar barrels, if it's been filtered through a very thin or slightly thicker gauze. Even the temperature matters. You can serve the same sake at a temperature of five or fifty-five degrees! When do I warm it up and when do I cool it down? Well, that depends on many things. The season. My mood. What I eat with it. In bars, they heat cheap sake to hide any shortcomings. Oh, will you look at that, I'm going on and on here, but the cups are empty! Pour some sake for our guest! After all, she won't pour it herself, come on now, where are your manners? Wait now, what happened after that?"

"What do you mean, Wataru san? You don't remember? Then rain started to fall in the city and the surrounding area. My dad picked me up from school and took me home. Laundry was drying in the yard. There were black, greasy streaks on my sister's diapers. Even in places far from Hiroshima, fish in ponds were floating belly up. We didn't know what was going on. A week had passed since the explosion, and perfectly healthy people were dying. No burns, no fractures. Suddenly, purple spots would start appearing all over their bodies, they would have nosebleeds and diarrhea, and their hair would fall out. We thought they had poisoned us with some kind of gas. That they dropped a virus. Or bacteria. People who would go into the city to look for their loved ones in the ruins a few days after the *pikadon* would get sick. Kasia san, I already told you that *pika* is a flash and *don* is an explosion? That's how we called what had happened. He was sick from the *pikadon*, he died of the *pikadon*. *Pikadon*. *Pikadon*. *Pikadon*!"

"Yoko san, perhaps a bit more of that sake from Kyoto? For my blood pressure. Go ahead, don't be shy!"

"My mom would tell me about the waves of death. People who were a kilometer away from the hypocenter were dying yesterday, those who were a hundred meters further away are dying today, while those who were a hundred meters further toward the hill will die tomorrow. Nobody knew when it was going to end. And whether it would end at all."

"It's true, Keiko chan, nobody knew anything. And when the Americans came into the city at the beginning of September, we were hoping that they would give us medicine. They didn't give us a damn thing. They just said that no one else will die of that any more. Even today, it's difficult to provide any official data. One hundred forty thousand people in Hiroshima and seventy thousand people in Nagasaki by the end of 1945, although there are no two statistics that say the same."

"Kasia san, please try this, it's sake from Kobe, it has a sharper taste to it and it's dry. In my opinion, it's the best in all of Japan. To our guest! *Kampai!*"

"*Kampai*, Kasia san! Do you know that we drink sake during wedding ceremonies? My wife and I got married near Tokyo, in a small Shinto temple. Yes, we all get married in temples, it looks so beautiful! Brides in white coats and the round hoods on their heads. And the men in black kimonos, makes them feel like a samurai. They sit in front of the altar, before the gods, and they drink three sips from the same cup. There are three cups as well, each one bigger than the other. What are they a symbol of? Some people say that it's heaven, Earth and the human. Or that it's love, wisdom, and happiness. Others, however, think it's hate, passion, and ignorance—our biggest flaws. I told my wife that I was a *hibakusha*. She knew where I was from. We never talked about it anymore. I had forgotten the word for fifty years. But then the cancer came . . . But you know, there are people who will never admit to it."

"It's true. In Japan, we don't really talk about this at all. People do not always understand. The stories I've heard about engagements broken off! Because the bride was from Hiroshima or from Nagasaki. Right after the war, wounds would heal in a strange way; they'd leave huge red scars. Nobody wanted to have these people with scars in bathhouses. Maybe it was contagious? Nobody knew what radiation was. When I was at summer camp and told everybody I was from Hiroshima, girls would spy on me in the bathhouse. It was as if I had been hiding scales under my clothes!"

"After all, we ourselves had no idea what was happening to us. I would feel weak. For no reason at all. I would have headaches and I couldn't walk straight. It would pass after three days. I knew people who couldn't find a job because of that. People would say that they were lazy. And tease them that they were *bura bura*. That's what we say when somebody walks around in circles without any purpose and wastes time. This sake is so good, let's order some more! The drink of the gods. Kasia san, do you know what the gods do in October? All of them, in harmony and without exception, all eight million of them, go to Izumo Temple; that's in Shimane, there in the west of Japan, on the opposite coast from Kyoto. They meet to decide what will happen in the following year: who will die, who will be born, and who will get married. But really, all they do all month long is drink sake. What's funny is that in Shimane, October is the 'month with the gods,' while in the rest of Japan it's the 'month without the gods.' Only one of them stays behind; Ebisu, god of the fishermen. He was born without bones, like a jellyfish. He can't hear the gong summoning everybody to the feast. Poor guy. All that fun he's missing."

"And do you know that nobody told us what really happened until 1951, or maybe 1952? The Americans imposed censorship. Photographers who would make their way in would have all their rolls of film confiscated. Likewise, movie crews would have their film stock taken away. The phrase *harmful effects of radiation* would never appear in newspapers. But they put us under medical observation. They created a special commission, back in 1946. The Atomic Bomb Casualty Commission. They were collecting information about the effects of the bomb. A long black car would come to pick me up. I'd never seen one like it before. They would take me to a clinic. They would listen to me with a stethoscope and take a sample of my blood and urine. They would take photos. I never received any medicine. It seems that the results were never even provided to Japanese doctors. They were sent to the States. It wasn't until Japan signed the peace treaty and paid out war reparations that censorship was eased. The occupation was over. We became friends."

"And that's when the rumors started. That something was wrong with our genes. And the feeling, Kasia san, that you know that something is not right, but you never know what it is. Will this have an effect? How, and where? Maybe your child will be stillborn? Maybe your grandchild will suffer from leukemia? Or maybe you'll die from metastatic cancer? An acquaintance of mine miscarried six times. My friend's daughter died having battled brain cancer for six months. Is it because of the bomb or was it a coincidence? We will never find out. But we will keep on asking ourselves this question until the day we die. And then our children will be asking themselves the same question. And so will their children. And their children's children. Oh well, just give me some more of that sake. And did you know that the kamikaze would drink sake just before their final flight?"

"And you are all just going on and on about the war. And what good did it do them that they drank sake? Meaningless deaths. They were young and stupid. So easy to manipulate. I was born one year after the bomb. And my son has cerebral palsy. And I think every day about whether I was right to get pregnant. After all, I knew who I was. And so what? I'd like some more of that dry sake, the one from Kobe, I liked it."

"Kasia san, let me tell you something about the horrible properties of nuclear bombs. Seven thousand degrees, a hot blast, which initially travels at a speed of four hundred meters per second, and the radiation that penetrates everything. Because the skin can stop some of it and light does not penetrate the skin, but that gamma radiation and the neutrons, well, they go straight through and right into the cells, and if they break the strand of DNA, well, then . . . do you understand now? Oh, and I didn't finish the story about that cancer. The doctor said that 'perhaps there may be a medical reason, but, Mr. Kobayashi, we can never state with 100 percent certainty that it was the bomb that caused the cancer.' However, I have the right to a governmental Victim Certificate. It's not the same certificate as the one that states that you are a *hibakusha* but it entitles you to additional free medical tests. The victim certificate provides a pension, ¥137,000 per month, a bit more than $1,200. I waited two years. It just takes forever, the criteria do not cover all diseases. You know, Kasia san, we are not that young anymore."

"Let's stop talking about this already. There are people whose job it is to tell these stories. In museums, at lectures. *Kataribe*—storytellers. It's one of our traditions that we have people who talk about disasters. Not only about Hiroshima and Nagasaki. About the Kobe earthquake. Now they're talking about the tsunami as well. Have you ever listened to a *kataribe*? You have? So you know that they are very precise in their storytelling. As if they were reading from a piece of paper. That's where you'll find the peeling skin and incinerated hair. The only thing you won't find there are emotions. After all, they have to protect themselves somehow. They say that they've forgiven? What else are they supposed to say? Oh well . . . it's all water under the bridge. No use in brooding over it. As long as it never happens again. Did we finish the sake? Uh, no we didn't. There's enough for one last cup for everyone."

"Terrible things are happening, Kasia san, you know? We're already hearing news about engagements being broken off. About mothers who move away with their children and leave the fathers on their own. And about flattened tires in cars with Fukushima license plates. We know what they can expect. Rumors. Anxiety. Fear. When you have a headache, you don't know if it's due to the radiation or because of fatigue. You're left all alone with the issue. Until the day you die."

"Now I'm all upset, yet we're so happy to have a visitor from Poland. Please come visit us again! You'll be most welcome whenever you'll be in Japan. We'll talk, eat and drink! And then talk even more, and eat even more, and drink even more!

We can't wait until you come back. It's always a joy for us to meet someone from a faraway country. Completely by chance, there was an article about Poland in the paper today. I even cut out a fragment of it. It seems you have a painting by Leonardo da Vinci there. A French scientist discovered that the painter had changed his mind several times; he couldn't make up his mind as to the cut of the dress and the color; initially, there was no animal in there at all, then a weasel appeared, and only later did Da Vinci change it to an ermine. Now that is very interesting. I've never been in Europe, maybe I'll go there one day. But until then, let's drink to your health! *Kampai!*"

## The Atom

In the first picture, we see two men sitting on swivel chairs. They are dressed in drill jackets with breast pockets and the collars turned up. You can't see their faces as they look at a wall full of buttons, lights, dials, and clocks. This is the control room of the reactor at the Tsuruga nuclear power plant, opened in 1970; one of the first three to be built in Japan. The men are carefully observing the gauges. They note data in thick notebooks. Everything is under control. Less than fourteen years earlier, in 1956, 70 percent of Japanese people associated the atom with something harmful. They didn't want to have anything to do with it. Not even Eisenhower's electrifying *Atom for Peace* speech of 1953 could convince them. And while the Japanese Government was interested in nuclear energy and the United States offered assistance, the Japanese people were unable to get rid of their nuclear-aversion. Especially after radioactive dust fell on the *Daigo Fucorn Maru* fishing boat following the detonation of a hydrogen bomb in the Bikini Islands in 1954 by the U.S. The Japanese fishermen were about 180 kilometers from the center of the explosion. From the boundary of the zone which was designated as dangerous—twenty-five kilometers. The entire boat was covered in white, snow-like flakes. The men loaded them into garbage bags with their bare hands. Two weeks later, they arrived at the port of Yaizu in southern Japan. They reported nausea and headaches. Their gums were bleeding and their skin was burned. The radio operator who had been reporting the event live as it was happening said they saw something bigger than the sun. He died six months later. Some of the men spent the entire year in the hospital. The Japanese were angry. Thirty-two million people, one third of the population, signed a petition against the use of nuclear weapons. But the Japanese government wanted to cooperate with the U.S. Research funding had already been allocated and commitments had already been made to purchase the technology. The Americans intended to build the first experimental reactor in Hiroshima. On November 1, 1955, in Tokyo, Shinto priests performed the *harae* ritual. It cleans that which is dirty and contaminated. Just as Izanagi washed his body clean of the infernal filth after escaping from hell, so the priests washed their hands and faces, and sprinkled salt on the earth. They recited the verses of the prayer. Using a wooden wand with strips of white paper attached to it, they cleansed all those gathered. They offered sacrifices for the kami—rice and sake. That was how the priests welcomed the return of the atom to Japan. The *harae* marked the beginning of a six-week exhibition at Hibiya Park in Tokyo called "Atoms for Peace."

Peaceful atoms produce energy, cure cancer, disinfect food, and power ships and aircraft. They support science and therefore help humanity develop. They never kill. Well, maybe only worms. The exhibition was also shown in seven other Japanese cities. In Hiroshima, more than one hundred thousand people visited it in the course of three weeks. That's nearly five thousand people a day. Newspapers with ties to the government wrote that atoms would reduce electricity expenses by two thousand times. And in the end, everyone will have their own power plant at home, since bars of uranium can be installed in basements. A series on how the atom could be harnessed was run on television, lectures were broadcast, and a live discussion was organized for the following year called "Let's Talk About the Atom." Japanese children would watch the Walt Disney feature "Our Friend the Atom," where nuclear power is portrayed as a powerful genie. He will fulfill our three wishes. We have to choose the wishes wisely though, because the power of the genie can be dangerous. How we use it is entirely up to us. So, the first wish is to have a source of energy that would never run out. The second wish is to have magic rays that will keep people healthy. And the third? Ensure world peace. The message was clear: nuclear energy is clean, safe, efficient and useful. In 1958, two years after the first survey, only a third of Japanese people associated the atom with something harmful. In 1966, Japan opened its first nuclear power plant in the village of Tôkai. The idea of building a reactor near Hiroshima was abandoned. In spite of the enthusiasm shown by journalists, power stations were built far from big cities; it was safer that way. Two more were commissioned in 1970. And more were being built. Today, Japan has forty-eight nuclear reactors in fifteen power plants. The second picture shows pipes. Big, thick, and glossy. At least one meter in diameter. And then you have air vents, fans, railings, industrial lamps, ventilation shafts, concrete stairs. The photo is shot from the perspective of the ground up, and it's hard to discern where it all starts and where it ends. It's actually an abstract presentation full of twisted lines. Metal and gloss. The inside of the reactor. In a nuclear power plant, it isn't the uranium or plutonium producing the power, but a large turbine. In one of the most popular types of reactor (boiling water reactor), nuclear fuel—or radioactive capsules arranged one on top of the other—is contained in bars coated with an aluminum alloy and zirconium alloy. The reactor core is made up of several hundred such bars placed next to each other; each bar can be up to four meters long. When uranium breaks down (this reaction occurs continuously), it produces radioactive isotopes that remain inside the aluminum bars. But the reaction also generates heat; the bars heat the water that circulates around the core to 285 degrees Celsius. Through a system of pipes, the generated steam passes into an adjacent room and powers the turbine. Then it condenses back into water and returns to the core. But before the water returns there, it needs to be cooled. A separate water circuit is used for this purpose. The pipes coming from the reactor wrap around the pipes from the water tank. That's why nuclear power plants are built near lakes or on the sea coast. This is to make sure that the supply of cooling water never runs out (it's important the water from the external tank never mixes with the reactor water; there are two separate circuits, otherwise radiation could easily penetrate the circuit and leak outside). The core is protected by a metal tank that can withstand high pressure (its walls can be up to twenty centimeters thick) and a two-meter thick reinforced shield. This final shield is approximately thirty meters high and twenty meters in diameter. Rising above the reactor is the reactor building, which usually has seven floors, two of which are underground. The entire reactor—with its reinforced concrete shield, cooling-pipe system, fire protection system, and ventilation shafts—is in the middle. There is also a fourteen-meter deep pool for spent fuel (usually located on one of the upper floors) that will continue to emit high levels of radiation for many decades (some isotopes, such as uranium, even take a billion years to decompose; the fuel is temporarily stored in pools until it is transferred to a radioactive-waste disposal facility). The water that the spent fuel rods are immersed in blocks any radiation. Stationed in the control room next to the reactor are technicians in drill jackets who observe the gauges. They note data in thick notebooks. They have everything under control. But you can't just seal the uranium in reinforced concrete shields and shut the door. In the reactor, steam is constantly hissing, the turbine is constantly rumbling, and the fans are constantly buzzing. Something breaks, something slips, something gets stuck. Something leaks, something cracks. All this machinery needs constant attention—it has to be maintained, replaced, and cleaned. Somebody needs to enter the reactor every day. When you look at it for the first time, it's hard to comprehend what exactly is going on in the third picture. On the right side of the photo, you have equipment on a wall with knobs and indicator dials; they look like radios. Kneeling near the equipment, with his back to the photographer, is a worker with a hood over his head. Two men are standing over him. Set on the floor are buckets and boxes, and a clock hangs on the wall. In the foreground we have a man looking in the direction of three workers exiting an oval-shaped tunnel in the center of the photo. They are pushing a cart. The core of the reactor is behind them. All the men are wearing protective suits, gloves, rubber boots, helmets, goggles, and air filter masks. The temperature rises to 40° Celsius inside the suit. The goggles fog up. The mask limits your field of view, although you can't see much in this half-light anyway. When employees shed their suits in the transition zone, they are drowning in their own sweat and gulp in fresh air. Each power plant needs fifteen hundred employees on duty daily. They check pipes, clean floors, remove leaking radioactive water, weld leaking tanks, or transfer nuclear waste. Once a year, the power plant is decommissioned for a mandatory inspection; at that time, the number of workers required increases to several thousand. The fourth picture shows a group of men wearing drill jackets and work pants, although some of them have on regular jeans or cargo pants. Dark skin, swollen eyes, and disheveled hair. Homeless and unemployed. Farmers, fishermen, builders, truck drivers, and former miners who lost their jobs after the country shifted from coal to oil and the atom. As well as those who are still *burakumin*—in the Edo era, these people were considered to be defiled, because they touched death (tanners, butchers, and gravediggers). And although they have enjoyed equal rights since 1871, some mothers still refuse to give their daughter's hand to a *burakumin*, whose grandfather had tanned animal skins over a hundred years ago. The bottom of the social ladder. Yet they are the ones who build the greatness of Japan. They are tempted by high daily pay-rates (¥10,000, about

$1,000) for easy work, for which no qualifications or diplomas are required. Sometimes, they work only two hours per day, wiping the floor with a rag. Sometimes they work eight hours doing minor repair work. They are not employed by the owner of the power plant, but by subcontractors. They are not full-time employees. They do not belong to any trade unions. They do not receive training. Some of them remove their masks and turn off their dosimeters inside the reactor. The beeping irritates them and the mask bothers them as they work. Nuclear power plants employ about seven hundred people in full-time positions—they are mainly engineers and upper management. The remaining people are hired by temporary employment agencies. Or through direct recruitment, like in the slums in Osaka, where solicitors show up every day before dawn. They have notes posted on the windows of their vans with the place of work and the daily rate. No one says a word about what radiation is. The annual permissible dose limit is fifty millisieverts (and one hundred millisieverts over five years).[1] Radiation is measured by dosimeters distributed to employees. Sometimes you can get this dose in three minutes, sometimes in a month, and other times you're able to stay well within the limit throughout the year. The system is quite straightforward—the longer you work, the more you earn. So it's better for you to lower your dose levels, because when you reach your limit, they'll fire you. After all, you're not a full-time employee. You're nuclear waste. But the next day, you can find a job at another nuclear power plant—just as if your radiation dose had been reset. People like that who migrate from one nuclear

---

1 These are pre-2011 limits. Japanese limits are different from international limits.

power station to another are referred to as nuclear nomads. And they are the ones who make sure that nuclear power plants operate without a hitch. In the fifth picture, you can't see much. Only black, thick, and swollen skin. In one spot you see a large mole with pimples around it. It's a photo of the right knee of Kazuyuki Iwasa, a plumber from Osaka. In 1971, he worked for two and a half hours at the Tsuruga nuclear power plant, one of the first, built in 1970. A blue tarp was lying on the floor. He was told that he should stay on it at all times and set any tools on it only. He worked close to the reactor core. The temperature was 40° Celsius. A red rash appeared around his knee. As if something had bitten him. Blisters appeared eight days later and the skin changed color. A dermatologist in Osaka stated, "It's radiation." Doctors at the hospital in Tokyo confirmed the diagnosis. In 1974, Iwasa sued the owner of the power plant, Japan Atomic Power Company, for which he had worked for two and a half hours of his life. The case constituted Japan's first ever claim for damages due to irradiation during work at a nuclear power plant. Weren't nuclear power plants supposed to be clean and safe? Iwasa lost the case. It was determined that it could not be unambiguously concluded that radiation was the cause of the disease—the dose registered in the documents was too low. There was also no evidence that the pipes and water in the bucket on that day had been contaminated. He appealed. And he appealed again. And again. In 1977, a young photographer, Kenji Higuchi, became interested in his case. For several months, he submitted requests for permission to go inside the Tsuruga power plant. His request was rejected every time. He wanted to get a job there, but employees are not allowed to bring so much as a pen into the plant. He stood at the gate for a week. To no avail. Finally, he wrote to the owner of the power plant that he would like to take pictures showing how the company cares about the safety of its employees. He was granted permission. In July 1977, he got in. He had three cameras and fifteen rolls of film. The photos he took inside of the reactor are among the first of their kind in the world. And the picture with the three workers pushing the cart taken right near the core (although that was clearly forbidden), is perhaps the only one of its kind in the world. The next picture is not really a picture, but a still from the movie "Nuclear Ginza," shot in 1995 by Nicholas Rohl for Channel 4 in the UK. The main character here is Kenji Higuchi, who visits nuclear power plant employees and slums in Osaka. In this still, Kunio Murai has a set of dentures in his hand. He did not work at the nuclear power plant for too long. He is a farmer from the west coast of Japan, where fifteen reactors were built one after the other. It was easier to find work cleaning the hallway at the power plant than planting rice. He would receive roughly one hundred dollars for two hours of work a day. While others refused to enter the reactor because they wondered why entry was safeguarded by a thick double door, Murai did not care about that at all. He believed that since he was working for a government company, he could put his trust in it. He had an easy assignment to do that day: a leak appeared in the turbine room, which had a maze of hundreds of pipes. He had to clean up the floor. He and his colleague grabbed some buckets and rags. They wore rubber gloves (Murai recalls that despite the fact that it was prohibited to carry out used gloves, workers felt it was foolish to throw away something that was still useful; so they would take them home and their wives wore them to wash the dishes). He didn't receive a mask that day. They put the wet rags in plastic bags. Their dosimeters were checked when they left the area. At first, the needle always shows zero, but then it jumps to a value between 30 and 50. This time though, the needle disappeared at the other end of the scale. Murai thought the device was broken. One month later, while eating lunch, his tooth crumbled to pieces. One tooth. Two teeth. Three. Pieces of teeth were falling out of his mouth. And then his hair fell out. And his joints began to swell. You can get dentures and you can simply be bald. But Murai was growing weaker. He couldn't get out of bed. "I became *bura bura*," he would say of himself. "I look normal on the outside, and my own brother looks at me and does not understand why I can't work. You're lazy, end of story. It's my fault, I was the one who wanted to have an easy job for quick money. I'm not complaining. But now I'm forty-eight years old,[2] and my wife has to support the family. I won't be able to do anything more in my lifetime. There is no cure for this." They came from the power plant with a check. Murai's wife agreed to $60,000. They never went to court. A few years later, Murai found out from the other employee who had been with him that day at the plant had received $20,000. He was supposed to refuse to testify if Murai sued the owner of the power plant.

The sixth picture was taken in color. It's 1994. A man in a beige shirt and black jacket holds a sheet of paper in his hands. Behind him are bushes, and in the background we see a water tank, square buildings, and a silo. It's the Tsuruga nuclear power plant and the man is Kazuyuki Iwasa, the first person to

---

2   In 1995, when the documentary was filmed.

sue a nuclear power plant for damages. The paper in his hands is a settlement that he was forced to sign after sixteen years of court battles. He received ¥6 million ($55,000) in six install-ments. He had to withdraw his lawsuit. When he entered the plant in 1971 for two and a half hours, he was forty-eight years old. He died on October 11, 2000. The official cause of death? Respiratory failure. Iwasa suffered from cancer.

## Boom!

**March 11, 2011. 3:27 P.M.**

Masao Yoshida, director of the Fukushima Daiichi Power Plant, did not see the first wave breaking up against the seawall. He is a tall, bulky man with short hair parted to the right, wire-rimmed glasses, and always sporting a friendly smile in pictures. But this time around he wasn't smiling. Instead, he was giv-ing curt orders. Forty-one minutes after the earthquake, over fifty-five hundred people had left the plant. Safety procedures remained in force even after the earthquake: every employee had to walk through the gate and turn in their personal dosim-eters to the guards. In accordance with the emergency action plan (practiced less than a week before), seven hundred people remained at the plant. Nearly everyone took cover in a quake-proof building that had recently been finished. It's situated on the hill, just behind the main office. It's reinforced, equipped with special filters, in-house power generators, and a separate phone line to the offices of the power plant owner, Tokyo Electric Power Company (TEPCO). On the second floor, in a room furnished with green walls, a conference table, and a row of screens, Masao Yoshida was gathering information about what was going on at the plant. The Fukushima Daiichi Nuclear Power Plant (Fukushima No. 1) was commissioned in 1971. It was built on the sea coast at the site of a former WWII kamikaze-training airbase. Perched on top of a hill were offices and a guest center, and even a sports field. At the bottom of the hill, ten meters above sea level, were the reactors along with the control rooms and turbine buildings. The ground level was specially lowered so the reactors would stand on granite rock and to reduce the distance to the ocean, from which the water to cool the cores was drawn directly. Spare sea water pumps and oil tanks were installed even lower, four meters above sea level. On that day, three of the six Fukushima Daiichi reactors, No. 1, No. 2, and No. 3, were in operation. No. 5 and No. 6 were shut down for routine maintenance. No. 4 was being repaired. For that time, the fuel rods were removed from the reactor core and moved to the spent-fuel pool on the upper floor of the building. During the earthquake, there were fourteen technicians present in the control room for reactors No. 1 and No. 2; the facility was a windowless bunker situated between the reactor and turbine buildings. The shocks threw the techs to their knees. What resounded in the room was the rattling of pipes hitting each other. And the screeching of the alarm and jarring sound of metal on top of that. But the men paid no attention to any of that. The only thing they cared about was if the lights on one of the panels were to change color; when all of the lights flashed red, they heaved a sigh of relief. Reactor No. 1 and No. 2 were automatically switched off. Control and emergency rods were inserted in between the fuel rods. Within a few seconds, the fission reaction was terminated. This is referred to as a scram. The earth was still shaking when the technicians heard yet another alarm, an annoying *Beep beep beep beep. Beep beep beep beep.* The lights on the control panels started to flash. The overhead lights went out. The power plant lost external power. The earthquake destroyed the power grid that provided Fukushima Daiichi with electricity. Then they heard the sound of the generators being triggered. These are large machines the size of locomotives with a diesel engine; the majority of them are located in the underground levels of reactor buildings. The lights in the control room flickered back on. The pumps supplying water to cool the bars in the core operated continuously, drawing water straight from the ocean (salt water was not pumped directly into the reactor—the steel would corrode, rendering the reactor useless; that's why the reactor water pipes and the ocean water pipes flowed in two separate, closed circuits wrapped around each other). The cover to the pipes routing the steam from the reactor to the turbine was closed. The core was cut off from the outside world. The emergency cooling and pressure monitoring system was activated. Everything was proceeding according to plan. Then another alarm was issued: *a tsunami is coming. It will be six meters high.* It did not even occur to the technicians that they should go outside. They stayed in the control room to observe the data coming from the reactors.

**March 11. 3:35 P.M.**

Yoshida didn't see the first wave breaking up against the ten-meter seawall. Nor did he see the second wave, which was almost fifteen meters high, as it stormed through the protective walls and carried parts of it toward the reactor buildings. It destroyed the ocean-water pumps needed to cool the core. It flowed into the basement through the ventilation ducts. It rose to four and a half meters and withdrew toward the Pacific. Employees receiving reports from the plant would run into the room with green walls, where Yoshida was stationed. *The tsunami washed away the spare fuel tanks! The water is throwing trucks from the parking lot against the reactor buildings! The direct-current switchgear has been flooded! The back-up batteries in the control room for reactor No. 1 and No. 2 have been flooded! Twelve generators have been flooded! Station blackout!* In the control room of reactors No. 1 and No. 2, the fourteen men who had been yelling over the noise of the generators for the past forty minutes suddenly went silent in astonishment. The roar of the machinery went silent. The ear-piercing alarm went off. The overhead light went out. They watched in silence as the indicators on the control panels went out, one at a time. In just one minute, the only light left in the room came from the green signs indicating the emergency exit. It was 3:37 P.M. The men consulted the instructions for crisis situations. However, none of the instructions anticipated a long-term loss of power throughout the entire nuclear plant. That's what the power generators were for. That's what the backup batteries, which were also flooded by water, were for. Generator trucks could be dispatched as a last resort. But no one anticipated that the roads destroyed by an earthquake and tsunami would become impassable.

**March 11. 3:40 P.M.**

When reactors No. 1, No. 2, and No. 3 automatically shut down just after the earthquake, they were still producing a small amount of heat—enough to heat the core to almost 3000° Celsius. After the scram, ensuring continued cooling was crucial. In theory, refrigeration systems should function without electricity, as they are driven by the steam into which the heated water is converted. But without being able to read the gauges, no one could be sure that these emergency systems were operational. If the fuel gets too hot, it will melt. Then the zirconium that provides the cladding for the fuel rod will react with the steam and produce flammable hydrogen. The tiniest spark is enough to blow up the reactor and spread radioactive particles all over the area. Maybe even all over Japan. After all, when the reactor in Chernobyl exploded, the radioactive cloud managed to reach Scotland. That's three thousand kilometers. That's more than the distance from the south of Kyushu to the northern tip of Hokkaido. Anybody who was at Fukushima Daiichi then was sure of one thing: they had to keep cooling down the reactors. Masao Yoshida was crushing a cigarette between his fingers. He made a snap decision. They would use the fire suppression system to cool the reactors. Inside each reactor building, there is a pump with an on-board diesel engine and a system of pipes running through the shield to the core. It would normally be used to extinguish fires; yet if the pumps were operational and if they would be able to hook them up to fire trucks, they would be able to get water to the core. Yoshida called the TEPCO Crisis Center in Tokyo. "I need fire trucks. And power generators," he said.

## March 11. After 4:00 P.M.

In accordance with the law, TEPCO had already informed the Japanese government of the situation in the power plant. Prime Minister Naoto Kan organized his own crisis team, made up of representatives of nuclear agencies and ministries associated with nuclear energy. Over the next few days, the crisis teams— the one in Tokyo and at the one at the power plant—would be communicating with each other. Not always successfully. After 4:00 P.M., the International Atomic Energy Agency was informed about the situation in Fukushima.

## March 11. Evening

The top priority was to determine whether emergency cooling systems for the No. 1 and No. 2 reactors were working (the backup batteries were working in the control room for reactor No. 3, and the gauges were reading as stable). Yoshida, holding an unlit cigarette in his hand, told his workers to find cars that had not been destroyed by the tsunami and to remove the batteries from them. If they could manage to connect the batteries to the measuring instruments, they would at least know where they stood. It was not yet 6:00 P.M. when two technicians from the control room approached the double door to the reactor; they were supposed to go in and start the fire protection system pump. Their dosimeters began to squeal. They had to go back to get protective suits and masks. At 7:03 P.M., Prime Minister Kan ordered the first evacuation, within a radius of two kilometers from the power plant. Around 8:00 P.M., power was restored in the control room of reactor No. 1 and No. 2. The first readings were collected after 9:00 P.M. But the pressure gauges weren't operational until 11:00 P.M. It was then that they discovered that the pressure in reactor No. 1 had long exceeded the permissible maximum. The radiation level was increasing. "Should I give my people iodine?!" Yoshida screamed into the receiver. "Yes or no?!" In Tokyo, 250 kilometers further south, they didn't know how to respond. "We're going to give iodine to everybody under the age of forty," Yoshida exclaimed as he pounded his fist on the table. "Do you hear me?! Can you give us the okay?! Make a decision, will you! We're losing time!" But the people at headquarters preferred to consult the Prime Minister's team and the Nuclear Safety Agency. By doing so, the decisions that Yoshida was asking for were taking forever. "Idiots," Yoshida said with grimace, while his friend, Hikita (who was one of the managers), put a tally mark on the sheet of paper before him. He would do so every time the director of Fukushima Daiichi swore. The sheet of paper was filling up fast.

### March 11. 11:58 P.M.

They knew that three things had to be done: hook up the reactors to a power source; supply water to reactor No. 1; reduce the pressure inside the reinforced shield of reactor No. 1.

### March 12. 2:33 A.M.

The tsunami washed away one of the three fire trucks that was at the power plant. The second one was next to reactor No. 6, in another part of the power plant, but the access road was impassable. There was only one fire truck left, which would normally be operated by firefighters sent by the subcontractor. TEPCO employees were not trained to use it. They got out the instructions. They worked in the dark. Right next to the reactor where the core was starting to melt. Surrounded by fragments of destroyed buildings. On roads where the asphalt had cracked, creating deep gaps between the tanks toppled by the wave. Everything was slippery and slimy from the sludge and the men kept on tripping over dead fish. Some were even half a meter long. The earth shook twenty-one more times during that night. Several tsunami warnings were issued; each time the men took refuge in the quake-proof building up the hill. At around four in the morning, they managed to connect the hose from the fire truck to the pump inside the reactor. Water finally started to flow inside. Though, unfortunately, with varied results. The fire truck was not designed to cool a room at high pressure. It was also not connected to a water tank. So every time it ran out of water, they had refill from a tank perched higher up. It wasn't until just before morning that two fire trucks from the cities of Fukushima and Kôriyama arrived. They formed a chain that provided a continuous flow of water into the reactor. The generator trucks sent by TEPCO also arrived that night. They were not able to drive up close to the reactors. The road leading down was blocked by a large oil tank. The employees found a DC switchgear not yet flooded near reactor No. 2. Long before sunrise, forty men began to string together dozens of cables. Each cable was two hundred meters in length, and each one weighed a ton. Another crew was busy lowering the pressure in the tank that held the core. They had to release the steam that accumulated around the core into the reactor building (where it would escape through the chimney). This would entail the release of radiation into the atmosphere. But the alternative was that the reactor would explode. No one knew to what extent the core had melted and how many radioactive substances were in the accumulating steam. Even before midnight, it became clear to everyone that they had to go in and manually release the valves that blocked the steam in the shield of the core. The instructions provided no information as to how they should go about this. They needed the building plans to determine exactly where the two valves they needed to open were located. The plans were strewn somewhere over the floor of the office where, due to the earthquake, the ceiling had collapsed and documents had poured out of the cabinets. More than nine hours passed before the first pair of employees entered the building of reactor No. 1. At 5:44 A.M., Prime Minister Naoto Kan ordered the evacuation of people within a radius of nine kilometers from the power plant.

### March 12. Around 7 A.M.

When the Japanese Prime Minister found out early in the morning that the ventilation process had not yet been started, he boarded a helicopter. At 7:11 A.M., the helicopter landed at the power plant. Yoshida was furious. They called from headquarters with orders to provide a gas mask and protective suits for the Prime Minister and his companions, while the power plant director was short on everything. Each time someone entered the quake-proof building, he had to remove the outer layer of his clothing, measure his radiation level, and change his shoes. When he went back out, he received a new set. "Why doesn't he bring something from Tokyo, they have piles of it all there!" he shouted into the receiver. And to his friend, he mumbled, "Idiots." The Prime Minister did not put on any kind of protective suit, but got off the helicopter and straight onto a bus that took him to the crisis management center. He did not allow the staff to measure his level of radiation: "This is not what I came here for," he snapped. He only changed his shoes and ran upstairs to meet Yoshida. "Why haven't you started the ventilation process yet? What's going on?" he demanded. Bearing a facial expression that was a far cry from the friendly smile seen in the pictures, Yoshida assured the Prime Minister that they were preparing a plan and that the suicide mission would start at 9 A.M. A reassured Naoto Kan returned to Tokyo. At 9:02 A.M., Yoshida was informed that the evacuation of people within a radius of ten kilometers from the power plant had been completed. The irradiated steam could be released into the air.

### March 12. 9:04 A.M.

In the control room, the two technicians who had volunteered for the mission swallowed their iodine tablets. They donned silver suits, strapped oxygen tanks on their backs and put on full face masks. They hung dosimeters around their necks. They took flashlights and big wrenches with them. They were supposed to have enough air for twenty minutes. They went through the dark building, lighting the way with their flashlights. The plans showed that the knob to open the upper valve was located on the upper level of the reactor. The knob had to be turned a few dozen times. They managed to open the valve one-quarter of the way. That was enough. They spent eleven minutes inside. Their dosimeters indicated that during this time they received a radiation dose of twenty-five millisieverts. That's half of the permissible annual dose in normal working conditions. In an emergency situation, the permissible dose is one hundred millisieverts. The next two volunteers put on their protective suits. These men were supposed to the open the valve in the basement, not on the upper level. They didn't even manage to get to it. They spent six minutes inside the reactor and had to back out. The dosimeters indicated that one of them received eighty millisieverts and the other ninety millisieverts. They had to abort the operation.

**March 12. 3:31 P.M.**

For the rest of day, they tried opening the valves using pressurized jets of air. Earlier, at 2:50 P.M., it seemed that the pressure finally dropped significantly. At 3:30 P.M., they finished laying the cables to reactor No. 2. Power would be restored shortly. Reactor No. 1 was being cooled by the fire trucks, and since they had run out of fresh water just before 3:00 P.M., Yoshida decided to use sea water. This meant that the reactor could never be used again. But who would worry about that? Definitely not Yoshida. Workers were pulling the hoses from the fire trucks toward the canal at the back of the turbine building next to reactor No. 3. The deep trench was filled with water from the tsunami. But it was too late. The tank shielding the melting core was already full of white steam. And hydrogen. A single spark was all it needed.

## March 12. 3:36 P.M.

The technicians in the control room, the windowless bunker where the measurements were being monitored, had already gotten used to the aftershocks. But that particular shock was different. It practically threw everybody up into the air. The lamps fell from the ceiling and crashed to the ground. Yoshida also felt the shock, though the quake-proof building and the room with green walls in which he had been sitting for the past twenty-four hours was four hundred meters from the reactors. Four minutes later, Yoshida was watching the building of the No. 1 reactor explode on a TV screen. The roof and the walls of the fifth floor had collapsed. White smoke was planned above the structure. The flying debris killed five people. And damaged the two-hundred-meter-long cables. And tore apart the fire hoses pulled to the trench filled with sea water.

## March 12. 3:41 P.M.

At the Fukushima Daiichi plant crisis center, people were saying over and over: *Oshimai da.* It's over.

## March 12. 6:30 P.M.

Prime Minister Kan increased the evacuation area to twenty kilometers. The entire population of Ōkuma, Futaba, Tomioka, Namie, and Naraha, as well as some of the inhabitants of Minamisōma (from Odaka), Tamura, Kawauchi, Kawamata, and Katsurao. Those who lived on the coast had to leave their homes already destroyed by the tsunami. All rescue operations were ceased. Firefighters and non-soldiers had to evacuate as well.

### March 12. After 7 P.M.

Everything seemed to indicate that the explosion destroyed the reactor building, but not the concrete shield. Although the core was melting, it was still inside the reinforced concrete casing. And it still had to be cooled down. Otherwise, it could melt through the shield and leak into the ground, along with the plutonium and uranium. And although no one was seriously considering the scenario of the 1979 movie *The China Syndrome* with Jane Fonda, Jack Lemmon, and Michael Douglas (melted nuclear fuel would have burned through the earth to China), the words "China syndrome" were repeated on many occasions during those few days. TEPCO called Yoshida with the following order, "Stop cooling the reactors with sea water until the government makes a decision."

"I understand," Yoshida responded, crumpling yet another cigarette in his hand. He put down the phone and looked at the workers gathered in the HQ. "Keep on cooling," he said. Hikita added a few more tally marks.

### March 13. Afternoon

After the explosion of reactor No. 1, problems started in reactor No. 3. The batteries needed for the emergency power supply had already gone dead, and, on top of that, the emergency cooling system had stopped working. The pressure was rising. Throughout the day on March 13, the ever-more-exhausted-workers tried to open the right valves. They did not go inside. Instead, they connected car batteries to the indicator and tried to open the valves remotely. The pressure would drop, only to rise again shortly thereafter. This back and forth lasted until the morning of March 14, at which time things got worse. One of the fire trucks ran out of fuel; the workers did not know how to refill the fuel tank. They had to consult the instructions. Then one of the trucks bringing in fuel from another city got a flat tire. Little details that were beginning to matter. For those few days, the border between life and death became as thin as paper: *giri giri*. Barely making it by. Yoshida had not left his chair for the past two days. When the pressure in reactor No. 3 rose to dangerous levels in the early morning hours of March 13, he ordered a temporary evacuation of workers who were laying cables and cooling the reactors with water. Yoshida recalls that when he saw the workers returning to the headquarters, a line from the *Lotus Sutra*, the most important text of the Tendai school of Buddhism, came to mind: *Upon the call of Buddha, the enlightened Bodhisattva will rise up to save the world*. And those were his employees—covered in dirt, drenched in sweat, disheveled, with ash in their hair and stubble on their faces. Coated in radioactive dust from head to toe. The saviors of the world. When he decided that the danger had diminished, Yoshida sent them back to the battlefield, as the terrain surrounding the reactors was already being referred to.

## March 14. 11:01 A.M.

Reactor No. 3 exploded at 11:01 A.M., destroying even more cables and fire truck hoses. The radioactive debris of the roof ended up in the trench of seawater they'd been using. When Yoshida told the workers to go outside, clear the debris from the latest explosion, and continue the cooling process, he bowed low to them and, in a tired voice said: "I'm sorry." Then he called headquarters. "We will do what is required of us, but the employees are in shock. We have a lot of work, and high levels of radiation on top of that, so people are getting nervous. Please take this into account." They responded, "We are considering sending out the additional ten people you have requested. We know that the situation is difficult and you are all working very hard. Please hang in there just a little bit longer. *Ganbare!*" This time, Hikita did not make any tally marks on the sheet of paper. Yoshida didn't even have the strength to swear anymore.

## March 14. 11:51 P.M.

Each subsequent explosion destroyed everything that the workers had put so much effort into since the first quake hit. They would get thirty cookies for breakfast. For lunch, they would be served canned food or ready-packed rice. Each had half a liter of water for the day. They worked in shifts. Those who had a break would just lie down as they were on the floor in the crisis center. Through the entire day of March 14, after the explosion of reactor No. 3, the major battle was to make sure that water flowed to reactor No. 2, where the control systems indicated that the pressure was rising and that the emergency cooling system, which had been working to that point had shut down. At one point, Yoshida got up from his chair. He sat on the floor and leaned his back against a desk. He crossed his legs and bent his head. He would later say that he was convinced they would all die. He entrusted everything to Buddha and the gods. He went to the smoking room to have a cigarette. The air was thick with smoke there. He offered his pack to the workers. On March 14, the government decided to increase the annual radiation dose for power plant workers from 100–250 millisieverts, following the example of the U.S.; such a dose is acceptable when actions of the employee save the lives of a larger population.

**March 15. Around 6 A.M.**

Yoshida received two pieces of news: the pressure in reactor No. 2 had dropped to zero. That was the first. And the other: someone heard the weak sound of an explosion. He made another decision. Only sixty-nine employees would remain on site; the group will include the technicians needed to read the gauges, pour water on the reactors, fill the fire trucks with fuel, and connect cables to restore power. Everyone else was to evacuate temporarily. Over six hundred people traveled sixteen kilometers south to the Fukushima Daini (Fukushima No. 2) power station, where they had just managed to regain control over three of their four reactors. The tsunami had also cut off power there, but fortunately one power line and one power generator were spared. It took the workers two days to lay the cables that they then connected to the reactors, and on the afternoon of March 14 they restored the cooling system.

### March 15. A little after 7 A.M.

Fukushima Daiichi was deserted. Sixty-nine men were looking at each other. Yoshida asked, "How about something to eat? They turned the cabinets inside out. Crackers, water, and iodine pills. "Great, I'm starving. I'll eat anything."

### March 15. Around 8 A.M.

It wasn't until half an hour later that Yoshida learned the sound of the explosion had come from reactor No. 4. But there was no fuel in its core. All the rods had been transferred to the spent fuel pool for maintenance. Nobody had really cared about it for the past seventy-two hours, because it hadn't posed a threat. Yet, suddenly, there was this explosion! They assumed that either the earthquake had damaged the spent-fuel pool or the cooling system had stopped working. This would mean that water was leaking or evaporating, thus exposing the radioactive rods. No one was able to assess how much radioactive cesium would get into the air if a fire broke out in the pool emptied of water. But everyone knew that if the rods had indeed been exposed, it would be very easy to ignite. In addition, the explosion removed the only barrier between the pool and the outside world—the roof of the reactor building. It wasn't until much later, when the situation at the power plant had stabilized, that they understood that it was not the fuel rods that caused the explosion, but the hydrogen from reactor No. 3, which had flowed through the shared ventilation system to reactor No. 4. But in March they had no knowledge about that yet.

**March 15. 8:25 A.M.**

White smoke started to rise from reactor No. 2. Twenty minutes later, it wasn't just smoke, but also steam. At 9 A.M. at the main gate to Fukushima Daiichi, radiation levels of eleven millisieverts per hour were recorded. Prime Minister Naoto Kan advised citizens living in a radius of twenty to thirty kilometers from the power plant to not leave their homes. Reactor No. 2 was being continuously cooled with water. It seemed that they averted the worst-case scenario; the one in which the fuel would melt through all the shields. The radiation level started to drop. In the afternoon, it fell to 0.2 millisieverts per hour at the exit gate. Yoshida called Fukushima Daini and said, "We need more people." Employees who left the plant on the morning of March 15 started to return that same evening. Following the explosions, the roads around the reactors had to be cleared of the rubble. Someone had to make trips to the border of the evacuation zone; drivers from Tokyo and the surrounding area had been bringing in the required fuel, but they did not enter the zone. They would leave the gas cans, tankers, and tanks twenty kilometers from the power plant. That's also where they left the fire trucks needed at Fukushima Daiichi.

**March 16**

A Japanese Self-Defense Forces helicopter flew over the power plant with one of the plant employees on board, who took aerial pictures of the reactors. With these photos, the team could see that the water in the pool of reactor No. 4 had not evaporated. The steam rising above reactor No. 3 had blocked the view of the pool. It wasn't until March 17 that they managed to dump water onto reactor No. 3 from helicopters. Non-soldiers dressed in special lead suits (each weighing at least twenty kilograms) made four flights in total. They dumped seven and a half tons of sea water onto the reactor each time. It didn't really help much, because the water dropped from a height of ninety meters splattered all over the surrounding area. "It's like a cicada took a piss," Yoshida would comment later. Finally, on March 20, fire trucks showed up that to pump high pressured water at the reactors directly from the Pacific. Concrete pumps appeared two days later; thanks to the long arms of their booms, water could be poured onto the reactors from above. The equipment did not pump concrete, as was the case in Chernobyl, but water. On that same day, power was permanently restored to the control room of reactors No. 3 and No. 4. On March 21, electrical power was restored to the control room of reactors No. 1 and No. 2. This was also when the SS *Kaio Maru* anchored near the shore. The sailors invited the employees of the power plant on board. For the first time in ten days, they were able to take a shower and have a hot meal. They ate chicken in teriyaki sauce.

### December 2011

By the end of March, the team knew that the temperatures of the cores were stabilizing. Yet a fully stable situation wasn't achieved until December 2011.

The core of reactor No. 1 had melted.

The core of reactor No. 2 had melted.

The core of reactor No. 3 had melted.

However, all of the molten cores remained inside the reactor buildings. No one knew exactly where, though. Although the Fukushima disaster released only 10 percent of the total radioactivity that had escaped into the atmosphere in the Chernobyl disaster, it still received the same, maximum level on the International Nuclear Event Scale (INES): level seven. In interviews given to the press later on, Prime Minister Naoto Kan stated that he had been developing an evacuation plan for Tokyo—the largest metropolis in the world with thirty-five million inhabitants. At the end of November 2012, Masao Yoshida was diagnosed with esophageal cancer. On December 1, he stepped down from his post as power plant director. On December 9, he came to the Fukushima Daiichi crisis center. "My cancer is in no way associated with what happened here; my dose did not exceed eighty millisieverts," Yoshida said. "Besides, esophageal cancer takes more than a year and a half to develop. It was likely caused by my smoking, which, by the way, should be prohibited in this building. I've already had my first round of chemotherapy and look, I haven't lost a single hair. So I still have more hair than our manager of general affairs," Yoshida added, pointing at a balding man standing in the first row. "It's going to be getting chilly outside, so don't you catch cold. I'll be back here in April," he concluded. "*Ganbare*, Yoshida san!" the employees of the power plant shouted. Masao Yoshida died on July 9, 2013.

## Kami

"Are you sure," Kaneta, the monk, asked, "that the fact that they brought the situation in Fukushima Daiichi under control is a triumph of technology, and not a warning? Because from my perspective, it's like this:

"The kami destroyed reactor No. 1.

"The kami destroyed reactor No. 2.

"The kami destroyed reactor No. 3.

"The kami spared reactor No. 4. Reactor No. 4 had the most fuel. If it had exploded, it could have destroyed all of Japan."

The kami are asking us: "So what will you do now?"

## The Future

Once the power plant was stabilized, it was time to put together a plan. Phase One would last until they started the process of disposing the spent fuel from the pools on the upper floors of the reactors (two years). That phase was completed on schedule, in 2013. Phase Two would last until they started removal of the melted fuel debris (ten years). Phase Three would last until the dismantling of the power plant was complete (thirty, perhaps forty years). "I don't rule out the possibility that in forty years' time there will be a seaside park here," said Akira Ono, director of the Fukushima Daiichi power plant. "But for the time being, there is no technology available in the world to facilitate the removal of molten nuclear fuel. But that's okay, we'll come up with a way. Forty years ago, we couldn't have imagined that we would be contacting someone who is hundreds of kilometers away from us using a device that fits in your pocket. We have the ability to create things we haven't even dreamed of yet."

## The New Japanese Bestiary

In the past, Japanese fairy tales were full of mythological creatures: skeleton whales that would tease sailors, malicious kappas, or amphibious demons that kidnap children, monsters, ghosts, and devils. Over time, increasingly grotesque monsters started to appear, including the mighty Godzilla, a mutated moth, or even a people-eating umbrella. Since 2011, a new set of characters has been appearing in Japanese tales.

**Cesium-137.** A playful, yet dangerous creature. Full of energy, it finds it easy to move around. It likes the water so much that he dissolves in it and travels with it over long distances. It can penetrate our body with ease—we swallow it together with food and drink. It is still young and very immature. It wasn't born until 1942. It was in that same year in Chicago that the first chain reaction on Earth was performed in the first experimental reactor. But really, Cesium-137 didn't start to widely travel the world until July 16, 1945, when the first ground test of nuclear weapons was carried out in New Mexico. From that day on, it has managed to break free every so often. In Hiroshima, in Nagasaki, during nuclear tests in the Soviet Union, and in the Pacific. It also enters the atmosphere when disasters occur at nuclear power plants. If you tame it, it can prove to be quite useful. It's used to calibrate radiation measuring devices. It's used in radiotherapy, as well as in flow meters and thickness gauges. It's also a rather decent sommelier. It's able to assess whether wine was bottled before 1945; it helps reveal counterfeits, often sold for tens of thousands of dollars. Since 1945, the year when cesium-137 made it world debut, it is literally everywhere—even if in the smallest of quantities. Including the skins of grapes used to make wine. If a corked bottle emits gamma radiation in the energy spectrum characteristic of cesium-137 (or actually, in the spectrum characteristic of barium-137, into which cesium-137 decays because cesium as such emits mainly beta radiation), this means that the wine was made after 1945. In minimal doses, cesium-137 seems harmless; at least for the time being. However, do not be led astray by its friendly personality or its love for water sports and good wine. Cesium-137 can be deadly. It disguises itself as potassium and integrates in the soft tissues of our bodies. Especially in the liver, spleen, and muscles. When taken into the body in larger amounts, it's quite poisonous. It can even kill you. Standing up to fight cesium-137 is Prussian blue, a compound of iron and potassium of an intense color that connects with cesium-137 and purifies our tissues from the insidious pollutant. However, if any cesium remains in the tissue, it can live to a ripe old age, as its half-life is thirty years. This means that, to this day, less than a quarter of the cesium-137 that was born in 1945 (half of it disappeared after thirty years; half of the remaining half after thirty years) is still circulating in the water, atmosphere, and in ourselves. But this remaining one-quarter is not behaving its age at all—it is still full of youthful energy.

**Cesium-134.** The stepbrother of cesium-137 is formed as a byproduct of the reactions taking place in the reactor, but never when a nuclear bomb explodes. It is younger than cesium-137 and rather naughty. It copies everything its older brother does. But it does not like wine. If it should get on our skin, we'll get a rash and sores, and may even develop tissue necrosis. It's pressed for time though because, unlike its older brother, its half-life is only two years.

**Strontium-90.** A bone collector. It usually appears in a dusty form. A nasty grouch with a crude sense of humor. Disguised as calcium, it fuses with our bone structure. And then the demolition derby starts. It causes bone cancer and leukemia. It attacks bone marrow and reduces our white blood cell levels. In addition, it's a real vampire, sucking out all our energy. It makes us feel tired; we're constantly catching colds, and we have blood issues problems. It's really not much fun. Though it can be quite ironic. If you tame it, it can treat bone cancer (although the less harmful strontium-89 is used for this purpose more often). It feels like an outcast though, since it doesn't give much even if it's forced to cooperate. That's why for the most part, it's quite simply treated as nuclear waste. Half-life: twenty-nine years.

**Iodine-131.** Elusive, ethereal, quick, and agile. It's all over the place. It lives a brief life, so it enjoys it to the fullest. It doesn't need to pretend to be anyone, it simply collects in the thyroid like its non-radioactive brother, iodine, also helping it to work properly. It goes about like a Shakespearean character. It gets its vengeance from beyond the grave. It's already been dead for long time (its half-life is only eight days), we have long forgotten that we had encountered him in the past, and suddenly, ten years later, we get a chilling diagnosis: thyroid cancer. Especially if we were minors on the day that iodine-131 attacked us.

**Tritium.** An aristocrat among radioisotopes. In small quantities, it is produced naturally, from a fiery misalliance between cosmic rays and gases in the Earth's atmosphere, and it is also manufactured artificially in nuclear reactors. Tritium is a hydrogen isotope, but unlike other isotopes, it has earned its own name, not just a number. As befits a real aristocrat, its movements are elegant and slow. It's a bit feeble and doesn't have too much energy. But it's all around us; it can enter our body through the skin, through the respiratory tracts, or through the digestive system. It penetrates tissue and can stay there for as long as ten years. In addition, when combined with oxygen, it creates tritiated water that behaves like normal water—the only difference being that it emits radiation and destroys our tissues. It takes about two weeks to remove it from the body. In larger quantities, tritium causes mutations, tumors and, cell degeneration. But it is highly valued. Although its half-life is relatively short, only twelve years, one gram of tritium costs $30,000. About four hundred grams of tritium are used annually in industries all over the world. It builds an exceptional relationship with phosphor: when both are next to each other, the amorous phosphor lights up. Therefore, sometimes they are sealed together in clocks and emergency exits signs. Tritium has yet another application: it is used to build hydrogen bombs, which can be up to four thousand times stronger than the bomb dropped on Hiroshima (like the Tsar Bomba, the most powerful nuclear bomb detonated in the world, which melted rock within a radius of ten kilometers from the hypocenter. If it were dropped over Greater Tokyo, it would turn the thirty-five-strong million metropolis into a desert in seconds.)

**Half-life.** The unit of time during which the number of atoms in radioactive elements is halved. It is very principled, but also quite independent, which makes it a great referee. You can't convince, deceive or bribe it. It will always be the same.

**Gamma radiation.** A semi-mythical animal that escapes our perception. We think it doesn't exist, because we can't see, smell, touch, taste, or hear it. But it is by all means present in our world, although much more gamma radiation can be found in space. It comes from the same family as radio waves, light, and infrared. It is an electromagnetic wave just like they are, only it has different, much higher energies. Its source is the decaying nucleus of a radioactive isotope (though sometimes it is created in a more romantic way, during a storm, and on occasion it comes from the stars). Gamma radiation is full of energy and it's difficult to stop. It can pass through a sheet of paper, through the skin, it can go through glass and even through a steel bar one centimeter thick! The only thing that can stop it is a three-centimeter-thick lead wall, or a concrete wall, but it needs to be three times thicker. It is this hard-to-stop energy that makes gamma radiation dangerous: when it penetrates our body, it physically destroys our cells. Naturally, an animal with such extraordinary characteristics as being invisible (and having brothers in space) also has exceptional abilities. Like the ability to clean bacteria off medical equipment and food. Or the ability to transform itself into a gamma blade and cut out cancer cells. Although it seems to be on our side, we must be very careful and we cannot forget that we are dealing with a wild animal. As soon as we show a bit of weakness, it will take control of us immediately. Often confused with its mysterious brother—X-radiation.

**Beta radiation.** An electron beam emitted by a radioactive isotope that moves at the speed of light. It is high-energy and easily penetrates air, paper, and skin. However, even a thin sheet of metal will stop it. It comes in two varieties: positive and negative. This makes no difference to humans—whether we are hit by its optimistic or pessimistic version, it destroys us in the same way; it tears our cells to pieces. If it destroys the DNA, the cell may mutate. A prolonged encounter with beta radiation can kill us. This agile, powerful, and penetrating beam can sometimes be tamed. It can be used to check the thickness of materials. Or it can be used in medicine—operating on the same principle that destroys healthy cells, it can also destroy cancer cells.

**Alpha radiation.** A malicious creature that moves at a speed of tens of thousands of kilometers per second. Fortunately, it is too big and heavy (made of two protons and two neutrons) to penetrate physical barriers. A regular sheet of paper stops it. Even air stops it. And so does our skin. However, the issue lies in when we swallow something that emits alpha radiation. Then it runs rampant throughout our body, and as it is really big and heavy, it tears apart the junctions of many cells. It causes acute radiation syndrome.

**Becquerel.** A useful unit of measurement that informs people how radioactive something is. Becquerels, named after Mr. Henri Becquerel (who, in 1903, received the Nobel Prize together with Marie and Pierre Curie), have a friendly attitude toward people. They live to warn us. They measure radioactivity in food, beverages, the earth, grass, or trees. If one atom in a sample decays in a second, emitting one alpha, beta, or gamma, we speak of one becquerel. If there are more decays, the number of becquerels increases. Becquerels usually appear in thousands (called kilobecquerels), millions (megabecquerels), billions (gigabecquerels), or even trillions (terabecquerels). One becquerel lets us know that what we are about to eat is fine, as do twenty becquerels. Danger is not determined by the number of becquerels alone, but rather by the type of sample. For example, for water, five hundred becquerels means: "Don't drink me." But in the case of spinach, it says: "Everything is okay." Only a reading over two thousand becquerels in spinach would be dangerous. Most governments work with becquerels as a unit. They use the abbreviation "Bq" when referring to it.

**Sievert.** Like the becquerel, it is a unit of measurement. It tells people how much radiation their body has absorbed at any given time. Sieverts are big and rude. They don't really care about people, their only task is to count the number of radioactive particles hitting the human body. They do not like to be disturbed while at work, they need to be focused when they're counting. It would be easier for them if they could count from one to ten, but instead, they count in fractions. If a person absorbed the equivalent of one sievert within an hour, he could get radiation poisoning and even die. That's why sieverts decided to present themselves in significantly smaller values to be able to promptly warn people of the danger. When they are divide into thousands, they are referred to as millisieverts. And when they divide into millions, microsieverts. Depending on their size, sieverts have different nicknames: "Sv," "mSv," and "μSv."

**Natural radiation.** Quiet as a mouse. We don't realize that it's with us at every step. Rocks, water, air, plants, our bones (containing the potassium 40 isotope), as well as outer space;

everything emits radiation. Natural radiation is measured in sieverts. On average, a human being receives 2.4 millisieverts of natural radiation per year. It shouldn't be confused with artificial radiation (also referred to as man-made radiation), which is produced by medical diagnostics, nuclear reactors, and nuclear explosions. The limits applied all over the world pertain to artificial radiation.

## The Island of Happiness

If the Japanese need to write a foreign word or emphasize something in a sentence, they use a special alphabet: *katakana*. The syllables are boxy and angular, as if they were slashed with a sword. When the bomb fell on Hiroshima, newspapers printed the name of the city using *katakana*: ヒロシマ. The characters held all the horrors of the mushroom-shaped cloud, incinerated human remains, skin separated from muscles, smoking ashes, hair loss, and our anxiety over falling victim to cancer. After March 2011, the name "Fukushima" was increasingly being presented in *katakana*: フクシマ. Residents of the prefecture protested. They did not want to be associated with the contaminated zone surrounding the Fukushima Daiichi plant. They prefer to use the standard alphabet: *hiragana*. *Hiragana* characters have soft, feminine shapes: ふくしま. *Hiragana* is neutral. *Katakana* suggests something extraordinary. Something foreign, something unknown. They also avoid using the Chinese characters (or *kanji*) for "Fukushima" (福島). The *kanji* have become contaminated in very much the same way as the soil in the Fukushima prefecture. In 2011, even foreigners were memorizing the *kanji*, to check labels on products. Nobody wanted to buy vegetables, fruit, or rice from Fukushima. *Fuku* means happiness. *Shima* is island. The Island of Happiness.

## The Most Beautiful Village in Japan

Hillsides, mountain streams, green rice fields, and river rapids in valleys. Wild boars, monkeys, and deer. The air filled with the scent of grass from pastures. Wooden houses with tatami mats and sliding paper walls. Even the cell-phone network was poor here. If you wanted to talk to a neighbor, you would take a walk through the woods rather than pick up the phone. Iitate. One of Japan's most beautiful villages.

But you're not allowed to visit it.

In the spring, bamboo shoots would pop up from the soil, ferns would sprout, the Japanese helwingia would throw out young leaves, and dandelions would appear. A short walk on your lunch break was all you needed to gather some food for dinner. Then you would take it all and cook it, blanch it, bake it, or dip it in batter and deep fry it. Every child was able to tell the difference between the succulent sprout of the ostrich fern and a slightly bitter bracken.

The sprouts are still growing. But you're not allowed to eat them.

In the summer, people would go to the river to catch *iwana*—a small, silver fish with delicate white meat. An ideal choice for a barbecue under the stars. Young people would go to the seaside; it's less than thirty-five kilometers away, but what a difference in climate! Unbearably hot, with monsoon-like humidity. So they would jump on their boards and surf the waves. Sometimes they'd have a bonfire and spend the night on the beach, or sometimes they'd return to the village, laughing loudly, carrying bags of fresh seafood.

The *iwanas* are still swimming in the river. But you're not allowed to catch them.

Fall was the time for mushrooms. The forests were full of *matsutake*; they have thick white stems, and small, smooth, brown caps. You pay as much as $2,000 per kilogram for them in Tokyo. They have a sharp, intense flavor and you can taste the pine forest in them. School kids would gather them for lunch during field trips, and nobody ever thought of making a fortune by selling them.

The mushrooms are still growing. But you're not allowed to gather them.

In the winter, when the temperature fell to minus 20° Celsius, strings of tofu, rice crackers, and white radishes would hang from the roofs, drying in the cold wind. They were kept there until spring. Men hunted, while women cooked pots of nutritious soups with carrots, mushrooms, and wild boar meat.

The wild boar still run through the forest. But you're not allowed to touch them.

Iitate fed its inhabitants. If you ran out of rice, you went to your neighbor, not the supermarket. In exchange for tomatoes from your garden or your homemade blueberry liqueur, your neighbor would give you a bag of rice along with a liter of fresh milk. Farmers from Iitate planted rice by hand and used natural fertilizers.

There is no more rice growing. Unplowed fields have become overgrown with bushes.

Four generations lived in houses built using traditional methods, with clay walls and sliding paper doors. Great-grandparents would watch cherry trees blossom with their great grandchildren. Grandmothers and mothers would prepare rice for lunch, grown by the grandfathers and fathers.

No one is looking at the blossoming cherry trees anymore. Houses are covered in cobwebs and mice live in the walls.

There's no one in Iitate.

The most beautiful village in Japan is empty.

## The North Wind

When we meet for the first time, Kenta Satō is wearing dark jeans, a cotton shirt with white and blue stripes, and a beige hemp jacket. He has a stylish haircut, probably trendy in Tokyo, with a jagged fringe falling across his forehead. He drums his long fingers on the tabletop as he shows me pictures of Iitate on his phone. A house with yellow walls and a gray roof. Blossoming cherry trees. Dogs on a country path. Daffodils. I catch a glimpse of the home screen on his phone. The mailbox icon shows 7,092 unread emails. For two years after March 2011, he would get up at six in the morning each day. He would work until midnight. Interviews, speeches, conferences, readings, and programs. He would respond to emails until three in morning and fall asleep with his phone in hand. He would eat only one meal a day; he didn't have time for more. Perhaps only a couple of *nigiri* rice balls, eaten on the run between one meeting and the next. His only moment of repose was when friends would take him out for a drink. Although sometimes they had to drag him out of bed to do that. They would start the evening with beer and grilled chicken kabobs. And then a bottle of sake. One. Two. Three. They would wrap up their nights in the bar with a bottle of whiskey. "Look!" they would cry, "this is how nuclear boys have fun!" This wasn't exactly the kind of life he had planned. It was supposed to be simple and predictable. In the morning, he would go to work at the family business; his father was the general manager and he was his assistant. The company stored metal molds used to cast concrete blocks that seawalls are built from. The staff of eight had more than enough work to do. At the customer's request, they would clean the molds, repair minor faults, and ship the molds to the site. Kenta appreciated the village and its tranquility. No, he would never move to the city. Many people living there had never set foot outside of Iitate. A neighbor (everybody is a neighbor here), Mr. Fumio Okubo, went to Tokyo for the first time ever when he was over seventy years old. He took the trip with a senior citizens group. Kenta knew something about life in the city. He had lived in Sendai, the largest city in the north, for a few years when he attended the automotive technical college there. He could have stayed there, but the eldest son always returns to his father. When he came back, all of his friends were already married; here, you get married when you're twenty-two years old. Only Kenta stood out from the crowd. Although all the single women were chasing after him (he was young, had a good job, had a big-city sense of fashion, and was dying his hair brown), he was in no rush to tie the knot. What good is marriage if they all end in divorce anyway, he would say to everybody. Just like his parents' marriage. His mother had been living alone in Fukushima for the past ten years, working at a catering company that serviced hospitals. Kenta's father lived in Iitate with his new partner. Kenta split his time between one and the other. In his planned life, he would have taken over the family company in a few years. And, well, okay, he would have gotten married, too, contrary to what he'd been saying to everyone. He would enjoy family vacations in Hawaii, the favorite islands of the Japanese. Kenta had gone there once, for his eighteenth birthday. He wanted his children to catch *iwana* in the stream, gather bamboo shoots in spring, and look for *matsutake* mushrooms in the fall. A great way to spend your childhood. On Friday, March 11, 2011, Kenta was removing rust from some metal molds. His father's workshop was a long shed with one of the walls open, so they could easily move heavy objects using cranes. The shed had hooks, strips, hoses, pressurized water, and an oven. And outside, in a big yard, was the mold depot. They would stack the molds one into the other and stand them up in tall columns, which rose much taller than people. The yard was surrounded by pastures and rice fields, and an artificial pond was down below. Perched higher up was the asphalt road, and further a paved drive leading to Kenta's family home. Kenta was just about to call it a day. He would still need to melt the steel and fix the forms in places where they had been eaten away by the rust. But that could wait till Monday. In his thoughts, he was already on the slopes of the Bandai volcano, a mountain located in the western part of Fukushima prefecture. Kenta was going snowboarding with a few friends. They were supposed to leave early Saturday morning. At 3:46 P.M., he heard a rumble coming from the mountains. That was immediately followed by an increasingly loud metallic sound. It came from the columns of metal molds.

"Quick! Earthquake!" shouted Kenta's father, a man with thin lips, deep furrows around his nose, and a short, military haircut. They didn't hear the warnings on their phones because they would never take them to work. The network in Iitate was poor. Kenta has no idea how and when he ran the three hundred meters to their house. His grandmother was sitting on the floor in the living room. The ninety-year-old woman had trouble walking. Kenta grabbed her by the waist and pulled her toward the door. He made it just before the heaviest shock, which sent the heavy wooden altar for Shinto gods crashing to the ground. It fell in the exact spot where they had been standing just a second earlier. When the quakes stopped, Kenta grabbed the keys to a small fire truck. He had been a member of the volunteer fire department for the past nine years, and knew exactly what to do in such situations. He drove through the area, assessing the damage from the earthquake. Some shingles had fallen to the ground, and cracks had formed in the ground in the pastures. But Iitate is situated on solid rock. There were even plans to store radioactive waste under the village from a nuclear power plant forty kilometers away. The idea was finally dropped, but Kenta has no idea why. He was never really interested in power plants. They've been around since long before he was born. Just a part of everyday life. The plant wasn't built for the inhabitants of Fukushima though, as all the power was sent to run Tokyo. Kenta went to the municipal office to file a report. It was there that he heard of the tsunami. Iitate is thirty-five kilometers from the sea, high up in the mountains. So people were worried about the lack of power, more so than about the tsunami. The temperature was dropping to freezing levels. Kenta had to make sure that nothing had happened to his mom in Fukushima. He got in his car and made it to the city within an hour. It wasn't until he got to Fukushima that he understood the magnitude of the earthquake. Strewn all over his mom's apartment were trinkets, plates, and books. Kenta helped clean up and returned to his father, to the village immersed in darkness and snow. They pulled out the gas heater and lit some candles. They went to bed in their clothes that night. But they couldn't sleep. Early in the morning, Kenta went to his car. He started the engine. And listened to the latest news about the tsunami. Later that morning, he drove back to Fukushima. The city had no water, but wells in Iitate were still working. Kenta's trunk was full of bottles. He wanted to get some gas, but the owner would sell no more than twenty liters per car. He had to pump the fuel himself. Kenta stopped at every station, and was sent away empty-handed every time. He brought his mom the water, took a bicycle (a piece of metal with three gears), attached some gas cans to the roof rack and went off to look for gas—for himself, for his mom, and for his father in Iitate. He would also make stops at every 7-Eleven; maybe they had some sandwiches, instant noodles, or yogurt left? No one knew when the next delivery would be, so vendors had to set limits on how much you could buy. His mom had the television on all the time. They were watching images from the tsunami. Kenta was looking for the faces of his customers based on the coast. Just before four in the afternoon, he found out that reactor No. 1 at the Fukushima Daiichi power plant exploded. The government ordered the evacuation of people within a radius of twenty kilometers. They saw an enormous traffic jam on TV; a string of cars stretching from the coast to the capital of the prefecture. Only ambulances and fire trucks were going in the opposite direction. His father's house was forty kilometers from the power plant. Too far, he thought. He got on the bike again and made another round through the city with gas cans attached to the rack. That was March 12. The wind was blowing toward the sea. Kenta spent the night from March 12 to March 13 in Fukushima. On March 13, he rode the bike around the entire city again. Water, gas, food. He created a Facebook account. Before, he wasn't interested at all in the internet, but now he could check which supermarket still had noodles and which gas stations were open. On March 14 at 8:00 A.M., he loaded everything onto his bike, fastened it all to the rack with cords, hung shopping bags on the handlebars and set off for Iitate. A difference in elevation of four hundred meters. Once he ran out of options with the gear combinations, he got off and pushed the bicycle up the hill. He made it home at noon. Reactor No. 3 had exploded an hour earlier. Kenta wasn't overly worried about that. There were rumors of radiation floating about, so he put on a face mask. The authorities are surely aware of what's going on. If the situation were dangerous, the inhabitants of the village would have been informed. On that day, the wind was also blowing toward the sea. Kenta didn't start to worry until the buildings of reactors No. 2 and No. 4 exploded on March 15. Weather forecasts for the afternoon called for rain and snow. People were saying that it could be radioactive. He had to warn his mom not to leave the house. When he arrived in Fukushima, it was already dark. He felt the first drops of rain on his face. The wind changed direction on the afternoon of March 15 and started blowing to the northwest. On March 16, Kenta's father woke up to find the village covered with snow. He grabbed a shovel and started to clear the road. The official measurement made by the local authorities in the center of Iitate (some thirty-five kilometers from the power plant) and reported on TV was 44.7 microsieverts per hour. Kenta didn't know what that meant. But just in case, he decided not to return to the village. Meanwhile, the authorities decided not to evacuate the area. And on top of that, evacuees from Minamasôma and Namie had arrived in Iitate on March 12. Village residents greeted them with wild boar stew, hot milk from local cows, and rice. One more person appeared in Iitate that day; it was the photographer Takashi Morizumi. Since the 1990s, he has been visiting areas associated with the atom. He had traveled to India where, in the village of Jaduguda, people worked in an open-pit uranium mine, and to the Bikini Atoll in the Marshall Islands, where Americans had conducted nuclear tests. And to Semipalatinsk (Semey) in Kazakhstan, where the Russians did the same. Morizumi had his own Geiger counter. On March 15, his device showed one hundred microsieverts in the north of the village. That was the maximum reading the counter could give. Following the photographer's advice, a few families, mainly those with young children, decided to leave, if only for a few days. The mayor of Iitate, Norio Kanno, announced that there was nothing to fear, and that radiation was not a threat to the inhabitants of the village. On March 19, the milk from Iitate cows was examined. A liter of it contained five thousand becquerels of radioactive iodine. In 2011, the permissible standard for liquids in Japan was two hundred becquerels. Farmers would milk their cows and pour the milk down the drain (one farmer calculated that, by the end of March, he had dumped eleven tons of milk worth $12,000). On March 20, the mayor announced a temporary voluntary evacuation for those people who felt uneasy. About five hundred people of the six thousand residents left the village in buses provided. The decision as to whether iodine tablets should be administered to children was made at a local rather than governmental level. The mayor of Iitate decided that it wasn't necessary. After all, there was no direct order. Rumors passed on by village residents claimed that the pills were at the municipal office the whole time, hidden away in a drawer. According to international standards, the average dose of radiation that people can receive per hour should not exceed 0.11 microsieverts. If people were to receive such a dose twenty-four hours a day, 365 days a year, the level of radiation in their body would accumulate to one millisievert.[3] This is a very conservative calculation, as one millisievert per year does not constitute a health threat. The World Nuclear Association provides one hundred millisieverts per year as the dose at which the risk of cancer increases. A dose of one sievert can cause radiation syndrome. A dose of four sieverts is considered to be lethal, although two sieverts can be deadly for some people, and six sieverts for others; one hundred microsieverts per hour amount to 876.6 millisieverts, or 0.88 of a sievert per year. On March 21, radioactive iodine was detected in the tap water: 965 becquerels per kilogram (the limit is three hundred becquerels). The authorities warned against drinking the water, while at the same time stating that the water in Iitate was suitable for dishwashing, cooking, bathing, and laundry. On the same day, Japanese government suspended the supply

---

3   As recommended by the International Commission on Radiological Protection

of spinach and Japanese mustard from the following prefectures: Fukushima, Ibaraki, Tochigi, and Gunma. Fifteen thousand becquerels of radioactive iodine were detected in the leaves of the plants. The government limit is two thousand becquerels. Also on March 21, Kenta's father decided that he didn't want to put off pending orders any longer. He had customers from all over the country—those who were not hit by the tsunami were waiting for clean molds to build seawalls. Kenta had no choice. He had to go back. He went to the municipal office to ask if it was safe. They said it was, but that he had to wear a face mask. A plain paper one would do. They're available at any supermarket. He kept on asking. What are becquerels? What are sieverts? What does half-life mean? What's the difference between radioactive iodine and cesium? How many sieverts are too many, and what will happen to me if I stay for a longer period of time in a radioactive environment? No one was able to provide any answers. The only thing Kenta knew about radioactivity was what he read in the manga about Hiroshima—*Barefoot Gen*. That was back in high school, and he remembered the part about skin peeling off of muscles and hair falling out. Will my body change too? Will I go bald? Will I have burnt skin? He looked for information online. On March 25, a professor from Nagasaki, Nobel Takamura, came to Iitate. A radiation expert. Six hundred people attended his lecture. It's all right, he said, there's nothing to be afraid of. You only have to follow the basic safety rules:

Wear face masks.

Wash your hands frequently.

Do not open any windows.

And stress is a greater threat than radiation.

Another expert, who was not invited by local authorities, Professor Tetsuji Imanaka from Kyoto, came on March 28. He measured the level of radiation at 130 locations in the air and on the ground. The measurements made at the south end of the village, which was closest to the Fukushima Daiichi power plant, indicated radiation levels equal to those inside nuclear reactors, which workers enter in special suits with dosimeters and which are closely monitored. Residents were hanging laundry out to dry, they were preparing the land for sowing, and children were playing outside in their yards. All this time, the authorities had not yet issued an evacuation order. Kenta opened a Twitter account. First entry: "I work in Iitate. We've been told 'it's safe here.' Everybody knows that our water, soil, and air have been contaminated with radiation." Second entry: "The government does not want to issue an evacuation order. People have to go back to Iitate, because otherwise someone would have to pay compensation for the land they lost. I work in a radioactive environment." Third entry: "In Iitate, children play on the banks of rivers. They eat vegetables that apparently 'have no impact on health.'" Fourth entry: "At this very moment, radioactive materials are being deposited in my body." Fifth entry: A picture of a wisteria in front of Kenta's house and a small yellow Geiger counter that he's holding in his long fingers: 5.92 microsieverts an hour—51.8 millisieverts per year. A few days later, he has fifty-seven hundred followers. From then on, each morning Kenta would drive up to a spot where he could connect to the Internet. He would check the latest information. And tweet. He would be in the workshop by nine. He would wear a thick hoodie and work in disposable gloves and a face mask. Instead of having lunch with his father, he would drive up to a spot that had coverage. He would check his messages. And tweet. After work, he would stop by the municipal office and ask questions. He lived with his father in the house with yellow walls and a gray roof. The smallest spark was enough to ignite a fiery argument. When, in early April, his father opened the windows and let some spring air in, Kenta couldn't bear it. He slammed the shutters, while showing his father the Geiger counter. "You see that?! See?! It says twelve microsieverts! And you're opening the window." His father simply shrugged. He did not care about the radiation. A few more experts came to Iitate. Dosimeters were delivered. People who had voluntarily self-evacuated came back. The school year began in mid-April, as, after all, the government hadn't said that it was dangerous. In one location, near the sewage system, somebody's counter indicated one thousand microsieverts per year. *Hotto spotto.* Such hot spots would also appear in Tokyo, and they didn't evacuate Tokyo, did they? If you repeat a hundred times that everything is all right, people will start to believe you. For this reason, when a complete evacuation order was issued for Iitate on April 22—nearly one and a half months after the Fukushima disaster—people were in no hurry to leave. Why now? The only people left are the 108 residents of the senior citizens' home. Evacuation would be more dangerous for them than the radiation. So to this day, caregivers go there for eight-hour shifts only. The elders can only listen to their grandchildren and great-grandchildren over the phone. Children will not return to Iitate. Kenta's neighbor, Mr. Fumio Okubo, the one who had left Iitate for the first time in his life when he was seventy, hung himself in his room. He was 102 years old. On March 15, the SPEEDI system reported that a radioactive cloud was making its way to Iitate. The system was created after the accident in 1979 at the Three Mile Island power plant in the U.S., when the reactor core partially melted due to a minor defect, design fault, and human error. They managed to restore cooling after sixteen hours, and the evacuation of fifty thousand people from Harrisburg, the capital of Pennsylvania, was avoided. But the reactor building itself was heavily contaminated by radiation. Decontamination work lasted fourteen years; the molten fuel was removed, contaminated water was cleaned and evaporated, and the nuclear waste and remains of the core were cleared away. The reactor building was permanently closed. The Japanese SPEEDI system cost ¥12 billion.[4] It measures how much radioactive material has been released into the air. It checks meteorological data and terrain maps. Based on this information, it foresees the direction and distance over which the hazardous isotopes will spread. It creates maps showing the areas that need to be evacuated. On the maps generated in March 2011, Iitate was marked red. The government later claimed that it was not aware of the existence of the system. The Japanese Nuclear Safety Commission explained in their defense that the initial data was only an estimation. No one was sure exactly how many radioactive elements were released into the atmosphere. The system, which was supposed to count it all and supply the data to SPEEDI, had been destroyed by the earthquake. When the maps finally made it to the crisis team, it was decided they should avoided creating panic. Evacuation within a radius of twenty kilometers was supposed to be sufficient. "SPEEDI was operated

---

4   In the 1980s, when the system was being built, it was the equivalent of $166 million.

by a bunch of idiots," one of the local politicians commented. "They had no idea what they were looking at. They thought that the direction of the wind only mattered in golf." Radiation does not spread evenly. Radiation is spread with the wind. And the wind was blowing north, in the direction of Iitate. For the past five years, Kenta has been participating in conferences and seminars, giving interviews, organizing workshops, and recording programs. He has given presentations all over Japan. He went to Chernobyl. He is invited to speak on the radio, television, and in newspapers—primarily foreign media. He never refuses. It is his duty to give interviews. Although evacuees are not responsible for the explosion, they are responsible for sharing stories about it. The government has already changed twice, and it will change again. Same thing goes for the top brass at TEPCO. That's why Kenta is founding a museum. For the time being, it will be housed in a single room leased from the city of Fukushima. And some day, if Kenta's dreams do come true, it will move into a building in a park. Just like the museum in Hiroshima. A place where people can learn about the earthquake and the tsunami and the radiation. Then Kenta will no longer have to talk about it. But for the time being, he has to tell the story. The biggest error was ignorance, he claims. He started learning English. Lying on the floor of his rented apartment in Fukushima are textbooks for first-grade elementary school students. Along with books about the effects of radiation. Kenta's daughter, Chiune, was born not too long ago. She was named after Chiune Sugihara, the vice-consul of Japan in Lithuania, who rescued six thousand Jews during World War II, and did so against his own government, which was allied with Nazi Germany. Kenta hopes that she will also make the right decisions. Although it's certain that Chiune will not fish for *iwana* in the rivers, or gather bamboo shoots, or *matsutake* mushrooms. Instead, she will know what a microsievert, becquerel, and half-life are. And that's why they will get her thyroid checked each year. "If something like this were to happen in France, in a region where some famous wine is produced, let's say in Champagne, the world would be totally pissed off," Kenta says as he drums his long fingers on the tabletop and brushes away the hair from on his forehead. "We can no longer live on our land either," he adds, "we can't produce rice, milk our cows, or harvest bamboo shoots. Yet the world remains silent."

## The Lament

My house had one hundred sixty microsieverts! My curtains had seventy microsieverts! My bed had fifty microsieverts! My garden had one hundred eighty microsieverts! They've poisoned us! They had us kill all our cattle. They were dairy cows, not for meat; we loaded them on a truck and took them to the slaughterhouse. My wife was running alongside the road, shouting, "I'm sorry, I'm sorry!" We've been robbed! We used to have houses and lives, now I can hear my neighbor through the wall. I know what he talks about with his wife, who visits him, and what he watches on TV. One hundred sixty-five thousand people. One hundred sixty-five thousand people who left their homes behind. We've been cheated! They told us it was safe, and they went on about technology, about Japan, about cheap energy. A neighbor returned to his empty barn and wrote a message on the wall: "If only there were no nuclear power plants! I don't want to live anymore." He hung himself on a supporting beam. They've poisoned us! We've been robbed! We've been cheated! My house had one hundred sixty microsieverts! My curtains had seventy microsieverts! My bed had fifty microsieverts! My garden had one hundred eighty microsieverts! We're being poisoned! Each city is building its own incinerator. They will burn radioactive garbage there. They say they have filters! But this is an experiment that we don't want to let happen. We're being robbed! Our children play in a sandbox inside the building. They don't go outside. They don't jump in puddles, they don't play in the mud, they don't roll down the hill toward the river. We're being cheated! We're farmers, but we no longer have any land to farm. We plant tomatoes in pots in temporary housing. We're fishermen, but we only go fishing once a week. Of the few hundred species that we were catching before 2011, we're only allowed to catch a few dozen now. We release the prohibited fish back into the sea. We're fleeing to Hokkaido, Kyoto, Kyushu, and Okinawa. We can't take this anymore. We're suing the government and TEPCO. There are already twelve thousand of us! We're being poisoned! We're being robbed! We're being cheated! My house had one hundred sixty microsieverts! My curtains had seventy microsieverts! My bed had fifty microsieverts! My garden had one hundred eighty microsieverts! *Fuck* TEPCO! Radioactive grass is growing in the cemeteries. Our ancestors have to look at it every day. It's only them; no one else is left.

## Yuna

My first name is Norio. My last name is Kimura. Do you want to hear about the day when the earth first shook, then the tsunami came, and then finally the nuclear power plant exploded? I'm ready to talk about it. Let me pour you some tea. Now listen. I was on the back of a truck, washing pigs with a hose. I worked on a farm in Ōkuma. The quake was so intense that I wasn't able to get off the truck. I squatted down and held onto guardrails. When the ground stopped shaking, I went to a phone to call my family. We never have cell phones with us, we leave them in our cars. But the line was dead. Since the forty-year-old buildings on the farm were still standing, my new house must be in one piece as well. My family is safe, everything is going to be alright, I thought, and started cleaning up with the others. The pigs had fallen into the cesspools, some of them were already dead. It took us over two hours to pull out the bodies. We heard about the approaching tsunami on the radio. I wasn't at all worried, the farm is situated high up. My house stood far from the beach, on the slope of a high hill. Everything is going to be alright, I thought. And I went back to work. At six in the evening, I got into my car. I had a ten-minute drive home. Only there was no home anymore. I looked up. Fifty meters further up, I saw buildings intact. Everything is alright, I thought. I'm sure they ran for higher ground when they saw the wave. I went to the evacuation site we had previously agreed on. No one there. Not my wife, not one daughter, not the other daughter, not my mother, not my father. Everything is alright, maybe they're at the hospital, I thought. They weren't at the hospital. I found my mother and my older daughter in a different evacuation center that evening. I went back to the place that used to be my home. I walked around all night, shouting, "*Otō san*, Miyuki, Yuna!" Nobody answered. Some people say that the tsunami passed through Ōkuma at fourteen meters high. Others claimed that it was twenty. What difference does that make? It was higher than the pine trees growing on the coast. My neighbors told me that they saw water flowing over the crowns of the trees. In the morning, the chairman of our municipality paid me a visit. He said, "The government has ordered an evacuation. You have to think about those who are alive, Norio." Although the power plant has "Fukushima" in its name, it's located in Ōkuma, my small town. There are four reactors situated on our side. And two on the side of Futaba. We were all proud of the power plant here. More people were working around the reactors than on the farm. My wife would sell lunches to employees. Thanks to TEPCO, we had a swimming pool and a ball field in town. One of the local courier companies was called Atomic Transport. At the train station, you could buy cookies shaped like the chimneys of Fukushima Daiichi—a souvenir from Ōkuma. And now we had to flee because of that very power plant. On March 12, 2011, my mother, daughter, and I got into the car and drove in the direction of Tokyo. The more news we heard about the power plant, the further we drove. Nearly one thousand kilometers. We went to my wife's family, to Okayama. That's where I left my mother and daughter. I went back to Ōkuma with my wife's sister. I did not agree to enter the closed area, although my sister-in-law insisted. "If they're alive, they're in one of the evacuation centers; no one will let them stay here,"

I explained. By the end of March, a full two weeks later, we had visited more than a hundred evacuation centers in the Miyagi and Fukushima prefectures. Not a trace of my father, my wife, or my younger daughter. My sister-in-law was running out of vacation days and I had to take care of those family members who had survived. On April 3, 2011, all of Ōkuma moved to Aizu Wakamatsu, a city in the northwest part of the Fukushima prefecture. I checked with my Geiger counter: the radiation there was three times higher than the permissible standard. And I was supposed to raise my older daughter in a place like that? I bought a house, high up in the mountains, in the Japanese Alps. Forty-nine days after the tsunami, they called me to come identify a body. I recognized him by the key chain which he had received as a gift from my mother. They found him in a rice field flooded with sea water. People say that they saw him going home, so the wave probably washed him away along with the building. And then he was thrown onto the field. He was a white mummy without any distinctive features. They had to do DNA tests. In May, they found a body floating in the ocean. Wearing a black T-shirt, 145 centimeters tall. They asked whether it was my wife. Impossible, I thought, Miyuki was 158 centimeters tall. They told me that if a body stays long in water enough, it could shrink. I didn't recognize her. Her identity was confirmed by DNA tests. I moved to the mountains with my older daughter, to live in a new house. When I need to heat it, I go to the forest to cut some wood. That takes time. And that's a good thing. Nowadays, when you want to turn on the heating, you just press a button. When you want to eat dinner, you go to the supermarket. People work hard to make the money that saves time. But that's a vicious circle. So you're earning money to spend it at a supermarket? Or maybe you could work less and have an extra hour to prepare lunch with your children? I will open a hostel in my house and show people that you can live without electricity. And maybe then they'll give some thought as to where the light in the light bulb comes from, and what the refrigerator, washing machine, or dishwasher need to work. Once a month, I return to Ōkuma. I stay there for eight hours. Together with a group of volunteers, policemen and firefighters, we put on white suits. We walk along the beach, we look under the remains of houses, fallen tree trunks, and piles of rocks. We aren't able to lift everything, but we can't get a machine into the contaminated zone for eight hours. We find photographs warped by the water, plastic toys, cutlery, and mugs. My house was three kilometers from the power plant. The radiation level there exceeds the standards by four hundred times. I am worried about the people who are helping me, but without them I have no chance of finding my youngest daughter. I named her after the quiet and peaceful ocean that we observe in the summer. Yet she was all over the place. Of the nine people who died in our town, three of them were my loved ones. Yuna's body was the only one that was not found. They suggested that I should have her declared legally dead. I would have received compensation, and Ōkuma would close its list of missing persons. But that missing "one" next to the name of the city keeps on reminding us of what happened here in March 2011.

## Clean Our Land

The Ministry of the Environment published guidelines for cleaning contaminated areas. To clean radiation in Japan, you use paper, rubber gloves, brushes, rakes, mowers, chain saws, trash bags, and water. It's an ambitious task. Cleaning contaminated soil with water and paper.

### CLEANING A HOUSE

**Tools:**

+ rubber gloves,
+ paper towels,
+ brushes,
+ pressurized water, if needed.

To clean the house, you need to start with the roof. Unless tree branches are hanging over the roof. Then you need to saw them off first. Leaves, moss, mud, and rotten organic matter should be removed by hand, without water, but you need to wear gloves. Then you wipe the roof with a paper towel. Anything that you could not remove by hand should be sprayed with water and scrubbed with a coarse bristle brush, paying particular attention to the areas where the fragments of the roof overlap. After these operations are complete, the radiation level must be measured according to the Ministry guidelines. If the level is still high, it means that radioactive elements have settled deep into the shingles and that rain will not wash it away. These elements thus need to be removed using pressurized water. Of course, while taking care not to damage the roof.

If this does not work, you need to replace the contaminated parts of the roof. Next, you need to wipe the walls of the house with paper towels, starting from the top and working toward the bottom. Discard the paper towels after each top-to-bottom stroke and take a clean one. If this does not work, you need to pressure-wash the walls, making sure that as little water as possible gets into the soil and sewage system. You also need to clean the soil within a radius of twenty meters from the house.

**CLEANING THE SOIL**

**Tools:**

- ◆ shovel,
- ◆ hoe,
- ◆ hedge trimmer,
- ◆ lawn mower,
- ◆ wheelbarrows,
- ◆ large garbage bags,
- ◆ uncontaminated soil (taken from mountain slopes, which need to be split open to dig up clean soil).

You clean the soil by removing the top layer with a shovel. Before you do that, you need to remove any leaves on the ground by hand. Mow the grass. Pull out any weeds. After the contaminated soil has been removed (usually a layer about five centimeters thick), you need to put it in the garbage bags. Then you cover the exposed soil with soil brought from a non-contaminated area. You can also decontaminate the soil by digging a trench thirty centimeters deep. The top ten centimeters—the contaminated layer—should be covered with a twenty-centimeter layer of uncontaminated soil. If there is any gravel in the garden, use a shovel to transfer it to a container and clean it using pressurized water. Then you can put it back, but first make sure the soil beneath the gravel is not contaminated. You need to clean yards, playgrounds, sports fields, tennis courts, parks, farms, and pastures in the same manner. You also need to remember to clean any barriers, fences, nets, hedges, and benches.

### CLEANING ROADS

**Tools:**

+ brushes,
+ highly pressurized water,
+ septic pump truck.

Pedestrian crossings, cracks in the asphalt, railings, and curbs all need to be thoroughly scrubbed. Wash the road using water at high pressure. If this does not produce the desired effect, you need to use an actual pressure-washer. Finally, use the septic-pump truck to collect elements removed from the asphalt.

### CLEANING THE FOREST

**Tools:**

+ rake
+ scraper,
+ saw.

Rake any leaves. Scrape the moss off of any stones. Remove mud by hand using rubber gloves. Cut off the branches of any trees standing on the edge of the forest. Pack the soil in garbage bags. Forests are cleaned only in a radius of up to twenty meters from buildings and roads. Cleaning a larger surface would result in far too many garbage bags with radioactive waste. Deciduous forests need to be cleaned once. Trees were not yet blossoming in March 2011, so any cesium-137 settled on the ground, not on leaves. The eternally green coniferous forests will have to be cleaned several times over a period of four years. Leaves and moss will be burned in specially built incinerators if their radioactivity does not exceed eight thousand becquerels. If the radioactivity turns out to be higher, they will be taken to a temporary storage facility.

## Cleaning Rivers

It is possible that cesium-137 and cesium-134 settled in the beds of rivers and streams. However, studies have shown that they do not contain any radioactive materials. Water acts as a shield and protects the environment from radiation. For this reason, no work will be carried out to remove radioactive deposits from rivers, streams, lakes, or water reservoirs.

These guidelines will be revised once cleaning operations have been completed. In April 2011, the Japanese government increased the annual permissible radiation doses from one millisievert to twenty millisieverts. In August 2011, it released special legislation—the "Act on Special Measures Concerning the Handling of Radioactive Pollution." The Act divides regions into more contaminated and less contaminated zones.

The government is in charge of organizing cleaning operations in the evacuated zone and in places where radiation levels exceed twenty millisieverts per year. The area includes eleven municipalities in Fukushima, from which 113,000 people had to be evacuated. And in places where radiation levels exceed one millisievert, municipalities can independently decide on any cleanup operations. The government will provide technical support and subsidize part of the expenses. But the final decision belongs to the municipalities. By June 2013, clean-up operations were deemed absolutely necessary for one hundred municipalities in eight prefectures. Fukushima was full of black garbage bags. When workers finish cleaning gardens, parks and forests, they set the bags on the side of roads, on school playgrounds, or behind houses. These are the initial temporary storage areas, before the bags make it to the second temporary storage facilities prepared in accordance with Ministry guidelines. These facilities must be properly secured. Their surfaces need to be covered with water-resistant tarpaulin. The bags are to be placed one on top of the other. Place bags with clean sand on the top and on the sides; these act like a shield. If possible, fence off the storage facility. These second temporary storage facilities are built on rice fields, in parking lots, and in the valleys of the cleaned cities and villages. The spaces filled up fast. It wasn't until March 2015 that a temporary, target storage-facility was opened on the border of Futaba and Ōkuma. The government is buying land from residents. For the time being, only eighty-two people out of 2,365 have decided to sell. The Ministry believes that by 2020 it will have bought up to 70 percent of the land it plans to acquire. The garbage bags containing twenty-two million cubic meters of contaminated soil will be stored for thirty years in an area of six square kilometers. Then the bags will be transferred to the final storage facility. Discussions are still ongoing as to where the final storage facility will be located. That's why black bags are still stacked around in the cleaned cities. In September 2015, northern Japan was flooded by heavy rainfall. The rain caused floods and landslides (people in the town of Jōsō were evacuated from the roofs of houses by helicopters). The river in Iitate swelled. The water washed away 395 black bags that were waiting for transfer to a temporary storage facility on a former rice field. Some of the bags were found as far away as the mouth of the river. One hundred fifty-three of them were empty. "I would like the black bags to become a souvenir of Fukushima," Kenta Satō tells me. In Japan, you can't come back from a trip empty-handed. You absolutely have to buy an *omiyage*, a small gift characteristic of the place you visited, for your family, friends, and even colleagues. It's usually something to eat. You can get an *omiyage* at any railway station; they can be cookies shape like a castle, fruit from a particular prefecture, or a sweet treat. From Miyajima, an island with one of the oldest Shinto temples and with the largest *torii* gate flooded daily by the tide, you bring cookies shaped like maple leaves. From Kamakura, the former capital, with its statue of the Great Buddha, you bring waffles shaped like a pigeon. Before the explosions at the Fukushima Daiichi reactors, you could buy *omiyage*—at the Ōkuma railway station, at the kiosk near the bus stop, and at the local supermarket—shaped like a nuclear power plant. "Now Fukushima will have a new *omiyage*," Kenta said, "black plastic bags. You can put coffee in them. Or cocoa. Whatever you want. As long as it looks like soil."

"And you know," Kenta added, "you can't decontaminate contamination. It can only be packed in black bags and moved somewhere else."

## Monuments

Three thousand six hundred monuments have been built in Fukushima prefecture. They are situated near stations, schools, preschools (where sandboxes have been moved inside the buildings), in front of town halls, shopping centers, and on major roads. White, semicircular poles with a black rectangular solar battery on top. Placed just below the battery is a monitor displaying red numbers. Three thousand six hundred poles that monitor radiation levels. They represent something everyone would just rather forget. You can't see, hear, or feel radiation. You can't smell or touch it. Some people say that it destroys relationships between people more than genes do.

## One Bowl of Rice

You get one bowl of rice to eat. With steaming, white grains and the aroma of sesame vinegar and sweet cooking wine. The waiter says that it's rice from Fukushima. It's been checked and has passed all the tests. Will you eat it? Now take one of the cards lying on the table. Other players do the same. You are a mother of two children. You live in downtown Fukushima. Your children have a thyroid exam once a year. Your daughter is fifteen years old; she is healthy and is category A1—no nodules or cysts. But your son, who is only eight years old, is an A2. They found a seventeen-millimeter cyst. If it grows to more than twenty millimeters, he will need to have additional tests, have his blood and urine checked, or even have a biopsy done. He will be moved up to category B. You recently read in a local newspaper that out of three hundred children who were examined, 115 were diagnosed with thyroid cancer. They also added that this was at least twenty-times the norm. Usually, thyroid cancer occurs in a few children per million. But maybe the results are due to very thorough testing?

*Would you serve this rice to your children?*

You are a farmer from the Aizu region in the northwest part of Fukushima. You're forty-two years old and have four children. You do what your father and your grandfather did, and you do it well. You do not use artificial fertilizers, you care about the high quality and flavor of your product. Although the contaminated cloud did not pass over your field, and the broken power plant is 150 kilometers and two mountain ranges away from you, no one wanted to buy your rice for a long while. Prices dropped three times. On the other side of the prefecture border, in Niigata (twenty-five kilometers from your field), they plant the same variety of rice. They sell it at the same prices as before 2011.

*Would you eat this rice?*

You are an IT expert from Tokyo. You remember how in March 2011, all the water bottles, instant noodles, and frozen pizzas disappeared from supermarket shelves. The only thing left were fruits and vegetables; no one wanted to buy food that could have been radioactive. To this day in stores the peaches from Fukushima are far cheaper than from other prefectures, although they are the best in Japan. In 2011, you went to Rikuzentakata as a volunteer and now you'd like to see what the situation in Fukushima is like. You join a group trip with a non-governmental organization. You enter Odaka, an evacuated district of Minamisōma. You can stay there for eight hours per day. The streets are empty and dusty bicycles are lined up in front of the station. You meet a retired farmer who continues to plant rice on contaminated land; he is experimenting between the difference of using water from a well and water from the river. He prefers to do things like this rather than sit idly in his temporary house. You talk to an older woman who, despite the ban, came back here for good and opened a weaver's workshop. And a young entrepreneur who wants to create a hundred jobs before the evacuation order is lifted in Odaka. So that people will have something to come back to. For the time being, he's opened a small restaurant, where grandmothers from Odaka work. They prepare meals for workers who clean radiation from the city. You go there for lunch. They serve vegetable tempura and rice.

*Would you eat this rice?*

You are the wife of a farmer from Fukushima. Your fields are fifty kilometers away from the power plant. You live in a large and spacious home together with your in-laws and your twins. You argue quite often after the catastrophe; you want to leave, get as far away as possible from the ruined power plant. Your husband and in-laws do not want to leave behind the land that had belonged to them for the past six generations. They repeatedly said: "You're obviously not from here." You review reports on radiation on several dozen websites every day. Each one says something else. Toward the end of May 2011, you pack up and leave, taking the twins with you. There are tens of thousands of people like you; they call it voluntary evacuation. Cowards—is quite often what people who stay behind say of them. Your husband chose the land. You chose the health of your children. But they miss their dad and grandparents. You sometimes come back for the weekends. For lunch, your in-laws serve pickles and rice that they have grown and prepared themselves.

*Would you let your kids eat it?*

You are a doctor from Fukushima. Just after the tsunami, you go to Minamisōma to help out at the local hospital. Part of the city was evacuated within the twenty-kilometer radius around the power plant, and part of it was destroyed by the tsunami. When you return to Fukushima after a few weeks, you and your wife make a decision: this place was not safe for small children. Your older son is five and your younger son is two years old. Your wife goes to Yamagata, about two hours by car. This is only temporary, you tell yourselves. You stay to work at the local hospital. You work on your specialization in liver cancer treatment here and you have your patients. It's safe in the city, the children could come back, but they're going to school in a different prefecture now, and changing schools in Japan is not an easy task. So for the past five years, you've been seeing your wife and children on weekends only.

*Would you eat this rice?*

You are the owner of a small hotel near the hot springs in the mountains surrounding the city of Fukushima. It's a traditional *minshuku*, a Japanese-style family guest house. You used to have regular guests. But people stopped coming in 2011. In the summer, they opt for southern Japan, most often Okinawa.

And in the winter they go to the Japanese Alps or to Hokkaido. "Even if rumors are only rumors, we prefer not to put our health at risk," they apologetically tell you as they cancel their booking. But for the past two years, guests have been coming back again. The traditional cuisine, the sulfuric water with its skin-smoothing properties, the forest landscape, and the low prices are what attracts visitors. You even have foreign tourists. They ask you about life in Fukushima and about the radiation.

*Would you eat this rice? Would you serve it to your guests?*

You are thirteen years old. You have just started middle school. For the past five years, you've been eating only organic rice from Kyushu. Your mom packs your lunch and forbids you to drink milk. One of your new friends invites you over to his house. His parents made dinner. You don't know what your friend's family thinks about radiation. You've never talked about it.

*Would you eat this rice?*

## Have a Good Cry

He comes to Fukushima once a year. He sets up chairs in the clubhouse of the temporary housing settlement and turns on the projector. About forty people come, some of them parents with their children. He dims the lights and plays short features. Each one lasts no longer than five minutes. Atsuko can't take it anymore when the missing dog finds its owner. Tears flow down her cheeks, as she looks through her bag for tissue. Makoto started to cry much earlier, when the father hugged his son, whom he hadn't seen for a long time. But when Mao

Asada, the figure skater, three-time world champion and silver medalist, who was the only woman to land three triple axels in one performance, announces that she is taking a break in her career—the whole room bursts in tears. Sobbing, blubbering, and weeping. "People get emotional in six kinds of situations," says Hiroki Terai, who organizes *ruikatsu*, or crying evenings. "Pets, especially dogs reunited with their owners, relationships between children and parents, marriages that last to a peaceful old age, grandparents with grandchildren, and, of course, sports and love stories. I don't show any catastrophes. The point here isn't to cry because you're terrified, but to release the stress built up in your body. Release the emotions. And the Japanese need that like no other nation in the world."

Hiroki Terai has been organizing the *ruikatsu* in Tokyo since January 2013. Before, he worked for a freight forwarder. But from time to time in the evenings, he would organize special divorce ceremonies called Happy Divorce. The divorced couple would read letters out loud and destroy their wedding rings with a big hammer. They would cry. And then they would shake each other's hand and leave with smiles on their faces (nine out of nearly two hundred couples decided not to go through with the divorce after all). Hiroki began to wonder if crying could make us happy. For the first session, he ran a Korean movie. A very sad story, a mix of serious health issues, love, family arguments, and misalliances. Two solid hours of ever-accumulating drama. No one cried. Hiroki changed his approach. He opted for lots of short feature films, so there'd be something for everyone. These included a Thai insurance commercial called *Silence of Love*, a short film about a teenager and her deaf father (it ended with the words: "There are no

perfect fathers, but their love is always perfect."), tributes to
dead pets recorded by their saddened owners and uploaded to
YouTube, a meeting of lovers after many long years, or a song
about unfulfilled love. He's been organizing these evening get-
togethers once a month for up to forty people. There is always
a full house. More women attend, but there is also a fair share
of men. The majority of them around fifty years old, although
twenty-year-olds and eighty-year-olds show up as well. Hiroki
estimates that about 85 percent of the viewers cry. Some sob
quietly, others a bit louder. For some people, it takes about ten
sessions until their first tears start to flow. Although there are
times when somebody breaks down and starts to sob uncon-
trollably. That's when the others go silent. As if they were suddenly reminded of the fact that they're sitting with strangers.
Crying evenings are free, but you have to bring your own story
of suffering or sadness. People write about diseases and about
parents whom they never really thanked because they ran out
of time. Just like that woman who had lost a dog when she was
a child. She missed him so much that she started writing letters to him. And the dog started replying; she would find notes
with messy handwriting on her desk. When she found out that
it was her father who was impersonating her beloved pet, she
felt cheated. She did not speak to her dad for several weeks.
Only later did she realize that her father did it out of love.
But she ran out of time to thank him. He died when she was
away at college. No too long ago Reisho Nakashiya, who tells
sad stories, joined Hiroki's project. He sets the mood before
Hiroki puts on his emotional movies. His performance is mod-
eled on the traditional art of *rakugo* (fallen words), where a lone
storyteller sits in front of the audience and tries to make them

laugh using only a paper fan, a piece of cloth, and his own voice. Without standing up from his position, the artist tells stories within stories. He indicates a change of characters with a turn of the head, tone of voice, or a small gesture. He's very serious, but the characters are supposed to be comical and their adventures incredibly funny. But Reisho decided to amend the style. Dressed in a coat with purple and gold stripes, he moves his audience to tears rather than laughter. He calls his performance *nakugo* (crying words). The sadder the story, the better. Reisho would like the country's wealth to be counted not in GDP, but in GDT, gross domestic tears. Perhaps if Japan were allowed to have a good cry, it would finally be a happier place. It's not only Tokyo doing the crying now. Kyoto is crying, Osaka is crying, Nagoya and Okayama are crying. New *ruikatsu* clubs are opening their doors. They choose their own movies and stories. Pretty soon, all of Japan will be crying.

"Maybe crying clubs will appear in Fukushima, too," Hiroki hopes. He adds, "In 1995, I lived through the Kobe earthquake; I was fourteen years old and lived in an evacuation center for two months. My friend died after a wall fell on him. For six months, I didn't cry, not even once. It wasn't until my grandfather died that something in me clicked. People here need time as well. But they're ready now. They can start to cry."

## Mr. Matsumura Does Not Feel Alone

All of Tomioka left on Saturday, in a hurry. They thought they were coming back the next day. Or in two or three days at the latest. They left an extra portion of food for their animals, but they had no way of leaving any water for them. The water supply system stopped working after the earthquake. They had practiced evacuation two years earlier. Buses transported them to Kawachi, a neighboring village. But when they really had to evacuate, they opted for their own cars instead. Maybe there were a few coaches, certainly in front of the hospital and the senior citizens' home. The patients had to be fastened to the seats with bandages, otherwise they would have fallen over. Several of them died during the escape. Although it's hard to call it an escape. When you're escaping, your heart pumps adrenaline, sends more oxygen to your legs, and expands your lungs. So you run with all your might, just like in the movies. But they were sitting in their cars. Stuck in a traffic jam. Moving at five kilometers an hour. When they stopped, they would shut off their engines. They already knew that they had to conserve gasoline. The temperature dropped to freezing. It started to snow. Naoto Matsumura did not leave. He was living with his parents in a house located halfway up a steep slope. Down below was a meadow, and further up were the woods and a road leading to town. They did not leave the house for two days. They insulated the window frames with blankets and did not open any windows or doors. He went out to check on the animals on Sunday. When the dogs saw him, they started to wag their tails like crazy. He fed them. The neighbor's dogs could smell the meat. They were baying, barking, and whimpering. He went to see them as well. Their bowls were turned upside down and the ground around them was clawed through, as if the dogs had tried to satisfy their hunger with whatever smell was left behind. He gave them water and fed them. And he set off to make a few rounds. Only in his neighborhood.

He walked along and whistled. In response, he heard barking from beyond all the gates. Yet when the third reactor went up in smoke two days later, he decided to pack his parents into the car after all. They drove to his cousin's, to the south. She didn't want to open the door to them. She only yelled out, "Why did you come here?! You're radioactive! Go away!" So he went back home with his parents. In an empty city, you can't go to the store, you can't have a chat with your neighbor, and you can't go to the pharmacy to ask for help when you have shortness of breath. You need to get water from a well, take a bath in a bucket, and flush your toilet with a bucket. They slept together under several layers of blankets. Three weeks later, his parents left for Tokyo, to stay with his sister. It was April 2011. Matsumura was all alone. He was fifty-two years old. Divorced. Two children. The population of Tomioka dropped from fourteen thousand people to one man with a dark complexion, patchy beard, and white hair. On April 22, 2011, when the government prohibited access to the evacuated area and set up barricades on the roads, it was already too late for Matsumura. He had dozens of dogs, almost a hundred cats, a herd of cattle, and two ostriches under his care. Friends were asking him, "Please take care of my Kimi. Please check on Shiro." He was covering an increasingly broader area of the city. He drove through town in a white car with a trailer. He would be greeted with the sound of barking. Dogs would recognize the hum of the engine. They would wag their tails. Why didn't people come back for their pets? But where would they live, if dogs and cats were prohibited in evacuation centers? People still believed they would be able to return soon. They'd apply for permits and enter the zone then to feed their pets; but permits were not issued on a daily basis. Some would take the animals and keep them in their cars. Sometimes they slept with them. People who had money would rent apartments. Fifty-eight hundred dogs alone were left behind in the evacuated zone. And then there are the farm animals. You can't take a herd of cows with you. Or a thousand chickens. Some people opened up the barns and let the animals out. Maybe they could make it on their own? In May, the government issued a decree. Any cows and pigs that were still alive had to be killed. With the consent of the owners, the animals were given lethal injections. That made Matsumura mad. Killing animals to eat them— that's all fine and good; after all, the role of these animals is to have humans eat them, he said. But killing them only because they have become radioactive and there's nobody around to take care of them? What right do we have? This is something he could not accept. So now he really couldn't leave.

Street lamps weren't working.

Traffic lights weren't working.

There was no running water.

He couldn't even turn on the television to listen to a human voice. He would get up in the morning, put a water kettle on the burner, and make some instant coffee in a thermos. He would pack a sandwich from the supermarket (they keep for three weeks) and go off to do his rounds. Every day in another part of the city. He was covering an increasingly broader area. Seven hours a day. Seventy dogs. At times, pigs would also appear whose owners had released from their pens before April 22, 2011. There were days when he would not utter a word. And when he would finally open his mouth, he could not make a sound. So he spoke to the animals. Sit. Beg. Down.

Shake. Wait. Even after a few months, some of the animals did not allow him to touch them. They would gulp down whatever he had brought—they couldn't wait—but after all, they had to protect their property. The police would come by at first. "Look, Mr. Matsumura, you don't have a permit," they would say. Then soldiers from the Self-Defense Forces would appear, saying "Mr. Matsumura, you can't stay here." To some of them he would say that he had an official government permit, so could they please just leave him alone. They wouldn't even ask for any documents. To the others, he would argue that sure, he'd be more than happy to leave, and that he wasn't at all interested in living in a radioactive house. But who would take care of the animals? Maybe they could? They didn't agree to it. But they left him alone. It was just him and the animals. The barns were the worst. Lying on the ground, with their heads in the troughs, were the rotting remains of starved cattle, covered in worms and flies. At the neighbor's, Matsumura saw a cow with her calf. The calf tried to suckle, but the cow did not want him to suck all the life out of her. She kicked him. He tried again. A second kick. The disoriented animal approached the udder once more. The third time round, the cow kicked so hard that the calf understood. The calf cried, sore and hungry. A piece of rope was hanging in the corner of the barn. He started to suckle it. Maybe it looked like the tip of an udder? The next day, both the cow and calf were dead. The smell of decomposing corpses was the smell of Tomioka in late spring 2011. Matsumura wanted someone to take responsibility for the death of the animals; a death by starvation. Preferably someone who had contributed to these deaths. He traveled to Tokyo three times. The first time he went to TEPCO headquarters with a demand: admit it, it's all your fault! But they said that they had to bring the damaged power plant under control first. Those were priorities they received from the government: first the power plant and then the dead animals. The same goes for compensation for people. They paid out partial compensation for the fact that they weren't able to farm their fields or go out fishing. They'd receive the remainder once the situation in the power plant is under control. Clever people, Matsumura figured. Instead of brains, they have machines. There were accidents before March 2011. Like the leaks that newspapers would report about. And when, together with the members of the voluntary fire department, he went to TEPCO to ask how the company intended to deal with this dangerous situation, the company pretended it had no idea what the situation was. Everything is fine. Power plants are safe. But they're not. When a fire broke out in the reactor building after the earthquake in Niigata in 2007, only a miracle saved us, Matsumura claims. And how about in 1999, when the employees of the Tōkai plant mixed the fuel in a bucket rather than in a special tank, to save time? Two of the three employees died. More than one hundred people were hit by radiation. So how can you talk about safety here? And look what's going on now. After all, Fukushima Daiichi is still leaking. Ground water flows through the reactors and flows back into the ocean, contaminated. TEPCO is building a wall of ice underground to stop it. But for the time being, 150 tons of contaminated water flow into the Pacific daily. For his second trip to Tokyo, Matsumura also went to TEPCO headquarters. He showed a letter from the States. Americans found out about the last man in the contaminated zone from the news. The *Guardian of Fukushima*, that's what the media liked to call Matsumura. They held a fundraiser and collected ¥300,000. Matsumura went to TEPCO. You won't accept the blame, but people all over the world see it. Look—these are the donations I'm receiving, and here are the letters of support. The whole world is supporting me. They answered. Every single time they answered: "We don't know how to read English." The third time, he joined Yoshizawa, a farmer who ridiculed the government when they told him he had to kill his herd. He stayed on his farm. No one is going to tell him what to do. Four years later, white spots appeared on the hides of his cows. Together with Matsumura, they loaded one of his bulls onto a truck and parked it in front of the Ministry of Agriculture. Why isn't the government investigating this? Why isn't it checking what impact radiation has? Why is it cleaning the soil and encouraging people to return? The police did not let them unload the bull from the truck. The three returned to Fukushima. It's been two years since the catastrophe, and the damaged power lines in Tomioka still haven't been fixed. Why, for one person only? Matsumura heats his house with coal. But not all of it. Only the living room where he set up his bed. He keeps two buckets of water next to the toilet, and another two in the bathroom next to the shower. He gets drinking water from a well, and he goes shopping for food for himself and the animals twice a month. Sometimes he catches fish in a nearby stream. In the spring, he picks young shoots, and in the fall, gathers mushrooms. In the evening, he lights altar candles. They're thin, though, and don't provide too much light. So he lights them in bundles of ten and opens a can of beans in tomato sauce.

A romantic dinner.

Mice prance all over him at night.

And then, given the fact that he was there and was being exposed to radiation, drank water from the well, ate fish from the stream, and mushrooms from the forest, scientists started asking him for help with their experiments. The first to call was a professor who wanted to see whether sunflowers were able to remove radiation from the soil. Matsumura planted an entire field of them. They don't. Yet another wanted to investigate whether the contamination could be removed by giving cows radioactive plants as feed. Instead of burning the plants in the incinerators built for that purpose, they could give them to contaminated cows, then seal their manure in cans and put the cans in the temporary storage along with soil from contaminated cities. Natural recycling. But the government didn't approve the project. Now Matsumura is thinking of studying bees. It's easier to observe the effects of radiation in insects. He's already in contact with one of the professors. Maybe they'll start researching the topic. Cesium-134 has already gone through two half-lives, Matsumura figures, so another four years and people could come back, if it weren't for cesium-137. But the town is being cleaned. In 2011, radiation levels there reached nearly eight microsieverts. Now it's three. His counter has long since broken. But he doesn't care. When he went to get his dosage measure, the doctor started to yell. But he didn't give him the results, and just stated that Matsumura was a radiation champion. And that he should stop eating those mushrooms and fish. If he doesn't, he'll have cancer in thirty years. By then, thought Matsumura, I'll be dead anyway. He sent one more letter to TEPCO. After he dies, he will give them his body for science. They replied that they weren't interested. Matsumura smokes cigarette after cigarette. He offers me some instant coffee. He still doesn't have running water and flushes his toilet with a bucket. But he does have power and his TV is on nonstop. I'll sooner die from these cigarettes than from radiation, Matsumura laughs. And he doesn't stop talking for the next five hours. He no longer has any neighborhood dogs to feed. All of them have been taken away. But he still has the cattle that he found wandering the streets. He keeps an entire herd on a field at the other end of the city. And next to his house, he has one ostrich, one pony, eleven cows (who don't like the pony), nine cats, and a dog. A meager little thing. Always hungry. But money doesn't grow on trees. The cost of the hay for the cows alone equals the monthly compensation he receives from TEPCO for mental distress. Each evacuated person receives ¥100,000. So does Matsumura, although he is not an evacuee in the technical sense. The payouts will end in 2018. That will be one year after all the villages and towns in the evacuated zone will have been cleaned of radiation, according to the government plan. That is, with the exception of Ōkuma and Futaba—Fukushima Daiichi borders those two towns. They'll figure out what to do with them later. Matsumura doesn't feel lonely. He found two cats in the forest. A white cat and a ginger tabby cat. They make the rounds of the farm together. Journalists, photographers, and filmmakers come here. Professors stop by. Even the Prime Minister's wife paid a visit. She signed her name on his wall. Matsumura says that if it weren't for the disaster, he would have had a normal life and would have died a normal death. He takes a good while to say his goodbyes as he stands in his doorway. In April 2015, the white cat gave birth to five kittens. They're doing alright. So if everything is alright with them, then maybe it won't be that bad for people either, Matsumura wonders as we part ways. In the evenings, he's all alone again. There are still no lights on the streets. Silence is strange here, Matsumura claims. It's too quiet. As if it were a tangible thing, something standing right next to you. It's much more than loneliness.

## Death in Tokyo

The session starts at seven in the evening, making it convenient to drop by after work. It all lasts no more than an hour and a half and costs ¥1,000 (ten dollars). First, there's a small snack with coffee and tea. Music mixed with the sound of ocean waves fills the background. The participants—six total strangers—are drinking tea. And they're talking about death. The youngest is twenty-six years old, the oldest is over sixty. "People younger than me are dying, my friends, my cousins," says Ms. Takamura, who recently turned fifty-nine. "I'm getting closer and closer to death." She gets up from the chair and stands in front of the coffin. It's a simple wooden box. The edges are decorated with a leaf pattern. The walls and the bottom are lined with glossy satin. Ms. Takamura lies down inside, exclaiming, "There's more space here than I thought!" The moderator covers her with a white blanket. He asks if everything is all right. He closes the lid, only leaving the glass window open. It's time for the photos. Ms. Takamura asks to have one taken with her phone. Then the glass window can be closed as well. Five minutes later, the moderator opens the lid and the woman opens her eyes. She smiles. "I was afraid it was going to be terrible. Tight, dark, cold. And that you can't hear a thing. But instead, I felt tranquility."[5] Tokyo has been preparing for death since 2009. In the beginning, it was mostly older people. More than a quarter of Japan's inhabitants are over sixty-five years old. That's thirty million people. They often live alone; their children have left, their spouses have died. They prefer to take care of things themselves. They figure, why should I burden others with my own funeral? In 2010, the Shukan Asahi Mook company sold half a million copies of its manual, *How to Prepare for Death*. The book has everything you need and addresses several issues—how do I choose a funeral home? What should a decent funeral look like? How do I make a good impression on the mourners? And, of course, know-how about the types of burials, graves, and cremation. Those who wanted to take things another step further would buy the *Living and Ending Notebook* published by Kokuyo Co. (the same publication came out with a guide on writing wills in 2009). It consists of sixty-four pages to be completed in your free time. Suggested questions include: what should my funeral look like? What do I do with my blog? What about my pets? Should my photos be burned or kept? What about the money they'll find in my wallet? What about my credit cards? What

---

5  Fragment based on the press coverage by journalists from Japan Trends (http://www.japantrends.com/shukatsu-prepare-death-coffin-experience/) and Bloomberg Technology (https://www.bloomberg.com/news/articles/2015-12-15/try-a-coffin-for-size-the-death-business-is-thriving-in-japan).

kind of farewell messages do I want to convey to my wife, my children, my bridge buddies? Kokuyo Co. is committed to the satisfaction of its customers. The paper is smooth and nice and easy to write on, and the notebook itself is easy to open and lie flat, because there's nothing more irritating than a notebook that keeps on closing. Once it's filled out, we should make sure to keep it in a visible location. When we die, whoever finds us will know what to do thanks to our notes. Over 360,000 people aged fourteen to ninety-seven bought the *Living and Ending Notebook*. Planning your own death already has a term: *shukatsu* (終活). It sounds similar to the word that means to job-hunt right after college (就活). The only difference is the first character. 就 means to "take a position," while 終 means "the end." Since 2011, more and more services have appeared associated with planning your own end. In Tokyo, you can even confront your own death in a supermarket. The largest chain of stores and shopping centers, AEON, runs a hundred seminars a year, during which death advisors explain how to write a testament, how inheritance is taxed, and how much a funeral costs. In Japan, the price tag is usually around ¥2 million (approximately $18,000). But AEON can organize a funeral for a quarter of that sum. Such a funeral is smaller (no more than fifty guests) and more modest than a funeral in a Buddhist temple. For an additional fee, you can invite a monk and rent elegant outfits for the mourners. After the session with the advisor, it's time for pictures. A photographer sets up the lamps and asks for a smile. Done. It's a good idea to have a photo for the funeral, one in which you are at your prime. All that's left to do is prepare the farewell letters and, finally, one at a time, the participants can try out the coffin. Today, you can check out a very elegant model lined on the inside with a slippery purple fabric. There's also a Hawaiian model with green leaves and a shiny rainbow lid. As well as an ecological model, made from cardboard. Preparing for death is like arranging a wedding. You have to choose what you'll wear, select the right makeup, and decide on the shape of the urn into which your ashes will be transferred. The next step is to plan everything that will happen after the funeral. Yahoo! can lend a hand here; the company established a special service called Yahoo! Endings. With its help, any e-mails, photos, and files you indicate will disappear from the servers after you die. After your body has been cremated, the farewell notes you've prepared earlier will be dispatched. "Dearest Wife, if you're reading this, it means that I've taken leave of this world . . . I promised you that I'd never die before you. I'm sorry. I was happy thanks to you. Thank you." That is one of Yahoo!'s suggested versions of such an e-mail. Of course, you can write your own customized farewells. The company will keep them on the servers until you die. The cost of the service? Two dollars per month. You can take things a step further and decide what happens to your ashes. Travel companies facilitate this task. They organize trips, during which bags of salt imitating ashes are scattered in various places in Tokyo. Where would you like you to be scattered? At sea? In the park? Or maybe from the top of a skyscraper? The article states that seventy-year-old Hatsue's heart beat faster when she scattered salt into the waters of Tokyo Bay from a small ship. She explained that her oldest daughter lives in the States. If they scatter her over the ocean, she can be with her daughter all the time. She is planning her death while she is healthy, because she does not want to become a burden for her children.[6] Similar trips are organized to visit cemeteries. Which one will you choose? The Ruriden is quite popular; it's an octagonal building in Kôkouji Temple. Mourners enter a room where 2,046 crystal Buddha figures illuminated with LED lamps line the six walls. Standing behind each of these figures is an urn with ashes. When the family enters their personal code, the corresponding figure will light up. The intensity of the light varies according to the time of day and the season. Yet another cemetery, Shinjuku Rurikōin Byakurengedō, was built in a skyscraper. The urns are kept underground. Just touch your card to a reader and soon, an urn with the remains of your grandfather will appear in the mourning room, along with his picture on a small screen. Burials in the shade of trees are also becoming increasingly popular, in common graves under a cherry tree. You don't need to maintain these graves, so the deceased family member or friend is no longer a burden to anyone. Families who opt for burial under the same tree get to know each other at meetings organized by *The Ending Center*; after all, you would like to know who you will be spending eternity with. They call each other *hakatomo*, or grave friends. But your life doesn't have to end at a cemetery. Alternative options were presented at the first Tokyo Death Fair, ENDEX. The event took place toward the end of 2015. It lasted three days. Over two hundred exhibitors and more than twenty-two thousand visitors. In addition to

---

6   Based on the article *Take a funeral portrait, scatter fake ashes: death tourism rising draw for Japan's elderly* reprinted in the *The Straits Times* November 7, 2014 (http://www.straitstimes.com/asia/east-asia/take-a-funeral-portrait-scatter-fake-ashes-death-tourism-rising-draw-for-japans).

vendors selling coffins, incense, clothing, caravans, altars, and stone tombs, there were companies offering more unconventional services (1.3 million people die in Japan each year, and the domestic funeral business is worth $16 billion). If you can't find your ideal final resting place, you can have your ashes converted into a diamond (red for warm extraverts, orange for the tenacious and curious, green for those who are well-balanced and confident, blue if you're honest and spiritual, or white for open and sincere individuals). Or you can send them into the cosmos (an offer from a U.S. company working with NASA). For $4,000, a rocket will take you into outer space. And $8,500 will give you the option of flying to Earth's orbit on board a satellite. Thanks to GPS technology, your family will be able to track your journey over the next 240 years. In turn, $2,200 will guarantee you a landing on the moon. Another company offers a service called the Falling Star; the urn will orbit the Earth, then drop back down, burning in the atmosphere. Cost? Twenty-five thousand dollars. People who have planned for their own deaths say they feel more at ease. Now they can really enjoy life to its fullest.

## Examine Yourself

To have the carrot examined, you must first fill out an application. Where was the carrot picked? On what day? Provide distinctive features of the farm (mountainous? in a valley? by the sea?). Provide the Geiger counter reading of the air, if measured. E-mail the application. Or send it by fax. On the day of the test, peel the skin from the carrot and cut it into five-millimeter pieces. Place it in clean packaging—a plastic bag or a plastic container. A full, one-liter container is needed for the test. One carrot will not be enough. On the day of your appointment, go to the Tarachine Radiation Measuring Center in Iwaki. Leave the sample. Go back to get the results. Take the sample home. Cost: $5 per food sample; $20 per liquid sample; $20 per breast milk sample. To test soil, fill out the application. Prepare a container of at least one-liter of soil from five different areas of your field—the center and the four corners. When taking a sample, dig to a depth of fifteen centimeters. Each portion should be the same volume. Take the sample one week before your appointment. Do not take any samples immediately after rainfall. Pick up the results. Take the sample home. Cost: $20. To have yourself examined, fill out an application. First name, last name, date of birth, weight, height. Wear clean and light clothing on the day of your examination. Remove your shoes for the examination. If necessary, we may ask you to undress. Take a seat on the chair. The examination with the detector takes five minutes. Sometimes it needs to be repeated. You'll get the results right away. If you want to have your children examined, remember that they must be over two years old, measure at least eighty centimeters, and weigh at least fifteen kilograms. Cost: $10. Free up to age eighteen. Free for pregnant women. Items that people bring to the Tarachine Radiation Measuring Center in the city of Iwaki include apples, cabbage, spinach, broccoli, radishes, lily bulbs, lemons, dried persimmon, mushrooms, rice, skin and bones of salmon, canned salmon, flounder, soy, seaweed, shrimp, oysters, dried bonito flakes, school lunches, instant soup, milk, cotton, tap water, well water, river water, garden leaves, ashes from the fireplace, dust from the vacuum cleaner, soil from the farm, sand from the beach, sea water.

## The Boundary

We're going to Iitate with Kenta. He's going to show me what he misses the most. The Ministry divided the evacuated zone into three parts. They are color-coded on the map. Green areas are ready to be inhabited. The annual radiation dose there does not exceed twenty millisieverts. You can go to the yellow zones for eight hours per day, but you're not allowed to stay there overnight. Once the cleaning of the contaminated soil and houses is completed (and when radiation drops below twenty millisieverts annually), these zones will be suitable for living. And then there are the red zones. You have to have a special permit to enter those. Nobody knows when, if at all, it will be possible to return there. Kenta's house is in the yellow zone. The Ministry guidelines are clear: they only clean up to a perimeter of twenty meters from buildings and roads. Workers hang white tape between the trees to mark the boundary between areas that have been cleaned and those that are still contaminated. Kenta feels uncomfortable in Iitate. There are seven and a half thousand men here during the day. Seven and a half thousand unfamiliar faces. Their accent is also unfamiliar. From Hokkaido, from southern Honshu, from Kyushu. They come here from all over Japan, attracted by the well-paid work. They wash houses with a hose and wipe them down with paper towels. They gather the top layer of soil and pack it into black garbage bags. The rice fields have been converted into a temporary storage facility, which is one kilometer long. The bags are placed one on top of the other and weigh one ton each. Mountains of nuclear waste. We walk into Kenta's house. His father still lives here; he doesn't care about the ban. The machines in the workshop cost a fortune, and he wouldn't want anybody to steal them. He lets the dogs out at night. Just recently, he obtained permission to reopen the workshop. The soil around it has been cleaned. Kenta's father turns off the TV. He goes to the kitchen and puts on the kettle for tea. Kenta shows me around the house. He built it himself. Fifteen years ago, he and his father laid the floors, finished the walls, and installed the window frames. After the earthquake, they picked up the Shinto altar that had fallen to the ground and reinstalled it up near the ceiling. Against the wall is a Buddhist altar with the *ihai* of Kenta's grandfather. Kenta lights the incense, folds his hands and bows his head low. And then he takes me for a walk. He swaps his elegant white shoes for a pair of felt-lined galoshes. We go through his home garden, where his favorite broccoli no longer grows, because nothing will grow on the sand that replaced the fertile soil during cleaning. A strand of white tape hangs between the tree trunks. The boundary. Kenta stoops down and crosses over to the other side. Firs, cryptomeria, cypresses, pines, maples, and oaks. The ground is full of wilted leaves that ruffle with every step. Kenta stops for a moment when a black snake slithers by his feet. He bends over to grab a stick. One bite is all you need to end up in the hospital. Better to have something to defend yourself with. The snow recently melted away, and buds appeared on the branches. Spring is in the air. It always comes a bit late to Iitate. The village is five hundred meters above sea level, and winters are long and severe. The ground is frozen solid from November to March. Kenta moves the leaves aside with the stick. He is looking for young bamboo shoots, you can barely see them above the forest cover. They are similar in shape to thick asparagus. But instead of bamboo, he finds a butterbur shoot; the thick husks conceal the flower buds inside. Instinctively, he picks it. Just as instinctively, he reaches for some sarsaparilla leaves and breaks off young buds from a branch of an angelica tree. "*Taranome*," he mumbles, "my favorite." He knows his way around wild plants. In spring, he would leave the house early in the morning, before he went to work. *Taranome, takenomo, warabi, fukinoto.* He would dip them in batter, deep fry them, sprinkle them with salt, or dip them in soy sauce. He would eat the bamboo shoots raw. Sometimes he would boil them in rice water with diced chili pepper. Or he would marinate them in grated radish. We come to the stream where Kenta and his friends would fish for *iwana*. He looks at the water for a moment. He turns back. We pass under the white tape hung between the tree trunks. We head toward the house with the sloped roof and yellow walls. Kenta toes the sand in the garden. The forest makes up 70 percent of the area of Iitate. Only the parts that fall within that twenty-meter perimeter are accessible. They don't touch the rest. If it were possible to go back to the way it was, Kenta wouldn't hesitate, not even for a second. But that Iitate no longer exists. Kenta opens the door and takes off his shoes in the hallway. You can only walk on tatami mats in your socks. He passes his father, who is waiting with the tea in a room used as an office. He goes to the kitchen. Opens the trash can and throws in the shoots and leaves he gathered that day. "Poisoned."

# The Zone

In the north of Japan, there is a story people pass on by word of mouth about a woman who got lost in the woods. The shadows were getting longer and she wasn't able to find her way home. She was turning onto different trails, but she kept getting the impression that she was still in the same place. Until finally, she saw a small trail covered with pine needles. She cautiously continued along the trail; it was getting darker and darker outside. She was just about to turn back when the rays of the sunset illuminated a wooden gate. But what a gate it was! It was decorated with relief carvings so beautiful that they seemed to be alive. The horses' manes were fluttering, apples were rolling on the grass, and dragons were flying out of the clouds. A small entry was ajar. The woman walked in. She stood in the garden, which was shining in yellow and red. Irises on a small pond glittered blue, and a blossoming cherry tree with pale pink flowers was hanging over a well, while alongside the wall was a persimmon with branches bowing down under the weight of its shiny orange fruit. She quietly called out. Only the wind answered her. It broke the delicate petals of the cherry blossoms and surrounded her with a pale pink whirl. The woman looked at the house. Smoke was coming out of the chimney. She slid the door open. A cast iron kettle was hanging over the hearth cut out between the tatami mats. Water was boiling for tea. The woman called out a little louder. Nobody answered her. She removed her shoes and went into the living room. In the ceiling beams, an artist had carved out figures of a rabbit and a frog. The doors to the inner garden were all made of paper—they only had glass windows at the bottom. If you knelt down, you could see moss-covered stones through them. Maybe the owners will come back soon? The woman walked around the house. Each room seemed to be more beautiful than the previous one. She'd never seen such cherry-wood bowls, such tea cups, or such ink paintings in her life. Had something happened to the owners? She walked through the entire house. Nobody was there. Bowls were set out on the kitchen table for dinner. She went to the garden. No one there. She went back to the decorated gate and ran down the pine needle trail. Her legs just carried her home. She has no idea how and when she made it back to the village. She immediately told her husband about the strange and beautiful house with no one inside. The men of the village set off to search for it. She showed them the way, but although they found the small trail covered in pine needles, the only thing at its end was a regular forest clearing. Standing in the middle of it was a wild persimmon, which would not bear fruit until the fall. It must have been a dream. But the next day, as she was washing her linens in the river, two cherry-wood bowls floated up to her. The same bowls she had seen in the house with the richly decorated gate. She fished them out of the water and took them home. The bowls were full of rice. And every time she emptied them, they would fill back up again. That's exactly how the *mayoiga* works. A lonely house hidden in the forest that seems to have just been abandoned by its owners. It brings good luck to those who visit it. Takamitsu drives me to the empty town. We see dusty shop windows, overgrown flower beds, broken telegraph poles, metal blinds twisted out of shape by the quake. Gaps in the asphalt—big cracks with grass growing out of them. It's hot. It's quiet. Takamitsu stops at the train tracks. He looks both ways out of habit. The tracks are covered in thicket. Even rows of homes with the straight lines broken in places by a collapsed roof or a buckled wall. But most of them still stand straight, only their windows are covered in dust. You can't tell what was inside. Grass is growing on the roof. Takamitsu explains, "This is a fruit and vegetable shop, here is a ramen restaurant, here you have a *ryokan*, or a Japanese-style hotel with tatami mats on the floors. Here is where the local doctor lived, that's where the gas station and cigarette shop was. That there was my school, this is where I would go shopping, and this is the park where we would go on dates when we were teenagers." I listen to a tale of a magic city. In this tale, the evil force has chased all the inhabitants out of their homes. Now the city is dead. A spell has been put on its history, sealed in these dust-covered windows and decaying buildings. Covered in bushes and wild grapevines. But there is one way to bring the town back to life. If somebody who used to live here shows up, if only for an hour, the town is revived thanks to this person's memory. For a brief moment, it goes back to what it once was. The air is filled with warm greetings, the smell of vegetable tempura, and the sound of automatic sliding doors. When the residents leave, and they do need to leave before nightfall, the city dies again. And if you come here on your own, without a guide, the only thing you'll see is a row of dusty houses that hold no meaning at all. Inside these houses, everything looks as if the owners are going to appear at any moment. Bowls are set on the table for lunch, slippers wait in the entryway, placed so you can easily put them on when you get home. An open newspaper in the living room on the couch. Only the pages of the calendar that haven't been torn off reveal that nobody has been here for a long time. March 12, 2011. In supermarkets, bags of instant noodles, bottles of water, and cans of food are strewn across the floors. Nobody picked them up after the earthquake. Thick spider webs span the aisles. In pachinko parlors, game coins wait near the slot machines. Computers covered in bird droppings line offices. In restaurants, you have bowls of rock-hard soy sauce. Shoes are still stashed in school lockers. Bushes have grown over a motorcycle that's leaning against a light pole to the point where you can barely see it. Bicycles have been parked in front of the train station for the past five years. Next to them is a telephone booth with a phone book covered in a thick layer of dust. Inside the booth, the bindweed has taken over, along with a spider as big as my fist. When I pick up the green telephone receiver, I hear a dull hum. They still have a signal here. But there are no more people. The cities have been taken over by animals. Packs of half-wild dogs run around the streets. Chubby wild boars and overgrown pigs break into food pantries. Crows fight cats and raccoons for food left behind by volunteers, who sometimes sneak into the prohibited zone via country roads. But the true kings here are the rats and mice. They have taken over houses, gnawed through cables, tatami mats, or paper doors decorated with ink drawings. They've arranged their sleeping quarters in thin futons. Their droppings fill the hallways. Ōkuma, Futaba, Namie, Tomioka, Iitate, Odaka, Naraha. Small towns full of lonely homes that no longer bring happiness to anyone.

## Homecomings

Their instinct tells them to come back. Every year, in the fall. But before they swim up the river, hopping through rapids and waterfalls, they wait a few days in the Pacific. Their bodies adapt to freshwater again. They won't eat anymore; their stomachs shrink. That leaves more room for the roe and milt. The fat they have accumulated in their bodies provides energy. Their meat loses its flavor and changes color from pink to white. Its texture becomes spongy. The skin color also changes from silver to rotten green. The jaw in males bends upward, creating a hook. The Pacific salmon is ready for spawning. They swim into the river. When they make it to their home stream, the females dig a hole in the gravel bed and lay the roe. The males deposit milt over the roe and cover it with the gravel. Both the males and females die. Their dead bodies flow back to the ocean. In spring, the young are big enough to go downriver with the current. They will return to exactly the same place in four years. Instinct never fails the salmon. Japanese fishermen take advantage of this fact. In the fall, they spread their nets along the rivers. They catch adult salmon, cut the belly open, take out the roe, take out the milt, and cultivate the young in special hatcheries. When they grow a bit, they release them into the river. Thanks to this operation, more of the fry survive. They will come back home in four years. Some of them will be caught in the ocean, when their meat is firm and pink. Meanwhile, the rest will swim up the river, where the nets will be waiting. Each spring, 56.5 million young fish were released into the five rivers of Fukushima prefecture.

Only Hokkaido and Iwate cultivate more salmon. And of the five rivers in Fukushima, the Kida River, which flows through Naraha, was the most fertile. No other river in all of Honshu would yield as many fish in the fall. That was before. The fishermen from Naraha had to evacuate. No one was catching the homebound salmon in fall 2011. And so, there was no fry to be released in spring 2012. It wasn't until 2014 that the local fishermen's union bought salmon fry in a different prefecture and released it into the Kida River. Each river is different. The salmon remembers the rivers. Their instinct tells them how long it will take for them to swim to their home stream; sometimes it's one day and sometimes it's fourteen. The bodies are resistant to parasites that live in a particular river. Will the fry from Iwate make it in the rivers of Fukushima? Will they come back in 2018? On October 18, 2015, a Shinto priest was standing on the edge of the Kida River. Using a wooden wand with strips of white paper attached to it, he performed the cleansing ritual. At 11:30 A.M., fishermen, dressed in rubber waders and in galoshes reaching half way up their thighs, went into the water with fishing nets. They walked along with the current, chasing the salmon to the nets set up on the bottom. They pulled them out with their bare hands and put them in buckets. That day they caught 120 salmon. Those were the fish that they had released in March 2011, before the earth shook, the wave flooded the coast, and the reactors at Fukushima Daiichi exploded. The catches lasted until the end of November. In total, 8,443 salmon were caught. On March 26, 2016, fishermen and preschoolers from Naraha gathered on the edge of the Kida River. Together, they released the young fry. During those six months, the fishermen had cultivated one million three hundred thousand fish. Prior to March 2011, they had been cultivating at least twelve million. "It will take us over ten years to go back to what we had before," is what Hideo Matsumoto, head of the local fishermen's union, told the *Asahi Shimbun*[7] newspaper. In the past, nearly eighty-five thousand salmon would return to Naraha in the fall (in 2009, it was 84,782). Now, less than 10 percent of them return. In September 2015, the evacuation order for Naraha was lifted. Out of five thousand inhabitants, two hundred returned.

## An Empty Sound

Keiko Takahashi is twenty-four years old and has had enough of being a victim. It's true, she still laughs nervously and has trouble sleeping, especially if she isn't sleeping in her bed. But how much longer are people going to look at her like she's contaminated? It started in 2011, when she attended the opening ceremony for the academic year in a mask. As one of very few who did. She said she was from Ōkuma. Some guy walked up to her in the hallway, asking, "Are you going to contaminate us, too?" Yet another one looked down at her, saying, "I feel sorry for the guy who marries you." Others would comment, "She's lucky, she gets compensation money!" As if they didn't know how radiation works. As if they didn't understand a thing. And on top of that, they were all from Fukushima! Keiko was educated by people from TEPCO. They would come to her school

---

7    The quote is from the article *Locally raised salmon released for 1st time since nuclear disaster* published in the *Asahi Shimbun* on March 26, 2016 (http://www.asahi.com/ajw/articles/ AJ201603260045. html).

once a year. They explained that everything was radioactive. The trees, the birds, the sky. Me and you. The children would wave Geiger counters on rocks they had brought to school. They would check the values. Radiation is a natural thing. And whatever is natural cannot be dangerous. After the disaster, Keiko visited her home twice. The last time was in 2015, in spring. She wore a white protective suit, gloves, and shoe covers. It was empty. It was quiet. Everything was overgrown with bushes. There is a piano on the first floor of Keiko's house. Her grandmother's beloved piece of furniture. Keiko touched the keys. A dull echo. A strange, unknown sound. She closed the fallboard. She will never go back there again. "I'm not a victim!" Keiko cries, "I've had enough of all this! I'm a student. I'm a girl. I'm human. I'm Keiko!"

## Questions

There's a lot of space here. And lots of hills that dominate the landscape. Hills covered in trees, with furrow-like valleys where the greenery is darker and denser. There are many rivers here with grassy banks. And streams with smooth stones. Trees with moss-covered roots. You see mountains even from the capital of the prefecture. They are tall and rocky. The setting sun colors them purple. I would like to be able to describe all this. But words fail to do the job; they're bloated, swollen, and mismatched. They lie. They lie when I describe the beauty of Fukushima. They lie when I talk about contamination. Because there's no way such beauty can be contaminated. And a contaminated place cannot be that beautiful. What does cleaning mean? The transfer of contamination to elsewhere. What does the demolition of mountains to bring clean soil to contaminated areas mean? Environmental destruction. What is reconstruction? The creation of completely new communities. The communities before 2011 can no longer be recreated. Pretty soon, people will be able to pack all the things they've gathered over these five years and return to their homes. Homes covered in grass, homes with gnawed-through wiring, homes reeking of mouse droppings, homes with windows broken by wild boar, and homes with a fox lair. You can clean up a house. Replace the rotted beams with new ones, repair the roof, and level out the walls. There are no clothes and no furniture either. Everything went to the incinerator. Renovating your house is easy. But those who are thinking of coming back are hesitant. They want to see how many neighbors will come back as well. Because how else could this work? Will I have to live alone surrounded by empty houses? And what if the shopkeeper doesn't come back? Or the sausage maker, famous throughout the area? You would go to his shop, chat for a few minutes, and make your choice of smoked lunch meat. And what if the nurse, who always had a small first aid kit at home, doesn't come back? And what if your favorite neighbor doesn't come back, the one you'd talk to by the fence as you were trimming your roses? What about the doctor? If not enough people come back, they won't reopen the hospital, and you'll have to drive to the emergency room in the neighboring city. What about the school? Will they open the elementary school? Because you can be sure that you'll have to commute somewhere else to middle school or high school. Where will the nearest supermarket be? And how about the nearest seafood market where you can buy fresh fish? Will children be able to play in the forest? In the stream? And what will happen if they pick berries, bamboo shoots, or mushrooms? And what about the snow? Apparently it's more radioactive. These are the questions that evacuees ask themselves. And I just keep asking myself: is it worth spending money to clean up villages when only one-fifth of the population wants to come back? Wouldn't it be better to spend it on building the lives of the other four-fifths in a new location? Is it worth risking the lives of the young workers working to decontaminate villages and cities? Can you prohibit someone from coming back if they really want to? Is there anything to come back to? Where is home?

## A Beautiful Sunny Day

It will be a beautiful sunny day. The air will have a certain lightness to it after the winter. Light will spread out on the streets in long streaks. On a day like that, you can't focus on anything else; you can only make plans for the future. People will go to the parks in the afternoon. They'll spread out plastic blue tarps on the ground, eat sushi bought at the supermarket, and catch some sun. And deep down, everybody will be wishing for a gust of wind. Then the delicate petals of the cherry trees will free themselves from their branches, dancing and twirling around the trees. *Hanafubuki*—cherry blossom blizzard. A sight that would be the culmination of this wonderful day. But instead of the petals, it's the ground that starts to dance. The entire park buzzes with the sound of phone alerts: *beeeep beeeep beeeep*. People will move away from trees and cover their heads with bags. They are relatively safe in the park. Things are harder for people who are in offices or in their homes. If the earthquake is really strong, objects placed on shelves can fall on their heads. The subway will stop automatically and people will wait underground until the shaking stops. They've gotten used to it. It can happen at any time. In the park or at work. At school, at a funeral, at a conference, or wedding. People can be sleeping, making love, eating dinner, doing homework, taking a shower, shopping, or watching a movie. They don't even notice most earthquakes. The weaker ones don't trigger phone alerts. The Japanese wait for mild tremors to end as if nothing really important was happening. But they never know whether or not the earth will shake again a few seconds later, giving way beneath their feet. Or whether there won't be a tsunami afterward. Or if a fire won't break out. Or a mudslide won't occur. This particular day doesn't necessarily need to be sunny. It can be freezing and wintry, the kind of day when your shoes creak in the snow. Or windy, when an approaching typhoon bends branches to the ground and the radio warns against leaving the house. It can be rainy and cloudy. And gray, as if the Japanese gods had sucked out all the light from the Earth. Or hot and humid, the kind of day when you sit still in the cold stream of air from your air conditioner. You know only one thing for certain: another earthquake, another tsunami, another volcanic eruption, tornado, typhoon, storm, landslide will happen. Death is inevitable. Simple as that.

# III

## The Workshops on Dying

There are twenty cards lying on the table. Five cards of each color: white, blue, red, and yellow. Carefully consider what's really important to you. Now take a pen. On the white cards, write down things you can't part with. Telephone? Computer? House? Car? Ring—a keepsake from your grandmother? Or maybe money? Don't worry if nothing comes to mind. You can also write down the things you simply like. Even your iPad. On the blue cards, write the places that you associate with good memories. And the places you love. The slope you like to whizz down on your skis. The village where you would spend your childhood vacations. The city you went to college in. Mountains. Seaside. Butterflies. On the red cards, write down the things you like to do. Your job. Hobby. And your dreams.

Climb an eight-thousander, write a book, give your children an education. Friendship? Yes. And love, too. On the yellow cards, write down the names of people who mean the most to you in your life. Even those who are dead. And pets. Mom, dad, sister, husband, child, grandmother, friend, lover, dog. You only have five cards. "Parents?" Uh-uh, no cheating. Now that you have written down everything that is important to you, close your eyes and listen to this story. It's a story about you. Or someone very much like you. It's a warm spring day. Cherry trees and forsythias are in bloom. Coming back from work, you get off one station earlier to take a walk in the sun. You open the door to your house and take off your shoes. You go to the kitchen. You pour yourself a glass of water. You get the rice going; the children should be back home from school soon. You open the fridge. Suddenly, you feel a piercing pain in your lower abdomen. You cringe. You count to ten, then to twenty, then to ten once again, and you wait until it goes away. The pain slowly subsides. You're left with a strange feeling of heaviness. Fatigue, you think. You close the fridge door. You go to the bathroom to get a pain reliever. You wake up very early the next day. The sun is barely peeking through the beige blinds. You sit on the edge of the bed. When you get up and straighten out, that strange feeling in your abdomen is back. Like a rock is weighing you down. Maybe it's just spring fever? You make some coffee, wait until the rest of the family wakes up, and you have breakfast together. You gaze through the window at what is still a tranquil city. Everything will be okay, you think. But the strange feeling persists for the rest of the week. You can't sleep. You can't focus on your work. It's exhaustion, you tell yourself. I need a vacation, you keep saying. But really, you know that something is wrong.

Open your eyes.

Look at the cards lying before you.

Select one. Crumple it up and throw it to the ground.

You tell your family that you're not feeling well. You're making an appointment for medical tests. They ask about your symptoms. Fatigue? Diarrhea? Weakness? And how about your family history? They take samples of your blood, urine and feces, and run tests. They prescribe additional X-rays and an ultrasound. Two weeks later, the doctor calls, asking you to come see him. It's getting warmer and warmer in the sun, the flowerbeds are full of flowers, trees are getting greener, and soon, the linden pollen will fill the entire city. You're going to your appointment. You knock on the door of the office. The doctor invites you to come in; he is wearing a white lab coat over his black jacket. He has a grave look in his eyes. Lying on the table before him are your test results. Cancer.

Open your eyes.

Look at the cards lying before you.

Select two. Crumple them up and throw them to the ground.

Over the next few weeks, your diagnosis is confirmed. They pierce your abdomen with a big needle under local anesthesia. Which stage is it? What treatment methods can we apply? Surgery? Chemotherapy? Radiation? You have a medical appointment every few days. You plan additional consultations. You're getting used to the increasingly intense feeling of heaviness in your abdomen. Sometimes you have episodes of piercing pain. That's when you hold your breath and count ten, then to twenty. You call your parents. You're anxious about how you should tell them. You can't focus on anything at work. At home you sit on the couch and count the days until your next doctor's appointment.

Open your eyes.

Look at the cards lying before you.

Select two. Crumple them and throw them to the ground.

Spring has long since turned into summer. The days are getting longer and hotter. The air is sticky and stuffy. Together with your family, you take a trip to the woods to get some fresh air, if only for a short while. Take a break from the heatwave. You go for a walk alongside a stream. The kids are fooling around, okay in the water, and splashing all about. You're holding hands. Everything is going to be okay after all, you think. But when you return to the city, you feel like the heat is sucking any remaining energy out of you. You don't feel like eating anything. You lose weight. You have more tests done. Your doctor says that it's not from the heat. You need surgery as soon as possible.

Open your eyes.

Look at the cards lying before you.

Select three. Crumple them and throw them to the ground.

They've removed the tumor. Now you have to monitor if any metastases appear. You feel weak, but that's normal after surgery. You're planning what to do next. As soon as you recover, you'll take your kids to the seaside. Your youngest is still learning to swim, you'll show him how to move his hands for the front crawl. And you'll teach your oldest how to play chess. You'll take your book with you, the one that's been sitting on your nightstand for several months. Finally, you'll have time to read. You'll spend the evenings together, the two of you—talking, watching movies and making love. And when you go back to work, you might still be able to join the tail-end of the project you'd been working on for the past six months. You'll drop by to see your parents over the weekend. And your great-aunt, whom you haven't seen since the previous holiday. You slowly regain your strength. You meet with your manager to find out which project you will be joining, maybe in as soon as two weeks? You're really planning a family vacation. Has to be on the seaside. You miss that smell. Your parents visit you every weekend. Your mom brings you pots full of your favorite foods. It's still hot outside, but the biggest heat waves are over. You're going out to do the shopping for dinner. When you get back home, you suddenly feel a sharp pain in your lower abdomen.

Open your eyes.

Look at the cards lying before you.

Select two. Crumple them up and throw them to the ground.

Your doctor has no doubts. The cancer has metastasized. He opts for chemotherapy and radiotherapy. You get oral chemo once a week, but radiotherapy sessions are five times a week for a month and a half. They don't take long—half an hour, tops—but you have to drive to the hospital every day. The only time you don't have to leave the house are the weekends. You suffer from nausea. You vomit after each treatment. And although your mom is preparing your favorite childhood foods, you have to force yourself to swallow anything. You have painful sores in your mouth. Even pressing a little too hard with your toothbrush causes your gums to bleed. Your fingernails are brittle. You have to be careful with everything. The diarrhea starts one month after you start radiotherapy. The skin on your belly is dry and sensitive. But you're happy, because your hair hasn't fallen out yet. You don't even know when summer turned into fall. The evenings are getting cooler. You go with your family to the park near your house to admire the fiery color of the leaves. The next day you have a runny nose and a fever. Just a brief moment outside is all you need to catch cold. Right now it's not only your abdomen that hurts—your entire body is in pain. You find it hard to get out of bed. You have no energy to do anything.

Open your eyes.

Look at the cards lying before you.

Select two. Crumple them up and throw them to the ground.

Your chemotherapy dosage needs to be increased. The doctor decides that it will be given by intravenous injection. As he gives you the shot you feel a cold sensation spreading throughout your body. The weeks pass. The sky takes on a gray hue. The pain is becoming hard to bear. You wake up at night screaming. They admit you to the hospital. They give you morphine. The world beyond the window gets dark more and more quickly. The rain banging against the panes wakes you up at night. As does the moaning of your neighbor. After a series of radiotherapy sessions, you have no hair, no eyebrows, no eyelashes. You whisper comforting words to your neighbor. Everything will be alright, everything will be alright. You doze off, but your sleep is broken. When you wake up, your neighbor's bed is empty.

Open your eyes.

Look at the cards lying before you.

Select three. Crumple them up and throw them to the ground.

You wake up in the middle of the night. You don't know where you are. You're cold and your teeth are chattering. You try to calm the convulsions. Your fingers slide across your protruding ribs. Increasing the drug dosage did not help at all. Your hair has long since fallen out and you don't get out of bed anymore. Only the morphine helps. The kids come by after school every day, but more and more, you sleep through their visits. The whole family comes by on holidays. They prop you up on pillows, and place beautifully wrapped gifts on your lap. You don't have the strength to open them. You look at the snow outside the window.

Open your eyes.

Look at the cards lying before you.

Select three. Crumple them up and throw them to the ground.

A ray of sun on your face wakes you up. The days are beginning to get longer again, you hear the chirping of birds outside the window; they're getting ready for spring. You look at the person sitting near the bed. Someone is always with you. You hear this person quietly say your name. Yet you do not recognize the voice or the face. You want to say something, but the only thing you can do is squeeze the hand tighter.

Open your eyes.

Look at the cards lying before you.

Select one. Crumple it up and throw it to the ground.

Then there comes the day when you no longer feel any pain. You no longer hear the voices of the doctor or nurses. You no longer see the trees outside the window. Breathe deeply three times. Really deeply. One. Two. Three.

Open your eyes.

Look at the last card on the table.

Crumple it up. And throw it to the ground. Now take one more deep breath.

Once you exhale, you'll die. "Which card did you leave for last? What is most important to you in life?" he asks in a quiet voice. All twenty of us are sitting in a dimly-lit room. We all die separately, each with our face to the wall. Over the last two years, more than one thousand people have died at the workshops of dying led by Tetsuya Urakami, a monk from the temple in Yokohama. Some have even died as many as four times. The hardest thing to do is crumple up and throw away people. That's why a person who is dying tends to fold the cards with the names of loved ones in half and gently set them on the ground. For older people, children are most important. Younger people choose their parents. Mothers more so than fathers. Then again, some people leave their glasses for the end: they can't see anything without them. Or their computer, because it holds their entire life in its memory. Others go with marriage, although they're single and put it down on the red card just because they couldn't think of anything else. Men who had chosen their girlfriends think of proposing, while people who had left their fathers for last and whom they haven't seen in a long time get in their cars to go see them. "Do you feel that you're still breathing?" the monk asks us. "You did not die. That was not your last breath. So what will you do with your life? And what will you do with the twenty treasures that are most important to you?"

# Acknowledgments

During one of my classes back in high school, my two best friends and I pretended that we knew exactly what truism was. We tried to convince our teacher that it had to have something to do with the Holy Trinity. Yet in fact, the truism here is that this book would not have come to fruition without the help of others. In Japan, a country whose language I do not speak, I encountered amazing acts of kindness and selflessness; this included things like offering me a place to stay or even traveling to another city only to help me with translating during an interview. There isn't sufficient room here to list every single person, but I wish to thank all of them, very much, for their support.

This book would not have seen the light of day without Tatsuya Yabuuchi, whom I met in September 2014. We sailed out to view one of the three most beautiful sights in Japan; the rocky islands in Matsushima Bay. A salty wind was blowing, and I was telling him how I'd like to write about Japanese reality after the triple catastrophe. Tatsuya just said, "I'll help you."

Without his involvement, energy, and downright pedantic approach to translation, I wouldn't have been able to conduct many important conversations (including my meetings with Kenta Satō, Naoto Matsumura, the mother who lost her two sons to the tsunami, the monk Kaneta, and Sadao Satō, whose family memories go back to the 1896 tsunami). Tatsuya's help didn't end in Japan; he patiently answered thousands of questions, arranged interviews, and translated, translated, translated.

Takamitsu Shiga from Namie, who brought the city's evacuated zone back to life for me, patiently answered my questions on statistics, and even called several fishing cooperatives to find out how many salmon returned to Naraha in 2015. Emiko Fujioka, who founded the non-profit organization Fukuden together with her husband, Toshiyuki Takeuchi, invited me for a two-day tour of the closed zone around the Fukushima Daiichi power plant. She shared her contacts with me, offered a place to stay for the night, and showed me what the traditional cuisine of Fukushima was all about. Yusuke Kato from Bridge for Fukushima helped in very much the same way; he found the time to go with me to talk with fishermen working for Fukushima Daiichi and hear the prefecture's most pressing issues.

Eri Kawai and Teppei Kobayashi took care of me while I was in Sendai. Without Eri's help, I would have never gotten to know Ishinomaki as well as I'd like, and wouldn't have had the opportunity to talk to Yasuo and Masaaki; the two men, husband and father, who learned how to dive. In turn, Justin Boley not only took me along for volunteer work in Minamisōma and helped me set up interviews in the evacuated district of

Odaka, but also accompanied me to the workshops of dying. Then Kakuho Aoe, a monk, agreed to be my translator for the interview with Testuya Urakami, who has been conducting these workshops for the past several years. It was Kakuho who was the first, back in 2014, to tell me about these workshops, during which you experience your own death.

Dean Newcombe, with whom I traveled a distance of over four hundred kilometers from Tokyo to Tōhoku in a charity rally (he ran, while the others and I went by bike): thank you for being such a role model. And for introducing me to Grandma Abe, whom I thank for teaching me that sometimes it's better to offer comfort rather than solutions. And I would like to thank Rebecca Irby for inviting me to the rally and becoming a close friend only five minutes after we met.

I want to thank Kaneta the monk for the long hours spent over cups of splendid green tea. And for inviting me to join in and complain at the "Café de Monk." On this occasion, I'd also like to thank Reiko Fujiwara for translating our second meeting, during which we spoke about ghosts.

My thanks to Kenta Satō for his time. Not only did he take me out to Iitate for the entire day, but he also never declined any of my requests for more detailed information about the story of his contaminated village. We talked for over twenty hours.

I also extend my thanks to Professor Masato Motosaka for the object lesson on "waves of books." And also how to ensure your own safety when the earth trembles. I would like to thank Professor Hikaru Amano from the Tarachine Independent Center for Radioactivity Studies for explaining to me, over and over again, how to magically test radioactivity.

Midori Namba rescued me at the very last minute (when the translator I had an appointment with got sick) by agreeing to translate my interview with Kenji Higuchi at his home full of books and pictures from inside a nuclear power plant. Dr. Sébastien Penmellen met with me several times to discuss death and the ways of commemorating the dead in Japan. Ali Dib, who showed me the world of Tokyo and shared curiosities about Japan, helped me in the translation of my conversation with Hiroki Terai; we both managed not to cry. And Amya Miller helped me during my conversation with Mr. Teiichi Satō. I want to thank Mr. Satō for a remarkable afternoon spent in a shed built from tsunami debris. And for serving me fresh cucumbers from his greenhouse served with *miso* paste.

I am very grateful to Atsuko Tanaka, a courageous and beautiful woman and my close friend, for providing me with a place in Japan that I call home. Even Yochan, the large tabby cat, has grown accustomed to me. I wish to thank her as well for translating my interview with Norio Kimura, back in March 2014. This all began with him.

I wish to thank Mikako Sawasa for leaving the key to the house in Kyoto under a flowerpot. As well as for the bicycle, which I would ride along the banks of the Kamo River, discovering the green, water-dwelling world of that exceptional city. My thanks to her also for introducing me to the nuances of Japanese culture. And I want to thank Mikako and Noriko Yamaguchi for the evenings in the best *izakayas* of Kyoto (both of them know the ins and outs like no one else; after all, they run newspaper columns about food). Thanks to them, I managed to take my mind off the heavy atmosphere in Fukushima.

Ganbare! Workshops on Dying

Noriko deserves separate thanks for her words in passing: "You know, there are shamanesses living in the north of Japan."

My thanks also go out to: Keiko Takahashi (for our conversations about ostracism), Shibuya san (for arranging accommodations for me in temporary housing), Ody Odybar (he traveled several hundred kilometers to translate my meeting with the *itako*!), Jeffrey Jousan (for our meeting and for the film *Alone in the Zone*, thanks to which I knew what to talk about with Mr. Matsumura), Yasuhiro Chiba (for our conversations about the *Save the Memory Project*, led by Ricoh), Ryoki Satō, Kyoko Hirano, Gan Iwao Nagayama, Tamao Yamamoto, Tetsuro Eguchi, Eijiro Toyota, Umi Kojima, Takanori Obayashi, Erika Nakajima from P@ct (which organizes volunteer work in Rikuzentakata), Yukari Ezoe from Ricoh, Kyoko Yukimoto, Akira Okayama, Mike Connolly, Satoru Mimura, as well as Saori Machimura and Satoko Noguchi from Habitat.

I didn't have the chance to personally speak with David Baxter, Sakiko Miura, or Itaru Sasaki. I would like to take the opportunity here to thank them for their stories.

And that's just the Japanese part. I've still got the no-less-important Polish part.

I wish to thank Dr. Beata Kubiak Ho-Chi for her thoughtful remarks, her correcting any errors and for broadening my knowledge. I'm happy that we share not only our love for Japan, but also for Vietnam.

Dr. Michał Kozub of ITME (Institute of Electronic Materials Technology in Warsaw) spent long hours with me, explaining what exactly this whole radiation thing is. He would patiently answer every one of my questions in such a fascinating way that I didn't notice how quickly time went by. In addition, I wish to thank him for the numerous consultations about isotopes, neutrons, and sieverts, as well as pasta pots.

Ms. Anna Król-Kuczkowska, a psychotherapist from the HUMANI studio in Poznań, met with me to discuss the differences between trauma and mourning. And about how different the processes of managing loss are.

And finally, the personal part.

I want to thank my mom, dad, and Zosia for always looking out for me, as well as for their patience and love. My thanks to my granddad for the learning experience and the thorough readings. I wish to thank my friends for not becoming discouraged by my silence. And that they learned the process together with me; things will be much easier with the next book. My thanks to Zuza, Dominika, and Ania for taking all the side effects of writing in stride. I wish to thank Agula for coming to see and understand my world. My thanks to Oleńka for always rooting for me, even two oceans away. My thanks to Alex for our conversations about evacuees and radiation, and for the overly long text messages sent between Poland and Japan when we were down. My thanks to Bhavik for the support and the funny animal videos. My thanks to Filip for always telling me that this is what I should be doing.

I wish to thank Ms. Agata Tuszyńska for having constantly repeated the same thing for over ten years: "Keep on writing!" My thanks to Wojciech Tochman for the fact that he had no problems with saying: "Let's do it together." I want to thank Paweł Goźliński, my editor, for his time and trust. For conversations that always lead to something. And for knowing when you have to say: "This is no joke."

I wish to thank Henryk Lipszyc for the stories within stories and for showing me that the love for Japan is a love for life.

And I want to thank my teacher, Aneta Pierzchała (who explained to me what truism is) for the fact that when we had been discussing Shakespeare, she showed us Kurosawa. It was she who, thanks to her stories about shadows in Hiroshima, instilled the love for Japan in me.

And—for the American edition—I would like to thank Antonia Lloyd-Jones, Sean Bye, Chad W. Post, and Kaija Straumanis for believing in this book. Special thanks goes to Mark Ordon for making it happen. Thanks to his commitment, determination, and years spent with the Polish version of *Ganbare*, you can read this book now.

# Sources

One of the major sources of information for me was the English-language daily, *The Japan Times*. This was where I would find short articles about the people I would later meet. Yet the *Asahi Shimbun* and *Mainichi* proved to be just as helpful. I read up on myths and legends in books by Jolanta Tubielewicz (*Mitologia Japonii* [Mythology of Japan], published by Wydawnictwa Artystyczne i Filmowe, Warsaw, 1986), Kunio Yanagita (*The Legends of Tono*, Lexington Books, Lanham, 2008), and Lafcadio Hearn (*Kwaidan: Stories and Studies of Strange Things*, Tuttle Publishing, 2015). I found out more about the history of Japan and economic miracles interwoven with economic crises from Andrew Gordon (*Modern History of Japan*, 2nd edition, Oxford University Press, New York, 2008). The classic work by Ruth Benedict, *The Chrysanthemum and the Sword: Patterns of Japanese Culture* ([1946]; Houghton Mifflin, Boston, 1989) and the more contemporary work by Joanna Bator, *Rekin z parku Yoyogi* (*The Shark from Yoyogi Park*; WAB, Warsaw, 2014) provided me with a view of the culture. I found out what Hiroshima looked like after the bomb was dropped from the journal by Michihiko Hachiya

(*Hiroshima Diary: The Journal of a Japanese Physician, August 6–September 30, 1945*, The University of North Carolina Press, Chapel Hill, 1995) and from the manga *Barefoot Gen* by Keiji Nakazawa (abridged English language version, Dino Box, Tokyo, 2013). I read about the disaster in Japan in 2011 in the works of two Polish journalists: Piotr Bernardyn (*Słońce jeszcze nie wzeszło. Tsunami. Fukushima* [The Sun Has Not Yet Risen. Tsunami. Fukushima], Bezdroża, Gliwice, 2014) and Rafał Tomański (*Made in Japan*, Bezdroża, Gliwice, 2013). Marie Mockett introduced me to the secrets of death the Japanese way in her book, *Where the Dead Pause and the Japanese Say Goodbye: A Journey*, Norton, New York, 2015. Journalists from the Ōtsuchi *Mirai Shimbun* collected eyewitness reports of the tsunami and published them as a book called *Life After the Tsunami* (Japan Center of Education for Journalist, 2013). The story of the earthquake, tsunami and explosions in the Fukushima Daiichi power plant were also told by Lucy Birmingham and David McNeill in their book *Strong in the Rain* (Palgrave Macmillan, New York, 2012).

I acquired knowledge about historic earthquakes from the *Studies on the 2011 Off the Pacific Coast of Tohoku Earthquake*, by Hiroshi Kawase (Springer, Tokyo, 2014). I read about the course of the catastrophe at Fukushima Daiichi in several publications (each describes these events a bit differently): The Independent Investigation Commission on the Fukushima Nuclear Accident, *The Fukushima Daiichi Nuclear Power Station Disaster: Investigating the Myth and Reality* (Routledge, London, 2014); David Lochbaum, Edwin Lyman, Susan Q. Stranahan, The Union of Concerned Scientists, *Fukushima: The Story of a Nuclear Disaster* (The New Press, New York,

2014); Ryūshō Kadota, *On the Brink: The Inside Story of Fuku-shima Daiichi* (Kurodahan Press, Fukuoka, 2014). I also used fragments of the questioning of Masao Yoshida translated to English by the *Asahi Shimbun* and published as *The Yoshida Testimony* (http://www.asahi.com/special/yoshida_report/en/). I read about the history of the atom in Japan in the work by Richard Krooth, Morris Edelson and Hiroshi Fukurai, *Nuclear Tsunami: The Japanese Government and America's Role in the Fukushima Disaster* (Lexington Books, Lanham, 2015), as well as the work of Benjamin K. Sovacool and Scott Victor Valentine, *The National Politics of Nuclear Power: Economics, Security, and Governance* (Routledge, Oxon, 2012). The beauty of Tōhoku was revealed to me by Matsuo Bashō in his book *The Narrow Road to the Deep North and Other Travel Sketches* (Penguin Books Classics, London, 1966).

## Miscellaneous

During work on the book, I also referenced a number of scientific studies, government documentation and publications released by non-governmental organizations. I am therefore listing only the most essential titles below, in chronological rather than alphabetical order.

Keiko Torigoe, *Insights into the Global Composition Taken at Three Stricken Places in Japan*, Soundscape, 2012-2013, vol. 12, no. 1, (p. 9-14).

Teiichi Satō, *The Seed of Hope in the Heart. March, 2014—Three years from "3.11,"* Rikuzentakata, 2014.

Munemasa Takahashi, *Tsunami, Photographs, and Then. Lost & Found Project. Family Photos swept away by 3.11 East*

*Japan Tsunami*, AKAAKA ART PUBLISHING Inc, Kyoto, 2014.

Peter H. Brothers, *Japan's Nuclear Nightmare: How the Bomb Became a Beast Called Godzilla, Cineaste*, 2011, vol. 36, no. 3, (p. 36-40).

Kenichi Hasegawa, *Fukushima's Stolen Lives: A Dairy Farmer's Story of How Nuclear Power Destroyed a Community and a Way of Life*, Reportage Laboratory Co. Ltd., 2012 (http://fukushima-diary.weebly.com/read-an-excerpt.html).

Reiko Hasegawa, *Disaster Evacuation from Japan's 2011 Tsunami Disaster and the Fukushima Nuclear Accident*, IDDRI, SciencesPo, Paris, 2013.

Hikaru Amano, Hideaki Sakamoto, Norikatsu Shiga, Kaori Suzuki, *Method for rapid screening analysis of Sr-90 in edible plant samples collected near Fukushima, Japan, Applied Radiation and Isotopes*, 2016, vol. 112 ( no. 6, p. 131-135).

Mark Willacy, *Fukushima*, Macmillian Australia, Sydney, 2013.

I also referenced the following information published in English on the webpage of the Japanese Ministry of the Environment:

*Decontamination Guidelines* (http://josen.env.go.jp/en/framework/pdf/decontamination_guidelines_2nd.pdf);

*Progress on Off-site Cleanup and Interim Storage in Japan*, (http://josen.env.go.jp/en/pdf/progressseet_progress_on_cleanup_efforts.pdf?160126);

*Act on Special Measures Concerning the Handling of Environment Pollution by Radioactive Materials Discharged by the Nuclear Power Station Accident with the Tohoku District*, (http://josen.env.go.jp/en/).

## Films

*Alone in the Zone*, directed by Ivan Kovac, Jeffrey Jousan, Japan, 2013.

*Nuclear Ginza*, directed by Nicholas Rohl, United Kingdom, 1995.

## Internet Sources

In a few cases, I based the stories told in the book on internet sources. Other sources helped me prepare for conversations with my protagonists and experts. I also used the sources cited below to verify stories I had heard, check some facts and find additional details that would enrich the story. The links are assigned to specific chapters. I list the most important ones.

### Garbage

www.tsunamireturn.com

https://m-kankou.jp/english/project/keimei-maru/

http://www.japantimes.co.jp/news/2012/06/14/national/owner-gets--back-float-found-in-alaska/

http://www.japantimes.co.jp/news/2012/05/16/national/eaterys-buoy-washes-up-in-alaska/

www.nhk.or.jp/japan311/tmrw2-return.html

https://indiecanent.com/movies/lost-found/

### What Lies Under the Water?

www.bbc.com/news/magazine-33294275

www.bbc.com/news/blogs-news-from-elsewhere-26169827

http://www.japantimes.co.jp/news/2014/03/11/national/widower-to-tsunami-dives-on-in-hope/

https://www.youtube.com/watch?v=0ey-4_iWEfU

## The Four Tsunamis of Mr. Satō

http://ngm.nationalgeographic.com/1896/09/japan-tsunami/scidmore--text

http://www.britannica.com/event/Chile-earthquake-of-1960

http://earthweb.ess.washington.edu/tsunami/general/historic/chilean60.html

https://www.youtube.com/watch?v=HQskwJSRecI

https://www.japantimes.co.jp/life/2011/06/12/general/heights-of-survival/

https://www.nbcnews.com/id/wbna43018489

## If People Were Dragons

http://earthquaketrack.com

https://en.wikipedia.org/wiki/List_of_earthquakes_in_Japan

## Mr. Frog Gives Warning

https://www.metro.tokyo.lg.jp/english/guide/bosai/index.html

## The North

https://markystar.wordpress.com/2013/04/23/go-kaido-what-are-the-5-highways-of-old-japan/

http://www.inboundtourism.com.au/pdf/japanese-tourism-history.pdf

## Cremations

https://www.tofugu.com/japan/japanese-funeral/

http://daily.jstor.org/history-japan-cremation/

http://traditionscustoms.com/death-rites/japanese-funeral

http://www.onmarkproductions.com/html/sai-no-kawara. html#datsueba

http://matthewmeyer.net/blog/2014/02/23/meido-the-japanese-underworld/

http://matthewmeyer.net/blog/2014/03/02/jigoku-japanese-hell/

## Survival Kit

https://sites.google.com/site/oliveinenglish/

http://www.bbc.com/news/mobile/world-asia-pacific-12733393

https://www.pri.org/stories/2011-03-13/japan-pm-calls-tsunami-worst-crisis-wwii

## Expired

http://www.soumu.go.jp/main_content/000370336.pdf

http://www.pref.iwate.jp/saiken/sumai/023870.html

https://www.pref.fukushima.lg.jp/uploaded/life/191221_427091_misc.pdf

http://www.pref.miyagi.jp/site/ej-earthquake/nyukyo-jokyo.html

https://www.japantimes.co.jp/opinion/2016/02/22/commentary/japan-commentary/wasteful-spending-tohoku/

http://www.japantimes.co.jp/news/2006/11/16/national/island-hit-by-1993-killer-tsunami-remains-vigilant/

http://www.theguardian.com/world/2014/jun/29/tsunami-wall-japan-divides-villagers

http://www.nytimes.com/2005/02/25/world/asia/behind-its-seawalls-japanese-isle-debates-their-value.html

## A White Spot

http://lostandfound311.jp/en/

http://www.ricoh.com/csr/savethememory/

https://blog.adobe.com/en/publish/2013/04/05/restoring-memories-with-becci-manson-a-different-kind-of-disaster-relief.html

https://petapixel.com/2015/03/11/how-ricoh-returned-90000-photos-to-victims-of-the-2011-tsunami-in-japan/

http://www.japantimes.co.jp/news/2014/07/11/national/nonprofit-reunites-photos-lost-tsunami-owners/

http://www.japantimes.co.jp/news/2011/05/27/national/fujifilm-helps-salvage-photos-in-disaster-zone/

http://www.huffingtonpost.com/2015/03/27/ricoh-japan-earthquake_n_6948960.html

http://www.npr.org/2011/08/19/139747453/in-japan-restoring-photos-for-tsunami-victims

http://www.cbsnews.com/news/year-after-japan-tsunami-precious-photos-saved/

## Call Me

https://sanichiichi-blog.tumblr.com/post/80042094470/phone-booth-in-garden-helps-bereaved-talk-to

https://recoveringtohoku.wordpress.com/category/iwate/otsuchi/

## Who You Will Become After You Die

http://yokai.com/

## Ghosts

https://hyakumonogatari.com/

http://www.reuters.com/article/us-japan-exorcist-ghosts-idUSBRE9240YZ20130305

http://www.lrb.co.uk/v36/n03/richard-lloydparry/ghosts-of-the-tsunami


## Kampai!

http://esake.com/Knowledge/Types/types.html

http://www.japansake.or.jp/sake/english/sake-basics/type.html

http://sake-world.com/about-sake/types-of-sake/


## The Atom

http://www.world-nuclear.org/information-library/country-profiles/countries-g-n/japan-nuclear-power.aspx

https://www.latimes.com/archives/la-xpm-1999-dec-30-mn-49042-story.html

https://www.washingtonpost.com/world/in-japan-newattention-for--longtime-anti-nuclear-activist/2011/04/05/AFMTG3GD_story.html

http://ncbj.edu.pl/bwr-wodny-wrzacy/ogolnie-o-bwr


## Boom!

http://www.world-nuclear.org/information-library/safety-and-security/safety-of-plants/fukushima-accident.aspx

http://www.tepco.co.jp/en/decommision/index-e.html

https://en.wikipedia.org/wiki/Japanese_reaction_to_Fukushima_Daiichi_nuclear_disaster

http://www.asahi.com/special/yoshida_report/en/

https://www.japantimes.co.jp/news/2014/10/09/national/remembering-fukushima-plant-chief-helped-prevent-catastrophe/

## The New Japanese Bestiary

http://c-navi.jaea.go.jp/en/background/remediation-
following-major-radiation-accidents/characteristics-of-
caesium-134-and-caesium-137.html

http://large.stanford.edu/courses/2012/ph241/wessells1/

http://toxnet.nlm.nih.gov/cgi-bin/sis/search/a?dbs+hsdb:
@term+@DOCNO+7389

http://www.geigercounter.org/radioactivity/isotopes.htm

http://www.npr.org/sections/thesalt/2014/06/03/318241738/
how-atomic-particles-became-the-smoking-gun-in-wine-fraud-
mystery

https://pubchem.ncbi.nlm.nih.gov/compound/5486527

http://www.atsdr.cdc.gov/PHS/PHS.asp?id=654&tid=120

https://pubchem.ncbi.nlm.nih.gov/compound/5486204

http://www.nirs.org/factsheets/tritiumbasicinfo.pdf

https://en.wikipedia.org/wiki/Tritium

https://nukleomed.pl/terapia-izotopowa-lagodnych-chorob-
tarczycy/

https://www.polatom.pl

## The Most Beautiful Village in Japan

http://shun-gate.com/en/roots/roots_36.html

## The North Wind

http://www.wsj.com/articles/SB100014240531119035549045
76458230766485092

http://www.spiegel.de/international/world/poisoned-fields-
the-painful-evacuation-of-a-japanese-village-a-765949.html

http://www.japantimes.co.jp/news/2014/04/11/national/
iitate-farmers--cautionary-tale-translated/

http://www.japantimes.co.jp/opinion/2012/08/11/editorials/speedi-report-deepens-suspicions/

http://www.nytimes.com/2011/08/09/world/asia/09japan.html

http://www.greenpeace.org/shadowlands

http://www.translatorscafe.com/cafe/EN/units-converter/radiation/24-22/microsievert%2Fhour-millisievert%2Fyear/

## Yuna

https://www.cbsnews.com/video/looking-for-yuna-a-fathers-steadfast-search/

http://www.ibtimes.co.uk/japan-dealing-radioactive-waste-four-years-after-tsunami-hit-fukushima-nuclear-power-plant-1491104

## Clean Our Land

http://www.reuters.com/article/us-japan-tsunami-widerimage-idUSKBN0M50HS20150309

http://www.japantimes.co.jp/news/2016/03/28/national/land-acquisition-fukushima-dump-site-may-reach-70-2020-ministry/

## One Bowl of Rice

http://www.ncbi.nlm.nih.gov/pubmed/26822892

http://www.mhlw.go.jp/english/topics/2011eq/dl/new_standard.pdf

http://www.fao.org/crisis/27242-0bfef658358a6ed53980a5eb5c80685ef.pdf

## Go Ahead and Complain

http://www.theatlantic.com/magazine/archive/2015/05/crying-it-out-in-japan/389528/

http://www.japantimes.co.jp/news/2013/06/22/national/participants-ease-stress-levels-at-crying-events/

http://tokyodesu.com/2015/04/30/rui-katsu-japanese-parties-where-people-go-to-cry-in-public/

http://www.japantrends.com/rui-katsu-group-crying-for-stress-relief/

## Mr. Matsumura Does Not Feel Alone

http://naotomatsumura.weebly.com/

http://www.boredpanda.com/fukushima-radioactive-disaster-abandoned-animal-guardian-naoto-matsumura/

http://www.dailymail.co.uk/wires/ap/article-2663401/Fukushima-farmers-appeal-Tokyo-live-bull.html

## Death in Tokyo

http://www.japantimes.co.jp/news/2012/09/04/reference/part-of-aging-process-preparing-for-the-end/

http://www.japantrends.com/shukatsu-prepare-death-coffin-experience/

http://www.ifcx.jp/en/

https://www.washingtonpost.com/world/in-rapidly-aging-japan-dyingis-big-business/2015/12/19/0f313244-a198-11e5-8318-bd8caed8c588_story.html?

http://www.straitstimes.com/asia/east-asia/take-a-funeral-portrait-scatter-fake-ashes-death-tourism-rising-draw-for-japans

https://www.bloomberg.com/news/articles/2015-12-15/
try-a-coffin-for-size-the-death-business-is-thriving-in-japan

http://kotaku.com/in-japan-living-people-are-lying-
in-coffins-729248895

https://www.washingtonpost.com/world/asia_pacific/
a-new-yahoo-ending-service-lets-users-in-japan-prepare-for-
the-inevitable/2014/07/20/d5751480-0866-4760-b41b-79a
ee25ad412_story.html

https://ending.yahoo.co.jp/

http://gizmodo.com/this-is-probably-the-most-high-tech-
cemetery-in-the-wor-1696153589

https://motherboard.vice.com/en_us/article/death-is-
a-high-tech-trip-in-japans-futuristic-cemeteries

http://www.kokuyo.com/en/csr/report/customer/
communication/st.html

### Examine Yourself

http://www.iwakisokuteishitu.com/english/index.html

### Homecomings

http://www.asahi.com/ajw/articles/AJ201603260045.html

https://recoveringtohoku.wordpress.com/2014/04/16/
salmon-fry-released-into-kido-river-in-naraha-1st-since-2011-
disaster-fukushima-minpo-41614/

**KATARZYNA BONI** graduated in cultural studies at the University of Warsaw and in social psychology at the SWPS University, as well as from the Polska Szkoła Reportażu (Polish School of Reportage). She publishes in travel magazines and the *Duży Format* magazine. Boni specializes in writing about Asia, where she spent over three years working in Japan, China, Cambodia, Thailand, the Philippines, and Indonesia. She is a co-author of *Kontener*—a book about Syrian refugees in Jordan, written together with Wojciech Tochman.

**MARK ORDON** is a writer and translator based in Poznań, Poland. His work has appeared in the English edition of *Przekrój* magazine and *The Thornfield Review,* as well as academic publications commissioned by the Polish Academy of Sciences. His focus to date has been on short fiction and non-fiction, as well as translations of academic papers and lectures, such as "On the Importance of Sadness," a lecture given by philosopher Tomasz Stawiszyński at A Night of Philosophy and Ideas in Brooklyn, New York in February 2020.